FATHER HORSE

FATHER HORSE

A Novel of Roman Britain

William Lewis

RESOURCE *Publications* • Eugene, Oregon

FATHER HORSE
A Novel of Roman Britain

Resource Publications
An Imprint of Wipf and Stock Publishers
199 W. 8th Ave., Suite 3
Eugene, OR 97401

www.wipfandstock.com

PAPERBACK ISBN: 978-1-6667-7179-4
HARDCOVER ISBN: 978-1-6667-7180-0
EBOOK ISBN: 978-1-6667-7181-7

VERSION NUMBER 051523

For Margo

and for Maia

CONTENTS

PROLOGUE

It was a hot summer's afternoon in northern Britain. This was not the Britain of today with its grey skies and clipped fields. This was the Britain of long ago, when it was ruled by the Romans and ended at a vast stone wall that ran across the island from east to west. Beyond that was foreign territory.

It was the summer of the year AD263, and two very grubby children were emerging from a small woodland, and making their way downhill to the sprawling complex of buildings that was their home. They had not been summoned by the urgent calling of their tutor, who stood wringing his hands in the gateway; nor by the anxieties of their mother, who watched for them from her own room; but by the insistent rumblings of their stomachs.

Their house was square, stout and built of stone. Three wings, arranged like a "U" surrounded a central courtyard. A three-story tower rose at one corner, its topmost room commanding a view of the fields and the hillside down which the children were tumbling. Across the mouth of the "U" ran a high wall with a mighty double gate at its center. It was there that the tutor stood, anxiously hopping from foot to foot, calling out their names.

The house itself was the center of a small cluster of buildings, for it was a working sheep farm and cloth factory. There was a barn to store the winter fodder, stables for the horses, a hen house, sheep pens and a large, covered area where the sheep were shorn. There were also two new timber buildings: one where the wool was spun, carded and woven into bolts of cloth; the other, a long, low barracks building to house the farm's slaves.

The children were a boy and a girl. Gini, the girl, was older and, probably, dirtier. Her face was streaked with grime, and her fingernails were black with dirt. She was eleven years old , too old to be a baby, but too young to be a grown-up. Her hair was fair, her eyes, a deep brown, and her skin, a natural Mediterranean olive. Her knees were scabbed with the remains of yesterday's grazes and scrapes, for her favorite things to do were stalking animals and climbing trees. Like her brother, she wore a tunic that had once been green and light-colored sandals.

Her brother, Gordi, was nine and looked much like a smaller version of his sister, except that his eyes were green, like their mother's. He had big front teeth, like a rabbit, that their mother assured him he would grow into, and his arms and legs were covered with he scratches of the brambles that he had fallen into that day. His hair was wild, for he seldom washed or combed it, but his face shone with the sheer joy of the day.

When the children reached the house, the tutor reached for them, rather feebly. They dodged his outstretched arms with ease, ran across the courtyard and all the way to the kitchens that served the needs of the big house.

The kitchen was the kingdom of the family's cook, Phormio, a slave who had come with them from the warm lands of the Middle Sea. He was a small man, with clever hands, a big nose (all the better to smell the food!), and a big bald spot in the middle of his head. He truly loved to cook and oversaw a small band of bakers, pastrycooks, assistants and cleaners. Phormio had fed both of the children for all of their lives. He loved them as deeply as if they were his own and he could deny them nothing. So it was that when Lydia, their mother, found them they were sitting at the big pine work table eating bread with cheese and honey.

As she came into the kitchen, she carried silence with her. The slaves who kept the benches wiped and pots scoured stopped their chatter and Phormio, who had been chopping some leeks, rinsed his hands, dried them, and came forward with a slight bow.

"Mistress," he said, waving at the children. "I think that you might be looking for these."

"Yes, thank you Phormio. I can see that they have helped themselves to their dinner. After the way in which they treated their poor tutor today, they can expect nothing more to eat until breakfast."

Then she turned to the children, who had put their bread down and stood also with their heads slightly bowed. They knew what was coming.

"Come with me," she said.

Her tone was not warm. They were in trouble.

When they were outside, she took each of them by the shoulder and turned them both to face her.

"First, a proper scrub for you both. I want the pair of you washed and in clean clothes in my room in half an hour. Now go. I am very disappointed with you both."

Lydia watched the children trudge off to the bathhouse to be seated, scrubbed and polished, with a mixture of affection and exasperation, then made her way up the stairs.

Her room was at the top of the tower. She had the whole floor to herself, and it was here that she spent much time reading, writing to friends and in her private religious devotions. The room was fitted out for her comfort with a writing table, wicker chairs, a long couch for her afternoon nap, a variety of small tables, and her greatest treasure, her library. Along one wall square wooden cubicles reached from floor to ceiling and each of these contained a varying number of scrolls. Two of the cubicles did not contain scrolls, but books: a new invention consisting of papyrus sheets cut into rectangles, sewn together down the spine and then glued between two wooden covers. This was Lydia's great treasure, of more value to her than the cloth business that had made her wealthy. This room was more than an office or a place to escape for an hour or two. It was a reflection of who she was, and she loved it.

The children came, received the expected lecture, and left. It was bed without supper again. From the way that the two received their punishment, Lydia thought that this might not be so terrible, and thinking that this might happen, the two had prepared some supplies.

Once they had gone, Lydia turned her attention to the real problem. She sat in thought for a time and then rang a little bell. Almost immediately, one of her maids came in, bowing her head as she entered the room.

"Please bring me that poor tutor. And a cool drink. Do we have oranges for juice?"

"Yes my lady. Tutor and juice. In that order?"

"I think so. He won't be here long."

A few minutes later, there was a timid knock at the door.

"Come in." Lydia spoke a firm voice, determined to be the strong mistress of the house.

The tutor shuffled in, his head bowed and his body slumped in defeat. He had tried. He really had. He had tried to tempt them with food, to excite them with bold stories from Homer; to discipline them with hard words. None of it had worked. They had ignored him, running off whenever his back was turned out the open windows, and up the hill into the little woodland that they truly loved for the adventures it brought them.

Lydia spoke, "I think that your time with us is at an end. I had hoped for better. You came well recommended and we spent good money bringing you here, but the result is a poor one. The children are more ungovernable that ever, and I fear that, under your tutelage, they have forgotten more than they had ever learned. You will pack and go. I will see that you are properly provided for."

"My Lady," he began...

"No," she interrupted. "There is nothing here for you to say. I am quite determined. There must be another way, and I will find it. But you are not the person who can teach my children. Under your care, they have learned only disobedience and a degree of dishonesty that I find most disappointing. Now leave. The steward will make the arrangements."

"But where will I get another post?" he asked.

"As I said, you will be provided for, but if you take my advice, you will find another way to make a living. Be a translator. Be a copyist. Teaching children is not for you."

With that, Lydia rose from her chair and gestured to the door. Crestfallen, the tutor took the hint, bowed and left.

Lydia sighed. She loved her children dearly, but they did frustrate her. This had not been the first tutor to fail to rein the children in, but she was determined that he would be the last. She sat in silence for a time, thinking over this problem. She did not want to teach the children herself, but she had not found anyone else who could do the job. As her questioning mind sought an answer, her eyes closed, her breathing slowed, and her lips began to move, speaking words below the level of hearing.

An idea seemed to strike her. Her lips stopped moving and she took a deep breath. Opening her eyes, she rose to her feet, went to her writing table, and wrote a letter.

CHAPTER ONE

FATHER HIPPOLYTUS GETS A NEW JOB

THREE MONTHS LATER, AND a long way away, a man with a long staff hobbled as quickly as he could with his bad feet through the crowded streets of a busy town. It was late in the morning when people were hurrying home for their midday meal. The day was already hot. The autumn was late; it still felt like summer with its clear skies and baking heat.

He was a small man with dark hair and a straw hat that covered a big bald spot in the middle of his head. He had sharp eyes and a beaky nose and he still had (most of) his teeth. He wore a tunic that came down to his knees. It might once have been white, but it was stained with travel (and a little food). His legs below his knees were wrapped in linen bandages and on his feet he did not wear sandals, like everyone else who had footwear, but covered slippers with hard soles. From the top of his staff, hung a little leather bag which held his few possessions.

The man was called Hippolytus and he was a Christian priest. He was on his way to meet with the bishop, the head of his community, and he was rather late. He had been summoned to this meeting and was anxious to obey.

The town was Myra, a place of middling size on the south coast of the ancient land of Lycia. It was an old town. As he walked along the road into the town he could see, carved into the cliffs above the theatre in which the people of Myra took particular pride, the houses of the long dead. Tier upon tier they rose, columns framing empty doors, doors opening onto empty, looted rooms. Those tombs, cut deep into the cliffs, both outside and inside the town, stared grimly down at the community, reminding it of its long past and daring it to do anything new. In the year 263, when Gallienus the

Roman Emperor was in the tenth year of his reign, the Bishop of Myra was called John.

Although John was a bishop, he did not have a big church building. At that time the Christian church was still quite small and did not have a lot of money. There was a house that belonged to the church where Bishop John lived, and it was here that the community met for worship on Sundays and young men learned to be priests. Hippolytus had studied there, before going into the countryside to lead the little churches in the villages of the hills and the bays of the nearby coast.

It was in one of these, Simena, a pretty town that word had reached Hippolytus that the bishop wanted to see him "as soon as possible." The word was in the form of a letter waiting for him when he arrived one afternoon after a hot and dusty walk from the next village. The letter had already been waiting for him for some days and that is why he was in such a hurry.

The swiftest way from Simena to Myra was by boat, but he had to wait for one. It was too late in the day to go, but early the next morning he found one loaded with dried fish for the markets in Myra. The breeze was good and, by mid-morning, the little boat had docked at the port of Andriake, that served the town of Myra.

He was hot and tired by the time he reached the bishop's house. His feet hurt and he did smell a bit because it had been a while since he'd had time to have a wash, or even to bathe in the sea, and he had just had a boat ride with a load of fish. As he knocked at the door he was cheered by the thought that there would be a familiar and friendly face to greet him.

Old Jacob opened the door to him. Jacob had lived in the house since before it had been the bishop's. In fact he and his wife Susanna were slaves, and it was they who kept the place clean, patched its leaks and kept its garden in order. They were both brown with the sun and creased with age. Their hands had grown hard with work, and they had both lost many of their teeth. But they stood straight when others were bent, and they were always kind.

One of Jacob's jobs was to greet callers when they arrived. He had been expecting Hippolytus for days and was looking forward to seeing him. They were old and dear friends, and, besides, Jacob had a little bit of news of his own. When he opened the door to Hippolytus, not only did the priest see his old friend, but he saw his old friend wearing a conical felt cap—the cap of freedom.

"Look, Father," he said, even before he said 'Hello.' "I'm a free man now. And Susanna is free too. Bishop John freed us when he arrived. He said to us 'The Church shouldn't own people.' So he gave us our papers and our freedom."

"Then, why are you still here?" asked Hippolytus. "You could go anywhere."

"But where would we go? Susanna and I, we've been slaves in this house all our lives. It's our home now, and so we choose to stay. Come in now. Father Timothy is eager to see you."

Father Timothy lived in the house with the bishop and helped him in his work. Years before, he and Hippolytus had studied together with Bishop Andrew (who had been bishop before John) and learned about being priests together. They had even become priests on the same day and they had been good friends ever since.

Hippolytus found Timothy reading at the heart of the garden courtyard. This had once been a place of ornamental flowers, but now vegetables grew in the garden beds; the scent of rosemary, thyme and oregano came from enormous orange terracotta pots; and cucumbers and grapes hung from vines that grew up on freestanding trellises. Timothy sat in the shade of one of these and his lips were moving as he read the words softly to himself. As Hippolytus approached, he stopped, looked up from his book, and smiled broadly in greeting. Soon they were sitting down together with some fruit and a cool drink and chatting away together as old friends do.

"Bishop John did not know when you would he here," explained Timothy. "He sent so many letters to lots of different villages where you usually call. One was bound to catch up with you sooner or later. But now he has gone off to see a sick family. He should be back soon."

"A whole family?"

"Yes. It might be the soldiers' plague that the army brought a few years ago. Or they might just have eaten something bad. Whatever it is, he is with them now, praying for their recovery."

"Is that why the bishop asked me here? Does he need help with the sick? I did learn some things in Caesarea that might help."

"No," Timothy replied smiling. "I think that he has other plans for you, although they might involve your studies in another way."

Years before, even before becoming a priest, Hippolytus had been sent to the great city of Caesarea in Palestine to study with the famous teachers there. He had always been a clever boy, and his parents thought that this would be the best way for him to make his way in the world. What they had not counted on was that one of his teachers would be the notorious Christian professor, Origen. It was through Origen's teaching that Hippolytus had become a Christian. This disappointed his parents greatly. They had expected great things from their clever son only to find that he had joined a religious group of which they did not approve, and whose membership was, at that time, against the law. Hippolytus had been thrown out by his family and forbidden to return home. The bishop had taken him in, and decided to put his learning to good use by making him a priest.

By now it was the middle of the day, and despite the fruit, Hippolytus' stomach was growling.

Hearing this Timothy mentioned it was time for the midday meal. "Would you like to help me with the lunch? Jacob and Susanna do like to have a little time to themselves in the middle of the day."

Hippolytus and Timothy went off to the kitchen at the back of the house. They put together a collection of fresh fruit and vegetables with bread, cheese and olives on three wooden platters. To these they added a great jug of water with a little wine and carried them all to the dining room. As they sat and waited for the bishop, they caught the hum of bees, the songs of birds and the fragrance of herbs and flowers.

Before too long the bishop came in and, when he saw Hippolytus, he smiled and held out his arms. It was a big smile for he was a large bald man with a fringe of white hair over around a happy round face framed by a white beard, and kind, deep brown, eyes.

"Greetings my son. It is good to see you!"

"Thank you," replied Hippolytus. "It is good to be back here in a place that holds so many good memories for me."

"Shall we bless the food and eat, and then talk?" asked the bishop, but it was not really a question.

And so they did, saying a grace together that they all knew well, and setting to work on the food with the hunger of people who have earned their meal.

None of the men spoke while they ate. This was not just manners. It was also the custom of the house.

After a while, Bishop John, having finished his food, emptied his cup in a long swallow, wiped his lips on his sleeve and said: "Well, Father Hippolytus, it's about time that I told you what all of this is about."

The bishop cleared his throat.

"I have a sister. Her name is Lydia and some years ago, she married a trader named Glaucus from the next town. Our parents were pleased enough with the match except that Glaucus was—is—not of the faith. But he is a clever man, and wealthy. Some years ago during the troubles around the coastlands, Glaucus took himself, my sister and their children, as far away as they could get, in fact as far as Britain. This was not just because these lands were suddenly dangerous, but also because Glaucus could see that there was a good opportunity to make money, importing dyes from here and then exporting dyed cloth to the markets of Gaul.

"Glaucus and Lydia have two children, a boy who would be about nine now and a girl who is a little bit older. Lydia has written to me to ask me to find them a tutor, one who can teach them Greek and Latin, how to speak properly, and so forth. Britain does have such people, but Lydia can find none that meet her requirements. Above all, she wants to find a very rare thing: a clever tutor for her children, who is also of the faith. This is especially important to her because Glaucus remains wedded to the old gods, and she thinks that a Christian teacher in the house will be good for him.

"You are one of the few priests under my authority who has a complete classical education, and even studied with one of the great masters, and so I am asking you to go be their tutor. This is not a matter of obedience. I understand if you do not wish to go. I cannot order you to do this, but I am asking you. There it is."

There was a moment's silence. Then Hippolytus stammered out the only question that he could think to ask: "But why me? Surely there are other, better priests whom you can send. There are certainly ones more clever than I am, better presented than I am, and who can make their way around without having to lean on a stick all the time."

"But my dear Father Hippolytus, that is exactly why I would like you to go. For years now, you have struggled on foot around the villages and farms of these coastlands. You have walked miles on those poor feet of yours. The Lord only knows what pains you have suffered for the sake of the gospel, just in going from place to place. But there is more. I am not just offering you a place in a house, a fireside to sit by, an opportunity to teach, and an end to your wandering. I am also asking you to take the Gospel of our Lord with you. There are not many of the Kingdom there. Perhaps your coming might bring some more."

Hippolytus was stunned. He had heard of Britain, of course, but never in his life had he thought of actually going there.

"But Britain?" replied Hippolytus at last. "It's so far."

"From where?" responded his bishop. "We know from experience just how unsafe these shores can be."

"But how will I get there? And has it not rebelled against our Emperor?" Hippolytus was searching for questions, anything to delay giving an answer.

"It might be a long journey," said the bishop, smiling. "But most of it is by ship. Glaucus imports many of his dyes from here, and so it is a simple matter for you to accompany the next shipment to Britain. And yes, it is true that the provinces of Britain declare loyalty to another emperor, but that is all politics. Trade continues. The ships move. Things are bought and sold in the markets and shops. Lydia tells me that little has changed."

Bishop John stopped and looked hard at Hippolytus. Then he said, gently: "My son, don't you think that you might deserve this, even just a little? You have labored hard and suffered much. You carry in your body the marks of your faith. I know that the little congregations around the coastal towns will miss you, but it is time to pass that ministry to another."

"My Lord," said Hippolytus, "I am weary with travel and cannot give you a good answer. Let me sleep awhile, and pray for guidance. I will give you a sure reply tonight after prayers."

"That is a good answer. I shall wait for your word," said the bishop, and as he did so, he knew in his heart what that word would be.

It was the custom of the house, as it was in some many houses around the Middle Sea, that lunch would be followed by an afternoon nap. In the bishop's house that daytime sleep would be followed by prayers, and then whatever work needed to be done while the daylight lasted. Timothy took Hippolytus to a little sleeping cell upstairs a room with a little hard bed and a chest for clothes.

Hippolytus did not bother to undress. He simply lay down on the bed. His feet were sore and his legs ached, and he could feel the tiredness swirling around in his head. He closed his eyes, said a little prayer and went to sleep.

After a couple of hours he woke, quite refreshed. The food and the sleep had done him a lot of good. The house was quiet but would soon be waking. It was the custom of the house to prepare a big pot of vegetable stew every day, and from it to feed those in need. It would be a while before the bell summoned him, and so he knelt down on the hard floor, cleared his mind and began to pray.

Hippolytus found the act of kneeling difficult which was why he continued to do it. Many people stood to pray, but Hippolytus had learned the discipline of kneeling when he was a student and had carried on, even after the injuries that he had suffered to his legs, perhaps to remind himself that the life of a priest was not an easy one and had already cost him a great deal.

Presently, the bell downstairs rang and Hippolytus struggled to his feet, knowing his decision. He straightened up and stretched, reached for his staff and hobbled down to join Timothy and the bishop.

They were already in the chapel by the time that Hippolytus arrived. This was a large chamber that had been created by knocking down all of the interior walls of one wing of the house to make one long, wide and lofty room. The walls were decorated with paintings (which were very bright but otherwise not very good) and there were benches against the two long sides. At one end, a table had been placed against the wall and, by its side, there was a chair facing the room.

Along with Jacob and Susanna there were also some women and men of the town whom Hippolytus knew to be regular members of the Christian community. The group sat in silence and rose when Bishop John came in, waiting until he had taken the chair at the far end of the room. Prayers and a short reading from the Bible followed. Then the company recited a psalm together and Bishop John blessed them and left. His departure marked the beginning of a certain amount of quiet chatter in the congregation but the two priests, along with Jacob and Susanna, did not remain for it. Instead they followed Bishop John out and crossed the courtyard to the kitchen where the next task awaited them.

The kitchen was already hot. The day was still warm, the lamps had been lit and burned with a fierce blue flame, and a fire glowed redly in the heart of the oven. It was a large room that had once served the needs of a considerable household.

This was Susanna's domain. There was a long food preparation bench along one wall, and shelves stacked with metal and clay pots. Working in silence, she went to a variety of baskets set under the bench and pulled out garlic, carrots, leeks, onions, turnips, some fresh parsley, a green cabbage from that morning's market, some barley and last of all, a pot of red beans that had been soaking in water. They all set to chopping vegetables, while Susanna took a deep pan, set on top of the cooking range and let it heat. For half an hour or so, there was no talking, only the sounds of chopping and frying. But then, it was done, and a pot of bean stew was simmering away on top of the range.

The rear door of the kitchen opened into an alleyway behind the house. The door itself had been cut in two so that the top half could be opened while the bottom remained closed. Timothy went and opened the top half of the door and there, in the alley, waiting patiently, was a line of men, women and children, all with empty bowls, ready to be fed.

"Peace be with you," called Timothy to the gathering. Some answered. Some didn't. Some just muttered.

"Now, who's ready to be fed with the Lord's food?"

The response was somewhat louder.

For the next half an hour or so, Timothy and Hippolytus doled out the stew into the bowls, while the women handed out hunks of bread that were in a wicker basket just by the door. When everyone had been fed, and the few cheeky souls who had gone to the back of the line, hoping for a second helping, had been shooed away, Timothy closed the door, and turned to Jacob and Susanna, making the sign of the cross over them in blessing. They then took a helping of the stew each and went off to their own part of the house.

The two priests ladled the rest of the stew into a smaller pot, and carried it into the dining room, along with some bread and a pitcher of watered wine. Bishop John was already waiting for them. He said grace and they settled down to eat.

After a time, when the most immediate demands of their hunger had been met, John turned to Hippolytus and asked: "Have you thought more on the offer that I made to you earlier?"

Hippolytus smiled: "My Lord, the word came clear to me when I was at prayer earlier. I am comfortable here. I do not mind the long walks between the little villages that I take all the time, and I love the folk that I meet, whether on the road or in the little churches of the hills and bays. To me, it has become an easy, and even a pleasant ministry. I do miss the world of learning. The peasants, the fisherfolk and the dye workers that fill my days have little time for learning—whether Plato or Moses—but they are kind and generous people, despite the hardness of their lives.

"That is why, my Lord, I will accept your offer. Not for Plato or Moses, but because I have done all I can here. It is time for another to walk those dusty roads. I feel the call of the Lord to Britain, and I feel it quite strongly. I think that those children, that family, and perhaps more people besides, have need of me. So I shall go."

Bishop John beamed.

"Thank you Hippolytus. One of Glaucus' ships has been tarrying here in port for this news. How soon can you leave?"

"Now, if you wish," replied Hippolytus. "My family has no interest in me. To them, I am dead. I have no goods to pack, no farewells to say, except in this place. I only wait for a fair wind."

"Let's take a day longer. If you are to be a tutor, you will need to dress as one. I will arrange for some new clothes for you. And, I think, for some books. You no longer have any, do you?"

"No, My Lord. I sold them all and gave the money to the poor."

"Well, you will need some now. And, I think, tomorrow, if you do not think it too sinful, we might send you to the baths for a good scrub!"

And so it was, that before dawn two days later, Hippolytus, the bishop and Timothy made their way to the docks of Andriake where Glaucus' ship, the *Pegasus*, was waiting. Two chests containing Hippolytus' new goods had already been taken on board. He had been scrubbed clean of the deep grime of the road and the lingering smell of fish and he wore a new robe.

He briefly embraced the bishop and his friend, and then turned, walked up the gangplank, and into a new life.

CHAPTER TWO

CAPTAIN COLOSSUS

WAITING FOR HIM AT the top of the gangplank was a busy-looking, red-haired man. A waxed tablet was tucked into the crook of his left arm and he held a stylus in his right hand. Where his left hand should have been was a stump covered in a little woolen sock. There was a list scratched into the wax, and as Hippolytus came aboard, the man asked him: "Are you Hippocrates, the Christian?"

"My name is Hippolytus."

"Oh, I had it differently. Never mind. I'll change it here, if you don't mind."

The man crossed out some letters, and added some others. Then he looked up at Hippolytus, gave a little grin and said: "Welcome aboard, priest. They call me Dexter. I look after the passengers, which in this case is just you. What do we call you?"

"Hippolytus will do nicely, or Father Hippolytus if you wish to be proper."

"Very good. Let me show you where you'll be. Have you ever sailed before?"

"Yes. I sailed to Caesarea once, and then home from there. I'm afraid that I wasn't a good sailor. I was sick a lot."

"That's what happens the first time. You get used to it so much that one day, you find yourself in a big blow, with the ship jumping and racing through the waves and all you can feel is the thrill of it."

"I look forward to it," said Hippolytus, smiling.

"Now, I expect that when you were on the Caesarea run, you were on a coasting ship and slept ashore a lot," remarked Dexter. "You'll find that the *Pegasus* is a completely different kind of ship. Those coasting ships are little floating tubs. When the wind blows, they hoist sail. When it doesn't, they row. Master Glaucus built the *Pegasus* partly for the trade and partly for his own use. The family sailed to Britain on it. That means that her hull is specially braced to resist those big seas outside the Pillars of Hercules, that it's fully decked to keep her dry below, and that there's a good sized cabin designed for the master and his family here in the deckhouse in the stern—that's the back end, sir. That's where you will be. We have the mistress' instructions to keep you comfortable and out of harm's way, and to feed you well! Normally we expect passengers to bring their own food, but you're a part of the household now, sir. It's nothing fancy, mind. We take our food at dawn, noon and dusk—on the deck in good weather, and wherever we can in a blow. Now sir, if you will, follow me. Can you manage on the deck, sir—I mean with your legs?" asked Dexter, kindly.

"If you can do get about this ship one-handed, I can surely do it with my bandy legs," grinned Hippolytus.

It was a brave statement, and more than once he needed Dexter to steady him as he nearly pitched over, especially which the ship gave a little lurch.

Dexter led him a few paces across the deck to the stern which was filled by what looked like a little house with a flat roof. The roof served as a kind of upper deck and, in the dawn gloom, Hippolytus could make out the enormous handles of the steering oars. The cabin to which Dexter led Hippolytus was surprisingly large. It was certainly much bigger than his sleeping cell at the bishop's house. The chests containing his belongings had been stowed against one wall and securely lashed there with a length of rope. There were windows, of sorts, which let in the growing light through thin panes of alabaster, a hanging lantern for a night light, along with a table, fixed into one of the rear bulkheads beneath a long, alabaster-paned window. In the middle of the little cabin, suspended from the roof by four stout ropes, hung a long, narrow box as long as a man with sidewalls two handspans high and filled with bedding.

"Is that where I sleep," asked Hippolytus, genuinely curious.

"Oh, yes. No beds on this boat and you have the best berth," laughed Dexter. "Here at sea, a fixed bed's not the best place to sleep. You move with the ship, and if there's a blow, you'll get thrown out. Better get used to sleeping in one of these. When the boat swings, you don't."

"Will it hold me?" ventured Hippolytus.

"It holds the Captain, and if it holds him, it will hold most men," Dexter replied with a wry smile.

It was full dawn now. Bright light seeped in through the portholes and the doorway.

"I'd best get moving," said Dexter. "The Captain will want to talk to me before we get under way, and he'll be in a hurry to hoist sail. He's a born sailor. He hates hanging about in port. I'm sure that he'll be here to see you soon. Best for you to stay here until we're at sea. You're not used to our ways yet and we don't need you underfoot."

Hippolytus realized that Dexter was trying to be tactful. In fact, the captain would be offering sacrifice to the gods for a fair voyage, and it was known that Christians did not approve of such things. It reminded him, just the same, of his own duty to pray, and so, using one of his sea chests as a rest for his elbows, he sank down onto his knees. He stayed that way for long minutes, his lips moving silently in prayer, until he felt the ship quicken and move.

As life came into the vessel, he heard the cries of the sailors. The faint rocking motion of the ship became more regularly up and down, as the unfurled sail caught the dawn breeze, carrying the *Pegasus* out of Andriake's little bay and into the paths of the Middle Sea.

Once the ship's course was firmly set, Hippolytus heard a polite, but firm, knock at the door. Before he had even called out, it opened and any light that came through it was blocked by a vast man squeezing his way into a cabin that suddenly felt very tiny. The man was as wide as he was tall , and mostly made of muscle. He had a bald head, a round broken-nosed face, and when he opened his mouth to speak, two front teeth were missing.

"So, you are the priest," he said, not unkindly. "Allow me to introduce myself. I am the captain of this ship and I am sometimes called Rhodius, that is 'the Rhodian.' I come from the island of Rhodes and, if you know the story, there's a really big statue of some old god, that they call 'the Colossus,' collapsed by the harbor. The sailors all know it well and, for some reason, they prefer to call me after that. I'm either Rhodius or Captain Colossus, whichever you like."

Rhodius' voice was surprisingly soft for a man of his size.

"Which do you like better?" asked Hippolytus.

The Captain grinned. "Colossus, of course. It's good for morale. Mine, mostly. So what do I call you, priest?"

"Oh, please, never call me 'priest.' It gives people the wrong idea. They think of temples and sacrificing animals. I don't do any of that. Just call me Hippolytus. That is my name and, unless you have Christians on board who have need of me, I can hardly be a priest. In any event, Captain, I do prefer to be called by my name."

"Fair enough," replied Rhodius. "We have all sorts on this ship. Sailors are a superstitious lot at the best of times. That means that we like to be able to talk to all of the gods, especially when the weather looks foul.

"Now Dexter should have given you basic instructions about the ship. There are only a few rules. The most important of these is that I am the captain, and when we are at sea, I am the law. We don't have council meetings or votes. What we have is me and, when I give an order, I want it obeyed and not debated. It's not because I like the sound of my own voice but because the sea does not forgive mistakes. This rule applies to everyone, including you, if the need comes. It may not, but if I call out for all aboard to help that will mean you.

"Two other things that you need to remember. Keep to your cabin in bad weather. My men will be too busy on the deck to look out for you. In really bad weather, I'll send someone in to lash you into your cot so you won't fall out. Lastly, and this is really important, never leave a flame uncovered. You will notice that everywhere the master has provided lanterns. We do not use oil, but good wax candles and, once they are lit, they are to go behind their covers. A fire at sea is a terrible thing and it can begin so easily. That's it. They're the rules. You can take your meals in here or on the deck with us, but you eat the same as us. When we're at sea for a few weeks it might get a bit boring, but it's better than going hungry."

"Captain," replied Hippolytus. "Just one question. I completely accept your authority, but surely all of the crew here must? Are not these sailors the slaves of the owner?"

"Oh, Great Poseidon, no. Unless you're the navy, you can't have slaves at sea. Sailoring's a dangerous living. No captain can rely on a slave crew. They'd sooner hide than take risks and they're no good in a fight. In fact they are downright dangerous because it's likely they'll change sides. Or they might mutiny anyway, take the vessel and go pirate themselves. A ship is a tight little kingdom, sir, and we can't have even the sniff of a rebellion."

"One more thing," asked Hippolytus, quietly. "Please tell me a little of the journey. I know that we are going to Britain, and it's a long way. How long will we be at sea?"

"It's a fair question. This is a blue-water ship, sir. We sail the open sea, rather than hug the coast like the little coastal freighters you might already have been on. So from here, we are sailing to Sicily. That should take between seven and fifteen days depending on the wind. We'll stop at Syracuse. That's a main port on the east coast, and get in fresh supplies. That will take a few days. Then another ten to fifteen days to New Carthage in Spain. We'll have four or five in port to get our land legs back, then a quick run to Gades to get ready for our long sail up to Britain to Portus Adurni. If all goes well, that should take us about eighteen days. I've done it in fifteen, but the winds and the sea have to be right. It's not the Middle Sea, out there. It's ocean and much less predictable. Then it's another few days sailing up to Petuaria, and that's where we finish. All up, we should be two months, wind and weather permitting. It's a big enough ship, the *Pegasus*, but it's not that big. We'll be seeing plenty of each other by the time we get there—gods' willing—oh, pardon me, I was forgetting, you only have the one."

He laughed at his own, poor, joke and Hippolytus, kindly, joined in.

"Now, I must go and captain this ship. We are coming out of sheltered waters now and into the main shipping channels. It may get a little bouncy. I'll send you in a bucket, just in case."

Colossus left and Hippolytus, suddenly a little queasy with the increasing swell, sat down heavily on one of his chests. The bucket arrived just in time.

Hippolytus stayed in his cabin for two days. On deck, the days were beautiful, bright, breezy with a fair wind from the north and clear skies. In Hippolytus' cabin, it was a terrible ordeal with the ship moving up and down with such apparent violence that Hippolytus could neither keep his feet on the ground nor his breakfast inside him. From time to time, he dozed off and that give him some relief. He was aware of Dexter's occasional visits to empty his bucket, swab his room, wash him down a little and feed him a little thin, wheaten porridge.

He woke up on the evening of the second day, after an afternoon doze, no longer feeling ill but feeling hungry instead. He swung out of his cot and stood up, balancing on the deck as it moved a little. He made his way, a little carefully across the room, opened the door and stepped out onto the deck. He was immediately conscious of the clean smell of the sea, the forward motion of the boat as it cut through the water, and the busyness of the crew around about him. He also became conscious of the fact that, because he had been stuck in his cabin for a couple of days without a wash and that he had been really ill, he smelt quite bad.

As he stood there, more than a little aware of his own stink, he felt the presence of someone behind him. He turned and saw Captain Colossus standing there, with a beaming smile all over his face.

"She's a beauty, isn't she?" said the captain, meaning the ship. "Fully one hundred feet from stem to stern, made from good Macedonian pine and solid oak. Sails sweetly, answers the helm like a dream. Turns on a coin. A lot of captains would give an arm to sail a ship like this."

Hippolytus would have liked to agree, but his view of the forward half of the ship was blocked by the vast mainsail, puffed full of the wind that sped them onwards. He chose tact instead.

"She seems very beautiful," he replied.

"Oh, indeed. And fast. Since we left Andriake we have had a good northerly wind which has brought us across the Aegean and, from sometime tonight, we will be in the open waters between Greece, Italy and Africa. We might be in Syracuse early, if the wind holds, although you can never entirely trust the sea. Only a fool takes her for granted. When we are out here, we are in the hands of the gods, or God, begging your pardon, F— Hippolytus. Now I will get Dexter to come and see to you. Now that you're up and about, you need to meet everyone, and, if you'll pardon me again sir, have a wash."

Almost as soon as the Captain had gone, Dexter arrived, pinching his nose with his only hand.

"Oooh, you don't half smell, sir. If you'll follow me up forward we have a special kind of bath on board the *Pegasus*."

As he made his way—still a little unsteadily—under the great taut, wind-filled sail, he saw the forward part of the ship for the first time. A second mast stood on the deck, its sail yet to be raised. Where the stern end of the ship ended with a square deckhouse, the forward part tapered to an elegant prow, at the tip of which was fixed the image of a flying horse, the Pegasus of Greek mythology. There were half a dozen crewmen, all apparently busy. They were all barefoot, brown from the sun, and wearing loincloths.

Hippolytus had been wondering what this special kind of bath might be. He thought that, given the nature of the ship, there might be some kind of tub or even more elaborate way of washing involving hot, cold and warm water. He found out soon enough.

"Bath time for the passenger, mateys," Dexter called out to the crewmen.

Then he said to Hippolytus, "Stand right there in the middle of the deck, if you would, sir. And try not to move too much."

Meanwhile, the crewman had fished out six buckets, filled them with sea water, and as Hippolytus tried to stay upright on the deck, he was doused with bucket after bucket of cold sea water.

It felt like it had gone on forever, but it was only a few minutes. After they had finished, he was wet through, and his tunic was wet through, and the bandages on his legs were wet through too.

For the crew, this was a risky moment. This was something that they did to passengers as a kind of welcome. Some passengers emerged from their drenching shouting and angry. Others were polite, but clearly felt ashamed and just as angry.

Hippolytus felt completely alive.

"Oh, that's just like being baptized," he laughed. "Do it again!"

Once more, six buckets were emptied on the now beaming priest.

"There you go," said Dexter. "The sun will dry you off soon enough."

"Not quick enough," replied Hippolytus, and he struggled out of his stained and sodden tunic and stood there in his loincloth and bandages.

The crewmen crowded around him and were soon joined by others, all asking him questions: questions about his health, his story, his journey, his background.

Two of the crew hung back a little. When a roar from the captain scattered everyone back to their jobs, these two remained, and shyly approached Hippolytus.

"If you please, Father," said one.

"We heard you was a Christian priest," said the other.

"Well, I am," said Hippolytus. "To those who need one. Otherwise, I am just Hippolytus."

"Well, Father, that's the thing," said the first. "Hooter and me, well, we're both Alexandrians and we grew up in the church. We might be sailors, sir, but we're Christians too."

"Hooter?" asked Hippolytus.

"That's me," said the second. He had a big nose, fleshy and red, with nostrils so cavernous that a small bird might have made a nest in it. "And this is Halfear, on account of him losing a part of his ear fighting pirates a few years ago." Sure enough, Halfear was missing half of his left ear, with a matching scar continuing on his left cheek.

"But what are your actual names?" asked Hippolytus.

"You mean our land names. We don't use them on board ship, sir. It's easier and quicker to use the names we make up for each other. We each have our own, see, and so when the orders are given, we knows exactly who's doing what."

"Well then, Hooter, Halfear, what can I do for you?"

"We'd be ever so pleased if you did us the bread and the wine, sir. Not every day, but we'll have a lot of Sundays at sea," replied Halfear.

"I would be doing it for myself, anyway, so yes, of course I'll celebrate the Thanksgiving with you. We can use my cabin. There's plenty of space."

"Thank you sir. Father. Thank you ever so much. We'd best be on our work now. Or the captain will give us a hiding."

Halfear and Hooter went off to their stations and Hippolytus turned to go to his own cabin. Almost immediately, he was joined by Dexter, who took his elbow, in case his sea legs were not quite steady enough. As Dexter guided Hippolytus back to the big deckhouse, he asked quietly, "What did those two want?"

"They want me to celebrate our Eucharist with them on the Sundays that we are at sea," answered Hippolytus.

"Is that some Christian thing? I thought those two were a bit different, begging your pardon, sir."

"Yes," explained Hippolytus. "It is our custom to come together on Sundays to share some bread and wine together, not as a regular meal as you or I might do, but to set the bread and the wine apart to be the body and the blood of our Lord."

"What?" Dexter seemed incredulous. "Body and blood? That doesn't sound the thing at all sir!"

"What do you know of our ways, Dexter?" Hippolytus asked gently.

"Oh, not much really. I've never had much interest until now and, besides, it was illegal to be a Christian until only a couple of years back."

They were at the cabin by now. Hippolytus felt completely dry, except where the wet bandages and loincloth still clung to his body.

"Should I explain it to you, some time?" he asked Dexter.

"I should like that, sir," said Dexter. "Especially the bit about the bread and the wine. That's got me fair beat."

"I'll do my best," Hippolytus replied.

CHAPTER THREE

THE STORM

Once settled on the ship and in his cabin, Hippolytus had not been idle. He opened and explored his two chests of new belongings. One contained a variety of clothes, including a white, woolen tunic. This was especially important because this was the uniform for his new job and showed to all the world that he was a teacher. There was also, tucked at the bottom, a small purse of good gold coins. The other chest was much heavier because it was full of books, all in the new form, with pages written on both sides, stitched together along the spine, and bound with glue. There were at least twenty different works in that chest, as many as Hippolytus had seen together in one place since he had been a student in Caesarea.

He spent much of his time at sea reading in his cabin in a kind of hanging chair that the sailors had rigged up for him. Dexter and Colossus dropped by from time to time for a chat, and Hooter and Halfear began to develop their own timid friendship with him. He took his meals with the crew, sitting on the deck in the forward section and eating freshly caught fish, or bread with cheese and dried fruit, all washed down with watered wine. He also made himself familiar with the ship. There was not that much to it. On the deck, there was the deckhouse at the stern in which he slept. It had a flat roof which served as the command deck for the captain and the helmsman. It was reached by a steep stairway that could almost have been a ladder. Hippolytus was careful not to go up there without invitation. If the cabin was his little realm, its roof belonged to Colossus and Deadeye, the helmsman.

Below decks was different. The single hold was like a vast treasure cave. The cargo was stored there: jar upon jar of olive oil, fish sauce and wine sat tightly packed together and cushioned with straw. In one part of the hold, hidden in plain sight, there were little multi-colored glass bottles: tiny flasks of raw dye, more valuable than gold. Swirling around it all, like heavy incense, there was an aroma of spices: pepper, cumin, saffron, cardamom, coriander and thyme. A half-deck above the cargo towards the ship's bows, served as the galley where the crew's meals were prepared and eaten if they couldn't eat on deck. It was also where they slept. Right at the back, against the stern of the ship and just below the deckhouse, were two cabins: those of Colossus and Dexter.

The sailing was swift and fair. After only seven more days they came to Syracuse, a large and ancient port city on the island of Sicily. It was to be a short visit. The ship was in port only to take on fresh water and food for the long trip across the Middle Sea, and so the crew were given a day's shore leave, but in two groups so that half of the crew would always be on hand on the ship. Hooter and Halfear arranged it that they were on different watches and could take turns looking after Hippolytus. Hippolytus liked the ship, and liked being on it, but not enough to stay there while the ship was in port. It was a famous city that he had read about in his books, so he was keen to explore it.

The first thing that he was aware of when he walked down the gangplank and stepped off the ship was that the ground was disturbingly stable. It did not shift or rock beneath his feet, but instead remained firm. It was he who felt the wobble, and it was Halfear who had to catch him, and reassure him that his land legs would be back soon enough.

"You know," he said to Halfear, as they pushed their way through the busy docks. "I have read so much about Syracuse in Thucydides' *History of the Peloponnesian War*. It's rather exciting to be here. You know, Plato came here too for a while, to give advice to the tyrant Dionysius."

"That's good sir. Them tyrants needs to hear a good word or two now and then," replied Halfear, smiling with the smile of one who had barely understood a word of what had just been said to him. "There's a church here Father," he continued, "and a group of our folk if you'd like to meet them."

Hippolytus was suddenly more excited. He was so used to being on his own that he forgot that there were other Christian communities with other Christian priests in other parts of the Empire and even far beyond it.

"I should like that very much," he said.

"This way then," said Halfear.

In the end, Hippolytus did not spend his two days ashore in Syracuse sightseeing, but with the Christian community. They were used to guests, because Syracuse was such a great port city, and treated them generously.

Like Myra, Syracuse had its own bishop. Hippolytus did not know him, nor had he even heard his name, but the bishop's house was opened to him. Although Hippolytus might have preferred to sleep on the ship, this kindness ensured that he ate better than he did at sea. And he was seldom without company. Two days of talking was more than enough for him. It was with a sigh of relief that, at sunset on the second day, he returned to the *Pegasus*, and the daily company of the crew.

Wind and weather continued to be kind, and the next stage of the journey took them around the southern tip of Sicily and then almost due west in a straight line to New Carthage in Spain. It was a long way, but now they were well provisioned and ready for the first of their two long hauls across the open sea. After a couple of days of clear sailing the wind's regularity ceased and it now often blew in from the west so that the ship had to change course constantly in order to make progress.

Hippolytus was happily unaware of this. He served as Hooter and Halfear's priest and, before long, Dexter asked if he could come along too, if only just to listen and learn. Colossus also made time, when he could, to sit and talk with Hippolytus, whose company he really enjoyed, not so much for his religion, but for the fund of stories his learning had supplied him.

As day slid into day, Hippolytus soaked in new experiences as he made new friends. The youngest member of the crew was an Arab from beyond Egypt. He had grown up sailing fishing boats on the Red Sea and the crew called him Perseus, or "the Persian" because he did not wear loincloths like everyone else on the ship, but loose trousers tied at the waist and ankles as the Persians do. One evening, as Hippolytus stood at the prow of the ship, watching the sun begin its descent to the horizon, Perseus came up behind him and said softly:

"Sir, may I ask you something?"

"Well, of course," said Hippolytus. "People are doing that all the time."

"Well, it's about your legs, sir. I saw that, even when they were wet through, you would not take off your bandages."

"That is true," replied Hippolytus. "My legs are…damaged. Perhaps it is a point of vanity, but I prefer to keep them covered."

"Well, sir," continued Perseus. "Where I come from, and even further east, men wear trousers like these. It's what we always wore on the fishing boat. It's more practical than a loincloth. They don't come loose and get in the way. Why don't you wear them, rather than those bandages, sir? They will be ever so much easier to get on and off, and to get dry when they are wet."

"Trousers?" Hippolytus was incredulous. "But that's what barbarians wear to ride horses!"

"Well, sir, I don't know much about that," responded Perseus. I just know that they seem to be sensible things to wear. And even if barbarians wear them, sir, well, I wear them. Am I a barbarian? Well, maybe I am, but does that make me a bad person?"

"But where would I get them?"

"Well, that's not so hard. Sailors sew, sir. We have to. There's a lot of it in our line of work. If you can get me the linen, sir, I can make them."

"But..." began Hippolytus, and then stopped.

He suddenly realized how foolish he was being. His mind went back twenty years, to the day in Caesarea when his teacher had laughed at something Hippolytus had said in answer to a question and then went on to say, "My dear Hippolytus, you think that the way to wisdom is to understand new things in an old way. It is not. The way to wisdom is to understand old things in a new way."

Those words had always stayed with him, but their full meaning now became clear.

He would wear trousers.

This stretch of sailing was much harder work for the crew. Both sails were up, and Colossus was constantly changing the way in which they were set, as well as the direction of the ship. This was so that they could make progress against a wind that seemed determined to push them back.

After fifteen days they sighted the coast of Spain a little north of where they meant to be and coasted down to the port.

New Carthage was, like Syracuse, a large port. The city sat on a headland overlooking a deep lagoon, although the port itself was on the seafront.

Colossus did not like to sail the ship into port, but to row it in so that he had better control of the vessel. The *Pegasus* stored long oars for the purpose. A pilot guided the ship to a jetty where it was tied up and secured. Around it crowded all of the vessels that traded at the port. There were large, stout ships to carry the silver ingots mined near there to the imperial mints; as well as smaller ships that carried pottery and fish sauce and great piles of dry grass. This puzzled Hippolytus, and he asked Dexter why dry grass was such a thing in New Carthage.

"Well, sir, this whole area is famous for it," explained Dexter. "It's a particular kind of grass called esparto, and it can be used to make all sorts of things: ropes, baskets, bags even shoes."

By late morning, he was walking down the gangplank with Hooter. As he staggered his way onto land, Hippolytus heard the voices around him. There were people calling out offering rooms in their houses to travelers, people selling roast chestnuts, people offering to hire out horses, people offering themselves as workers to unload ships. As he stood listening, Hippolytus realized that this was the first city that he had ever been in where the only language that he could hear was Latin.

Hippolytus had spoken Greek for all of his life. He had learned Latin, as all educated young men did, but he had not had much reason to speak it for a few years, and so his ears and mouth were rusty in its use.

"Well," he thought to himself. "I suppose that there is no better way of getting back into a language than going to the marketplace and bargaining for things."

"Have you been here much before," he asked Hooter.

"This will be the fifth time. It's my third run to Britain, and we always stop here on the way out and the way back."

"Where's the marketplace?"

"Oh, follow me, Father, it's this way." Hooter headed off into the crowd and Hippolytus followed.

Finding the market was surprisingly easy. This was a Roman town with straight streets that led to the great market square in the middle of the city.

It was about midday when he reached the marketplace. There was color and noise everywhere. As was the custom in all cities, trades stuck together. Hippolytus and Hooter made their way through past sweet-smelling spice booths, a clutch of cheesemongers, fruitmongers, pork butchers and wine merchants. There were booths on which wares made from esparto grass were on display, and a dozen stalls where eager sellers pointed out the many advantages of owning one of the dozen sad-eyed slaves that sat shackled to a post. Finally, Hippolytus found what he sought: a cloth merchant with a bolt of Egyptian linen. Now he had to test his Latin.

"How much per foot?" he asked in a sentence that he had been practicing in his head since he woke up.

The merchant named a truly huge price.

Hippolytus was practiced in the ways of bargaining.

"Thank you," he said. "But I was looking for something a lot less expensive."

"It's very good cloth, sir. It's the best that Egypt can produce: grown on the banks of the Nile, spun and woven in the mills of Pelusium and then brought all the way from Alexandria to this very shop. You'll get none better." The merchant was insistent and persuasive, but Hippolytus had heard it before.

"I'm sure that it is all that you say," he replied, "but at that price, I could barely afford an inch. And besides, I hear the Spanish linen is very good too."

They laughed, and the real haggling began.

Half an hour later, Hippolytus walked away with Hooter following, carrying his newly purchased linen. He was most pleased. Not only had he arrived at a price that was a little less than he thought that he might have had to pay, but his Latin proved up to the task, and he had even sharpened it a little during the discussion.

The ship stayed in New Carthage for four days. Once he had his linen Hippolytus was not much interested in going ashore until he had an idea. Taking Hooter, he went back to the market where he found just what he was looking for: shoes made from woven esparto grass. He had seen many of the locals wearing these in the markets and down at the port. The soles were strong like thick rope, while the uppers covered his feet and heels. These were far better than the flimsy slippers that he had been wearing, and, using one of the gold coins from his trove (a whole gold coin!), he bought not just one pair that fitted him well, but as many as he could get. In the end, he went back to the *Pegasus* laden with six pairs of new shoes. That would last him a very long time.

When the *Pegasus* finally put to sea, Hippolytus had a whole new look. Perseus had made him a pair of linen trousers, and with the new shoes, he looked very different from the Hippolytus who had come on board four weeks before. He rather liked his trousers and shoes and they made dressing in the morning a whole lot quicker and easier. He had also increased his small congregation. He had begun with Hooter and Halfear. Dexter had also taken to dropping in on the group, as well as two of the other sailors, Hamhands and Squint. They all preferred to use their ship names and so Hippolytus never learned what their actual names were. Hamhands and Squint were not Christians, but they liked Hippolytus so much that they became interested, and so he became a priest after all. He sat with his little group on the deck, in their off hours, answering their questions and telling them stories.

It was a two day run down the coast from New Carthage to the Pillars of Hercules, the strait that separated the Middle Sea from the ocean. On the second evening, Colossus invited Hippolytus to dinner. The Captain normally took his meals alone. It was not that he disliked his crew—he liked them very much—but he was not one of them. It was both his view, and the custom of the sea, that since the captain's word had to be obeyed swiftly and without question, he could not become too friendly with his crew. He demanded respect and obedience, not love and affection.

Colossus had a low table set up on his deck—the roof of Hippolytus' cabin—and some throw cushions on the floor so that they could both lie down to eat, as civilized people did in Roman times. Baconbones, the ship's cook, brought them up a steady stream of dishes from the galley far below.

"I took the opportunity to stock up when we were in port. Let's eat it while it's good and fresh," he had said, by way of invitation to Hippolytus. The meal began with bowls of bitter Spanish olives and sliced boiled eggs in fish sauce, and before he began, Hippolytus crossed himself and said a quiet word of grace.

"Was that some Christian thing?" asked Colossus, picking up a tiny olive with massive fingers.

"It is our custom to give thanks whenever we eat, whatever we eat," replied Hippolytus. "One can never be too grateful for the gifts that God supplies us."

"Well, your God has been good to us. Or the sea gods have. We've made good time, and the weather has been kind. It won't last, of course. If we don't get foul weather before we leave the Middle Sea, we're sure to strike some on the ocean. The sailing out there is very different. The tides are bigger, the seas are bigger, and the weather is bigger. Please keep giving thanks, and maybe that will all work to our advantage instead of sending us to the bottom of the sea."

The courses came and went, all small plates of things rather than big bowls of food. As they ate, Colossus and Hippolytus talked about sailing, about studying, about being a priest, about being a captain.

Colossus, it turned out, had been born to the sea, as so many sailors were. Coming from an island, he had sailed since he was a boy—fishing boats, small coastal trading vessels, even the run from Alexandria to Rome and back on a huge grain tanker, twice the size of the *Pegasus*. The *Pegasus* was his first real command. Glaucus, who owned the ship, had begun his trading career buying and selling goods in the small ports of the eastern Middle Sea. It was then that he had met Colossus and learned to trust his sailing instincts. He had sailed for Glaucus ever since, and when Glaucus had the *Pegasus* built, it was only natural that he offer the command to Colossus. A child of the sea in so many ways, Colossus had a home in Rhodes where he tried to spend the winter months with his wife and growing family.

"It's not a safe life, though," he said to Hippolytus as they finished with a bowl of chestnuts. "Any trip could be my last. And there is a change coming." He sniffed deeply. "Oh yes. It's in the air. Best go below, Father. We'll have a blow before the dawn comes."

Whether it was the captain's words, or that he really felt it, Hippolytus thought that he too could sense a change: a stillness in the air, and then a breath of wind, not from the west this time, but from the east. He went below, said his prayers, climbed into his cot and went to sleep.

He woke up suddenly in the predawn darkness. His cot was swinging from side to side as he felt the ship lurch through the rough waters. He could hear the rain pelting on the roof of his cabin and, more distantly, the cries of the crew as they called to each other, shortening the sail, and keeping the ship from going over on its side. He dared not get up. He did not trust either his balance or his legs on the tilting floor. Instead, he stayed just where he was, and did the only thing that he could. He prayed.

By dawn, the *Pegasus* seemed to have settled into some stability, running before the wind. Hippolytus ventured to swing out of his cot and stand up straight. He found that, so long as he held on to something, he would be all right. Step by step, he made his way across the cabin and opened the door. Immediately, he felt himself pelted with rain. In the dull grey light, he could see that the Pegasus was speeding through the waves at a rate that he had never seen before. The big square mainsail had been hauled up so that only half of it was in use, and that was bellied with wind. He heard a voice above him and looked up.

Colossus was calling down to him. He was standing, clinging to the railing of his own deck, and his face shone with a fierce joy.

"Beautiful, isn't it. I love a breeze like this. It's taking us where we want to go. You'd best go back inside, Father. I'll have some food sent in, by and by."

In fact, he stayed in there for two days. He read, slept, prayed, ate the food that came in to him, and waited until he could be back on deck. He missed the great spectacle of the Pillars of Hercules, and Calpe Rock, and when he finally came back on deck, the ship was far out on the vast and choppy ocean.

"Come on up here and see," Colossus called to Hippolytus The priest struggled up the steep stairs, clung to the rail and looked up. The rain had gone and the sky was now clear. They were a little sheltered from the east wind that had brought them so far so quickly, but Colossus still headed westwards rather than hug the coast. He explained that he had intended to stop at the port of Gades for one last rest before pushing on to the far north, but they had made such a swift passage, and the wind seemed so good, that he decided to press on.

"Then why are we still heading west?" asked Hippolytus?

"We need sea room," answered the Captain.

"What?"

"At some point, we are probably going to hit a storm that will come to us from the west. That will push us towards the coast. The closer we are to the coast, the more danger we're in of striking a reef, running aground or being smashed against cliffs. So I want to get well out to sea before we head north."

"I thought that we just had a storm," said Hippolytus.

"That was not storm. A good wind, yes. Tell me, were you sick?" asked Colossus.

"No." Hippolytus was secretly rather proud of that.

"Then I make my case. Your belly will tell you when we hit a storm."

"Is a storm so much worse?"

"Oh, yes. Even the mild ones."

"Well, let us hope and pray that we are spared the experience."

It was not to be. Four days later, the storm came.

The day began well enough. For days, the wind had come consistently from the south which enabled them to make good time. During the night, Colossus judged that they had enough sea room and changed course to head north. As they did, they picked up speed since they now had the wind directly behind them.

As Hippolytus emerged from his cabin for breakfast, Colossus called him up to his own deck to join him. It seemed a good day. The sky was clear except for a smudge of cloud on the western horizon, and the wind was steadily propelling them northwards to Britain. Colossus held out a bowl of lentil stew.

"Get that into you. You're going to need it."

"Why?"

"A storm's coming."

"How do you know?"

"See those clouds on the horizon?"

"Is that what they are?"

"Oh yes. They'll be with us in a couple of hours with all the wind and rain that Poseidon can send. Begging your pardon, Father. I'm going to send you one of your friends to make sure you and your gear are secure. We'll take everything off the floor, mind. That door may be strong but it ain't watertight. Oh, and lay in some food and drink."

Hippolytus ate his lentils while Colossus turned to the deck and bellowed out orders. The sails were all to be taken in except for a tiny scrap at the top of the foresail. Everything tied down and , even the crew had all been secured to the ship with ropes because if someone went overboard during the storm there would be no going back to get them. Colossus himself took the helm and kept the prow pointed resolutely to the north.

The smudge on the horizon grew and grew. Soon, it was a wall of cloud, dark and lit from time to time with flashes of lightning. Thunder rolled across the sea.

The south wind ceased as the first drops of rain arrived. That was when Hooter, who had been sent to look after him, closed his door, checked that his travel chests were securely tied to the cabin walls, and suggested to Hippolytus that he might like to take to his cot. When he did, Hooter wrapped a couple of lengths of rope around him to keep him in, and slipped out, saying, "I'll be back to check on you when I can."

Hippolytus lay, listening to the sound of the rain and the thunder. And then the wind struck: great gusts from the west, wild and savage. He felt the ship shudder, as if struck and then begin to buck like an angry horse. He did not know it, but this was a good thing. The ship was upright and breasting the swell as it came, sinking into its troughs and then rising with each great wave. He did not know it because the movement of the ship had thrown him back into the misery of seasickness. The swell that flooded the deck also rushed under his door and washed the floor clean, but he was beyond caring.

He did not know how long it lasted. It might have been a day, a week, a year. It felt like forever. He dozed as much as he could. He prayed with all his might for it all to end. From time to time he was aware of one of the sailors slipping into his cabin, checking on him, giving him a little dry bread soaked in wine, checking that his gear was still secure and dry and changing his bucket.

Then, finally, he woke from a doze. It was light, but it might have been morning or afternoon. What he was aware of was that the rain beat less furiously, the wind no longer screamed its fury, the waves had lessened, and he no longer felt ill. He struggled out of his cot, slipped on the wet floor and finally found his feet. As he stood, clinging to the ropes holding the cot for support, his door opened and Colossus stood there. He looked exhausted. There were dark rings under his eyes but there was a beaming smile on his face.

"Now that," he said. "Was a storm."

CHAPTER FOUR

HIGHTOWER

It was the early afternoon. The *Pegasus* had fled before the tempest for four days, and for all of those days Hippolytus had been wrapped in the misery of seasickness. Now the storm had gone to spend its fury in the fields of Gaul.

Colossus was completely exhausted. He had little sleep, little to eat and constantly on watch, ensuring that the ship stayed afloat and reasonably dry. But he still seemed full of energy as he stood there in the doorway, hollow-eyed and beaming.

"Well" he said. "That's given us a good push to Britain. Not long now!"

"Where are we?" asked Hippolytus.

"That storm blew us a long way west, so it was as well that we had plenty of sea room. It blew us a long way north too. We are well north of Hispania. Gaul is not far beyond the horizon to the east, and Britain is due north of us. Just how much and where, we'll find out when we see some land. I'm not sure whether we'll see Gaul or Britain first. Now I'm going to have a sleep. Deadeye can steer from here."

With every passing minute, there was less rain, and finally, none. Soon, a break in the clouds admitted a feeble sun. The wind still blew, sharp against the skin, but filling the great mainsail which had now been unfurled and tied down hard. One by one, Hippolytus' friends came to visit him.

"Oh, it was fine to be in," said Hooter. "We flew before the wind with only a scrap of sail. And no damage to the ship, no real hurts to the crew. We think it's a bit of a miracle, sir."

"There's some in the crew who said that you was praying for us and that's what kept us safe," added Halfear.

"Well I spent most of my time either sleeping, trying to sleep or being sick," responded Hippolytus." I did pray that it would all go away more than once, though."

"There you are!" said Halfear, triumphantly. "I told you. We was saved by the prayers of a Christian priest."

Many of crew actually came to believe that Hippolytus' prayers had kept them safe and his little congregation grew again.

Twelve days later, they slowly made their way up the long, deep river mouth of the Abus. They had made steady progress since the storm, although a little more slowly than Colossus would have liked. It had been a good time for Hippolytus. Day after day, he had sat out on the deck reading his books and thinking about the task of tutorship that drew steadily nearer. He was approached, from time to time, by members of the crew, many of whom were now in awe of him. They brought him drinks, fish that they had caught, anything that they thought might please him. He gave them time, accepted their gifts with grace, and shared whatever they had brought him.

Colossus looked down it all from his post on the command deck with contentment. Hippolytus had impressed him. He had been a good passenger: never in the way, helpful when needed, and accepted by the crew. He had made a happy ship even happier, and to a captain, that could only ever be a good thing.

The journey had been mostly uneventful since the storm, if slower and with less reliable wind. The only point of tension had been when they had been sailing into what Colossus called "the Germanic Sea." They had left the tall white cliffs of south-east Britain behind and were sailing north past some shoals that they needed all their skill to avoid.

As they made their way, not far from the coast, two ships came into sight. They were sleek, had sharp, fierce rams and cut through the water with the all power of two hard-rowed banks of oars. All of the crew had experience with pirates and they knew when to be on guard. Swords were fetched and bows were strung, and the two ships drew ever nearer.

Suddenly, Colossus let out a roar. He had seen what his crew had not, the men on board the approaching vessels wore familiar uniforms.

"Don't worry, boys! It's the navy."

Hippolytus, who had been sent to his cabin when a pirate attack had been feared, came out onto the deck.

"Come up and look," Colossus called down to him.

Hippolytus joined the captain on the command deck and watched, marveling, at the precise movements of the two navy ships. One hung back, and then took up a position past the *Pegasus*, while the other sliced swiftly through the water, water spraying back from its bronze-sheathed prow. When it was almost alongside the *Pegasus*, the oars were all pulled inboard and the craft glided gently until the sides of the two ships were almost touching. This was sailing of great skill, and the product of constant training and practice.

Both ships threw lines to one another, and soon, they were secured to one another, with a gangplank in place between them. Only when that had been done did a cheery, round-faced young man stride boldly across from the naval ship, and announce to Colossus, who had come down from his command deck to meet him, "I am Mausaeus Carausius, Captain of the Imperial warship *Minerva*, at your service," he announced.

Colossus introduced himself equally formally. "I am Demetrius of Rhodes, sometimes called Rhodius or, more often, Colossus, captain of the private vessel *Pegasus*, at yours."

"Captain Colossus," Carausius addressed the whole crew, as he spoke to Colossus. His voice was loud, assured, used to command and be obeyed. "These are difficult times and you must understand that there are many pirates and other dangers in these seas. The emperor has decreed that all trading ships must pay a tax in order to keep the navy in the water. I must look at your cargo and assess its value so that the proper amount can be worked out. Do you have any passengers?"

"Yes," replied Colossus. "Just the one, Hippolytus of Myra, a priest."

"Of which god," asked Carausius with a little smile.

"He is a Christian priest. Now that our Lord, the Emperor Gallienus has ordered that Christians may move and worship safely, he is come to Britain to be a tutor to the family that owns this boat."

"Do not say the name of Gallienus too loudly here, my friend. Here, we recognize the rule only of our Emperor Postumus. Remember that. Still, a Christian priest here. That does not happen very often. Where is he?"

Hippolytus, who had been standing in the shadow of Colossus, moved forward.

"I am he," he said. "I am honored to meet you, captain."

Carausius looked him up and down, and snorted: "You don't look much like a priest to me. Well, watch your step. We don't hold much to Christians around here, whatever your emperor might say. Now, captain, let's see a list of your cargo."

Dexter was almost immediately there, offering Carausius a scroll.

As he did, Carausius looked down at Dexter's missing hand, and then looked up at his face: "Did that happen in the service?" he asked.

Dexter nodded.

"It was in a fight with the Goths up by the Black Sea a few years ago."

Carausius passed the document to one of his officers who sat down on the deck with a wax tablet and stylus. As he worked out the amount, Carausius walked the deck with Dexter, chatting amiably, like two old comrades.

When the work was finally done, the officer with the list went to Carausius and presented it.

Carausius turned to Colossus.

"Some very valuable stuff here. The dyes in particular. I think that twelve in gold would be a fair toll for you."

Colossus looked stunned. It was a vast fortune, a year's wages.

"We don't have that kind of money on the ship. You could bill the owner, Publius Glaucus."

"Or we could hold you here, and send him a message, and keep you until the money arrived. Still, that's a lot of trouble and delay. I could reduce it to ten, on account of Dexter here being a veteran. Surely that's fair?"

Colossus still looked uncertain. He knew that if he did a whip-round of the crew and himself and collected all of the ready money that they had, it would be barely half the amount.

Then Hippolytus took Colossus aside.

"Captain, if the navy could be content with nine gold pieces, then I think that we might be on our way."

"What?" said Colossus.

"I was given ten for my pay, and I have nine whole gold pieces left."

Colossus turned to Carausius who now stood, a little less cheery, a little more impatient.

"Sir, we can raise nine gold pieces here. Can you be content with that?"

Carausius beamed. It was more than he had hoped.

"If you can provide us with the cash, you can be on your way."

And so it was that Hippolytus went back to his cabin, found the purse deep in his travel chest and paid the navy their toll.

As the naval ships pulled away, Colossus turned again to Hippolytus.

"Once again, sir, we are in your debt. That was a year's wages that you gave to them."

"And what would I buy with it?" replied Hippolytus. "I have all that I need. That money is better used keeping us all safe and on the move."

The Abus was part river, part deep inlet. The water was chocolate brown with silt and, when the tide went out, the exposed mudflats stank of rotting seaweed. The little port of Petuaria sat on its northern bank, timber jetties reaching out far across the tidal flats to the deep water where ships could float.

"I know it's not beautiful," said Dexter to Hippolytus as they used their oars to make their way up the river. "But it's not home, neither."

"How far, then?"

"Oh, we'll hop off here, unload and have a spot of shore leave. Petuaria's not much of a place, but it's all we have here. There will probably be a load of dyed cloth for us to take on to Gaul. You'll go with the cargo, on the wagons, to Hightower, Glaucus' house. It's a little less than a day north of here. I'll come with you as well so that I can make a full report to the master."

Hippolytus was sorry to leave the ship and the crew were sorry to see him go. On the day they were due to disembark, Hippolytus invited all of his friends to breakfast on the deck outside his cabin. There was Perseus and Halfear, Dexter and Hooter. The food was nothing special, just the usual salted porridge, washed down with a little watered wine. But there was the sense of an ending. One journey was over; another was beginning. Halfear and Hooter both had gifts for the priest. Halfear was a skilled sculptor in wood, and he had carved a leaping fish from a piece of old pine. Hooter, having seen the way that the rope-soled shoes had been made in New Carthage, had crafted a pair for Hippolytus from odd bits of ship's rope.

"We know it's not much, sir," said Hooter, as he handed over the gifts.

"It is everything," replied Hippolytus. "This are true gifts of the heart and I have little by way of farewell gift but the words that I have shared with you. Dexter here can read and write, and so I give this to him to read to you when you need it, or when you come together."

He passed Dexter a small scroll.

"This is a little book about Jesus, and it is by a man called Marcus. Marcus might even have been there, with Jesus, and we know that he was an important member of the first church. Have it with my blessings and use it well."

Petuaria was a small town that was a naval base, a port for the local farms and a market center. The *Pegasus* moored at one of the long jetties thrust out into the river. Two soldiers waited for them on the pier and came aboard as soon as they had docked. Even though the day was becoming warm, they wore the red cloaks that marked them as Roman soldiers.

The soldiers clearly knew Colossus. There was an ease in their manner, and a simple directness in their questions. Hippolytus knew what would come. He had met men like this before. Beneath their friendliness was a cold and brutal efficiency. They were not on the ship to catch up with old friends. They were there to do a job. He heard them ask for a list of the ship's cargo and passengers, and so came forward to be questioned.

"I am the passenger, Hippolytus," he identified himself to the soldiers.

"Just some questions, if you please," said the one who seemed to be in charge. "What is your business in Britain?"

"I am come to be the tutor to the children of Publius Glaucus."

"Where have you come from?"

"From Myra, in the province of Lycia and Pamphylia."

"Have you come directly?"

"Yes, sir. I boarded this ship in Myra, and have not strayed far from her since."

"The captain tells me that you stayed off the vessel in Syracuse. Why was that?"

"I am a Christian priest, sir. I was visiting the community of the faithful there and they offered me their hospitality."

"A Christian?" The officer's voice raised slightly. "We don't hold much with that sort of thing around here. Be very careful, Christian, or you will find yourself up before a judge before you know it."

Although Christianity was now legal, Hippolytus knew better than to argue.

"One more thing, sir. If you have any money I should change it with the military office in the walled town, and not the rogues outside. You will get a better rate.

Hippolytus was intrigued.

"Is not my money good here?"

"You come from Myra. There you recognized the authority of a different emperor and his head is on the coins. Here, we recognize Postumus. Old coins are good, and coins bearing Postumus' likeness, but nothing with your old emperor's head on it. Postumus is your emperor now. Remember that."

The officer turned his back on Hippolytus and that was that.

Soon Hippolytus was back on solid ground, feeling once more the strange sensation of standing on something that does not move with the sea. He turned and saw the hatches in the deck of the *Pegasus* opened wide, and the work of unloading her begin.

While all of the goods were being taken off the ship and carried down the jetty to a warehouse that huddled underneath the wall of the fort, Hippolytus stretched his legs along the waterfront. Years before, military engineers had made a proper stone quayside to make easier the loading and unloading of goods. It was about twenty feet wide and not very long, perhaps two hundred feet or so, and lined on the landward side with warehouses. Most were old timber buildings, but Glaucus' was made of solid stone.

The place was quiet: the *Pegasus* was the only ship unloading that day. The air was still and the day was muggy with the damp heat of summer. All around him were the smells of a working port: salt water, oyster shells and rotting seaweed. Now and then, a cat crept by in search of fish scraps. Hippolytus ambled on, deep in thought. So, this was Britain.

He turned when he heard his name called. Colossus was calling to him and beckoning him over.

"It's a day or so from here to Hightower," explained Colossus. "We'll load up the cart tonight and doss down in the warehouse so that we can get going first thing in the morning. There's an inn in the town if you want a softer bed."

"No, Captain. We have come thus far together. We shall go on together. My bed will be soft enough at Hightower, I think."

"Well then, let's at least go, change our money and get a feed in the town. I know where they do a good fish stew.

While Petuaria was a walled town, it was not quite like the kind of walled town that you might have seen. Its walls were not of stone or brick, but rammed earth, and they were topped by a wooden barrier of upright logs with sharpened points. Inside its timber gates, the place was strictly Roman. The streets were straight; the buildings regular and made from brick and seasoned wood. This was the kind of fortified town that Roman soldiers had made across the empire. Outside the walls, it was different. This was where many of the local Britons lived in huts with mud walls and thatch roofs. The streets were unpaved and crooked, with odd and unexpected turnings. Strangely, Hippolytus noted the remains of a stone theatre but this was clearly now a quarry for stone to strengthen the earth wall of the fort. Hippolytus also noted the number of soldiers either in uniform and clearly on patrol, or out of uniform and out to relax and enjoy themselves.

They equipped themselves with local coin, and found Colossus' fish stew outside the walls in a tavern where off-duty soldiers sat in one corner, while the local Britons sat in another. All of them were drinking beer, something that Hippolytus had not seen before.

"We are a long way from home, Hippolytus," Colossus observed. "Rome has ruled our coastlands for hundreds of years and we know no other, or better, master. They have not been in this place for quite so long, and the memory of a free people remains. This is not the heart of empire, where we are from, but its edge. You will not go far in Britain, especially this far north, without seeing soldiers. And native Britons."

Towards dusk on the following day, Colossus and Hippolytus were both perched on top of a cart as it came over a ridge that gave onto the little valley where Hightower sat. The driver paused, reining the horses in.

"There she is sirs. That's Hightower. And a fine place she is too."

"Well come on, let's get down there before dark," replied Colossus, now impatient for the end of a cart ride which had been far more uncomfortable than any sea trip in any weather. The cart had bounced and jolted with every rut and pothole in the old road. Hippolytus hurt all over, particularly his rear end, and he was most impatient to be at his journey's end.

Hightower seemed huge. The tower from which it was named loomed over the landscape, rising to three or four storeys. The wings of the house seemed impossibly long, and the great gate, at which they eventually arrived, was big enough for the cart to go through.

Waiting for them, in the courtyard, was a tall, slim man, dark-haired and bearded with a grey-streaked beard. He wore a simple tunic of good cloth and his feet were bare. "Septimus, you rogue," Colossus called out. "How goes it with you?"

"Well enough," came the reply. "We did not expect you for some days more, and so we were all surprised when the rider came from Petuaria this morning with the news that you were to be expected tonight."

"We had good winds," replied the captain. "And we had the fortune to meet a storm that blew us just as far as we wanted to go. The gods were truly with us this time, although my crew thank the little priest here."

Septimus looked fully at Hippolytus for the first time.

"I had heard the mistress was getting a Christian. So this is the new tutor?" Septimus' tone was amused rather than hostile.

"Yes," said the priest. "That is me. It has been a long journey and I am most glad to be here."

"Perhaps you will change your mind when you meet the children. Still, the mistress will want to see you straight away." Septimus then turned to the captain. "Colossus, will you see to the unloading. I must see to this matter now. I will be back with you when I can."

More than a little painfully, Hippolytus climbed down from the cart. He was so stiff that he needed his staff to help him walk. Septimus stood back while he found his feet and then, when he had straightened, he spoke to Hippolytus directly:

"I am sorry, my manners have deserted me. My name is Septimus, as you heard from the captain. I am the steward of Hightower. I run the house and the household for the master and mistress, and so if you have any questions or need anything, please ask me. The master and the mistress are kind people who would not wish you to be uncomfortable."

"Thank you, I shall. Tell me," said Hippolytus, to make conversation, "Have you been with them long?"

"Only since they have been here at Hightower, sir," said Septimus, placing stress upon the "sir." "I have been the steward here for many years. In fact, I was born here. When the master bought Hightower, he bought me and all the other slaves with it."

"So you are…"

"Yes sir, a slave. If you would be so kind, there is no need to speak of it further."

Septimus led him inside, and his new life began.

CHAPTER FIVE

FATHER HORSE

Septimus led Hippolytus up to the tower room. Stiff and sore, he limped up each staircase, leaning on the banister. The tower was solid Roman brick, as were the stairs that were hard and cold under his feet. On each floor, there was a landing with a door leading off it. On the first and second levels, the doors were closed. On the third, it was open, and soft evening light streamed through.

Septimus gently knocked at the door, signaled to Hippolytus to wait and went in. The priest only heard the soft murmur of two voices before the steward emerged to usher him inside. Lydia was sitting in a wicker chair in the midst of her private room. A large table against one wall was covered with papers and scrolls, and the light came in from two large, open windows, one looking west, the other south. These were tightly screened by fine linen that let in the light but not the insects that swarmed at dusk.

Hippolytus took all this in in an instant before he turned to Lydia, who was already covering her head and rising from her chair. She looked over Hippolytus' shoulder to the steward and said, "Thank you Septimus. That will be all."

Hippolytus saw a slim woman of his own height, wearing a finely woven woolen gown of pale blue that reached to her wrists and ankles. There was a sash of pale yellow about her waist, the end of which she had hastily thrown over her head just as Hippolytus had come in. Her eyes were fierce and intelligent, her face, broad and kind and the smile that she turned upon him was light and happy.

She spoke in Latin.

"Father Hippolytus," she said, softly, in greeting.

"My Lady," he replied with a slight bow.

She offered him a seat and he sank into one of the wicker armchairs with a sigh.

"You have had a good journey?" she asked.

A courtesy, he thought and a kind way to begin the conversation. "My Lady, it was long, but not so long as it might have been. If there were discomforts, they were made easier by your kind provision for me, and the company of the crew. I made good friends there, and they taught me much."

"I am glad to hear it," she replied. "The overnight courier brought me a letter from the captain with a full report. Oh, don't worry, he wasn't spying on you, it was just what a kind of a passenger you were. I have to say that he was very full in his praise, something that happens rarely enough. He also mentioned how you helped to get out of a difficult situation."

Hippolytus thought for a moment and responded. "The captain was most kind to say so. I did only what was needed and was pleased to be of help."

"It was so much more than mere help," Lydia said. "You gave a year's pay—not some trifle—to help keep the ship afloat. You will be sure that my husband will hear of it."

"There is no need to trouble him with this, surely," Hippolytus protested.

"There is every need. Now I wish to talk about two things with you: your place in this household and the children.

"As my brother will have told you, I am a Christian, as were our parents. My husband is not. It has always been that way. Our marriage was arranged by our parents, and I always knew that I would be 'unequally yoked' as the scripture puts it. But yoked I am, as Glaucus is to me. He is not a bad man indeed, in many ways, a good one and I have come to love him, as he has come to love me. We were both from the city of Tarsus and, while we lived there, there was no difficulty with this. There are many in Tarsus who follow the Way, and a large group met in my parents' house. I remained a member of that community until a terrible war came.

"We had a lovely house, but it was outside the walls. When the enemy came, there was no one to protect us. Glaucus was arming himself when we were attacked by some of our household slaves. Fortunately, he knows how to use his sword and spear. We escaped with the children, and most of the rest of the household, and fled to the *Pegasus*. Some of the others were killed; the rest plundered our house, burnt it to the ground and deserted to the enemy. It was a terrible time. We have nothing left there now.

"I tell you this so that you understand some things about the children. We came here to put a deep distance between ourselves and those dreadful, horrifying, events. But we all carry the scars of those few days with us. Our memories of Tarsus are, in a sense, painful to us because they remind us of what dear friends and family we have lost. I love my children and know there is no wickedness in them, but there is much hurt. They have made life very difficult for those who have come before you because the war made them question why they needed to learn at all. As far as they are concerned, that kind of life ended when we sailed away from Tarsus. It is your task to bring that back to them, and to make learning a worthwhile thing once more.

"Of course, I did not have to ask for a priest to do this. Indeed, none of those who came before you are priests, or even, Christian. I'm not quite sure why I asked for a priest. The idea just seemed to come to me. Perhaps I asked my brother to send you as much for myself as for my children. As I said before, Tarsus was a place with many believers. We cared for one another, in our gathering, and for those who came to us in need. At Hightower there is just me and some of the household. The nearest priest is Bishop Moguntius in Eboracum, and that is a day away. He has been here once or twice, and I try to stay in touch with my sisters and brothers in Tarsus by letter, but that is not enough. Perhaps I need the conversation of a learned man as much as I need the counsel of a holy one, and so you are here to be my chaplain as much as to tutor the children." She paused and smiled a secret, private smile. "But do not tell my husband that," she added.

She looked up and gestured at the paper-strewn table. "For him, my faith is a different country, and he would not travel there. Instead, he allows me—and for this I am grateful—my books, my letters and my ...views. This is not a deception, simply something that he would not entirely understand, not having come to my country, even for a while."

"As my lady wishes," replied Hippolytus, bowing his head slightly.

"In private, Father, I am not 'My Lady' but Lydia, your daughter in the faith. That brings me to the last thing. You are in the household, and a part of it, but not a servant. You will dine with the family, and not with the slaves. Your room shall be here, in this tower, which is my domain. For you to have any authority over the children, they must understand that you are my friend, and not my servant. That is a mistake that I have made before and will not make again. I would be glad, too, if you would lead worship for those of us who follow the Way on the Lord's Day.

"By now, your things should be in your room, which is below this one. There should also be some food set out for you. You must be hungry and tired. Tomorrow should do for everything else. We break our fast an hour after dawn (the sun rises early here). One of the slaves will fetch you. Is there anything that you would like to know for now?"

"Yes, daughter. We are in Britain and the language of the land is Latin. I think, though, that your mother tongue, and that of the children is Greek?"

"This is a Latin-speaking house, Father. Most of our slaves know no other language, and if the children are to make futures here, then they must be as comfortable using Latin as Greek, if not more so. Given the books that you will be using, I would expect you to move easily between Latin and Greek with the children. They need both languages equally."

Hippolytus swayed suddenly, as a wave of tiredness hit him.

"Oh, Father, how thoughtless of me. You are tired from your journey and I have kept you here, talking. I think you must eat and take your rest now.

"I would be so very grateful if you would bless me before you leave me."

Hippolytus stood and Lydia knelt before him. Softly he traced the sign of the cross on her forehead with his thumb and said the words of blessing. She stayed kneeling for a moment, and then stood, head slightly bowed and said, "Until tomorrow, Father."

"Until tomorrow, then, my daughter," replied Hippolytus and he turned and left the room.

Hippolytus' chamber was almost a copy of the one above it. There were alcoves for his books, a chest for his clothes, a table for his work and a bed for his rest. The same two windows, with linen screens let in the dim light of a sun now resting on the western horizon. Lamps already burned with their blue-orange glow and plates of cold food were set out on the table, with a jug of wine and some water. He had never felt so tired, so hungry, or so welcome. He fell upon the food; then fell upon the bed, closed his eyes and slept."

He woke the next morning to the sound of a gentle tapping at his door. The light was streaming in through the east window. He shook the sleep from his head, sat up on the bed and called for whomever it was at the door to enter.

The door opened a little and, shyly, a small boy of eight or nine slipped into the room and stood with his head slightly bent and eyes looking down.

"Are you Gordi?" Hippolytus asked, puzzled at this unexpected visit.

"Oh, no, master. I'm Simon. My father's the chief cook here and the mistress has sent me to look after you."

"Look after me?" Hippolytus asked puzzled.

"Yes. Pick up after you, put your things away, make sure your clothes are washed, run messages and errands for you, that sort of thing."

"And why could I not do these things for myself?"

There was a pause. Simon looked confused. "But why should you do those things when you have me to do them for you?"

Simon looked plaintively at Hippolytus, and Hippolytus, looking carefully at the boy, understood something for the first time.

"You are a slave, aren't you?"

"Well yes, most of the household is. That's how things work," replied Simon, almost defiantly.

Hippolytus had realized that slaves like Simon had no choice about what tasks they were set, but that Simon really wanted this one. And if he said no to Simon, then he could well be set to less pleasant work.

"Simon, I will be glad of your help. But please note, I do not answer to 'Master,' but, because I am a priest, I do answer to 'Father.' Could you do that?"

"I don't understand."

And there, Hippolytus learned another lesson. This was not the clever child of a wealthy family who had grown up surrounded by books and talk. Simon was a slave boy, born into slavery, and who had learned only the skills needed to fetch and carry.

"You will in time, child," Hippolytus said quietly. "Now I must wash and dress for breakfast."

"That was why I was knocking on your door, sir. I brought some warm water from the bathhouse but it might be cold by now."

It was but Hippolytus made the best of it. Then he put on his trousers and the white robe of his profession, and followed Simon down to breakfast.

It was quite a walk. From the bottom of the tower, Simon led Hippolytus along a covered way beside the courtyard to a large room in the middle of the western wing. It was separated from the walkway by large folding wooden shutters, which were wide open, so that the dining room looked like nothing more than a very large alcove. The walls were brightly painted in red and yellow panels, some framing painted garden scenes. The floor was a carpet of black and white mosaic tiles set in a chequerboard pattern. Lydia was already there, as was Colossus, eating a chicken leg that looked like a twig in his hand. A table was set in the middle of the room, with a variety of foods: bread, oil, honey, apples, nuts, hard-boiled eggs, olives, and the chicken that Colossus had taken to himself. Lydia was seated at one end of the table and there were a number of places set.

"Forgive us Father, but we only recline to eat on formal occasions. Otherwise it is as you see it," said Lydia, rising as he entered the room. "I would be most glad if you would say a blessing for us."

Colossus put down his chicken, a little sheepishly, while Hippolytus said grace.

"Help yourself Father. We prefer to do that here. The children will be along in a moment. I think that they are being scrubbed until they shine."

Hippolytus helped himself to some bread, honey and fruit. He was finishing this when the two children came in quietly and without ceremony. Their clothes were clean and their faces and hands were pink with scrubbing.

"Father Hippolytus, it is time that you met my children. My son, Gordianus and my daughter, Verginia."

Hippolytus did not know what to expect. Lydia had briefed him well enough but now he was face to face with his task. As he looked at the two children, Gini boldly in front and looking directly at him, Gordi half a pace behind and hiding behind his sister more than just a little, he suddenly felt a sense of great peace fall upon him. A weight of unspoken worry fell from him and a fierce joy awoke in its place as a voice, unbidden, said in his head *this is what you were born for.*

Gini saw someone quite different from those who had tried to teach them before. To be sure, he was dressed as they had been, in the white gown of his profession, but she felt, somehow, that he was worthy of it. She felt his own gaze with such acuteness that it was as if he looked into her rather than at her. For the children most grownups were just grownups different from them, but not so much from one another. Perhaps she caught something impish, something childlike, in Hippolytus' face and she thought to herself *I might learn from this one.*

Gordi, peeping out from behind his sister saw little, except—because he was the smallest—his eyes were below the level of the table and so he noticed something that caused him to cry out in a rage, "You're wearing trousers. Mama, he has trousers, he's a barbarian!"

"Hush Gordianus," said Lydia.

"But they burned our house!" he bawled, hiccupping the words with emotion and then jamming his fists into his eyes to stop the tears.

"Yes Gordianus, they did," started Hippolytus, softly. "But not because they were wearing trousers. Surely it is not the wearing of trousers that makes a barbarian. Many here wear trousers. It is their habit. I have seen many Britons wear trousers, even some of the soldiers, our soldiers. Spend some time with me today, and you can tell me if I am a barbarian, if I might have burned your house. Will you allow me this day?"

His words were gentle. As he spoke, Gordi calmed. He stood there, a little ashamed of his outburst, occasionally stifling a sob that seemed to come from nowhere. Then, with the eyes of the room upon him, wordlessly, he nodded.

"Sir," said the girl with plain politeness, "We would love to spend this day with you. If you don't mind, Verginia and Gordianus are our proper names, but we prefer to be called Gini and Gordi."

"Gini and Gordi it is, then. And I am Father Hippolytus. We shall get to know each other better by and by. For now, I think that you might be hungry and ready to eat? I never yet met a child that didn't want at least two breakfasts. Afterwards, with your mother's permission, perhaps you could show me around the house? It seems very large and, unless I have help, I might easily get lost."

"That is an excellent idea, Father," said Lydia. "Children, you may eat."

Only then did the two begin to take food from the table. Hippolytus noted that both chose carefully, only taking what they could eat and not too much. For the next few minutes, the only sound in the room was that of eating.

At length, Colossus stood, bowed and excused himself, leaving only Hippolytus and the family. Then, abruptly, Lydia stood too.

"I have work to do now. I leave the children with you. We take a meal at midday. The bell will ring to tell you that it is to be served."

Just as quickly she was gone, leaving Hippolytus with the two children. His work had begun.

Hippolytus waited for the children to finish. As he did, he thought about how he might approach his task. Gordi had given him an idea, but the time for it had not yet come. Instead, as they wiped their faces, he rose. Simon, who had been waiting somewhere, was beside him in a moment.

"Shall we see the house now?" he asked and, wordlessly, they left the room.

It was Gini who took the lead, easily chatting to Hippolytus.

The house was vast, although the design was simple enough. It was a large rectangle of rooms around a central courtyard. On three sides, there was a covered walkway alongside the courtyard between it and the rooms. In each corner there was a different but important structure: at the northeast, the kitchens; at the northwest, the bathhouse; the family's private quarters were at the southwest corner, and the tower, where Lydia's room and Hippolytus' own room lay, was at the southeast corner. Glaucus' office and the room used by Septimus for his work were both on the ground floor of the tower. The public rooms of the house were together on the eastern side; the guest rooms on the western side; while the quarters of the senior slaves were on the north side. There was no rooms on the south side, but it was here that the outer wall was pierced by a gate large enough to admit a horse and cart. There had once been a gatehouse there, but that had gone, although two buttresses for the wall still stood on either side of the gate. Instead, there was a large, stone-floored area, with bins for storage and big clay pots against the wall. The entrance courtyard was separated from the central courtyard by the covered walkway between the family quarters and the tower.

The courtyard itself was part ornamental, part practical. The whole space was divided into four large, raised garden beds with a paved path between them. The two garden beds at the back, nearer to the kitchen, were devoted to herbs and vegetables; those at the front to ornamental flowers. It was evident that Lydia had a taste for roses as many different varieties were on display there. At the heart of the courtyard, where the paved paths met, was a circular podium about four feet high and seven across. Once it might have supported the statue of a god; now it held an enormous pot with a fig tree in it. Hippolytus noticed a small door in one side. On either side of the door were two large empty pots.

"That's where the garden tools are kept," explained Gini. "Those pots don't fit through the door. I think that they are going to put some trees in them or something."

The morning was drawing to a close. All through the tour, Gordi had said little, and, when he could, clung to his sister. There, by the podium, Hippolytus sat down on the coping of the raised garden bed and said to Gordi, "Let's talk about trousers."

Gordi remained stubbornly silent.

"You don't like them, do you?" asked Hippolytus.

"No" said Gordi, unwillingly.

"Because men with trousers burned your house?"

"Yes," the response was quiet but very clear.

"Gordi, I'm going to tell you something that my old teacher taught me many years ago, and then we shall talk again about trousers. He said that the path to true knowledge was not thinking about new things in old ways, but in thinking about old things in new ways."

"I don't understand."

"Was it the trousers who burned the house down, or the men?"

"The men."

"And you have seen many other people wear trousers, some of them friends?"

"Yes."

"Well, if it is true that all barbarians wear trousers, does it follow that all who wear trousers are barbarians?"

A light seemed to come on in Gordi's eyes.

Hippolytus continued. "People wear trousers for lots of reasons. The man who suggested that I wear them was a sailor, who told me that it made it easier for him to move around a boat. Some sailors wear them, some soldiers wear them—"

"To keep their legs warm in winter, interrupted Gini, laughing.

"Or to hide scars, or other unsightliness," continued Hippolytus.

"Or to ride a horse!" shouted Gordi, excited at catching on.

"That's right," said Hippolytus. "It's not the trousers that do bad things, but some of the people who wear them. See, old things in a new way!"

Gordi thought for a moment and then, suddenly, said, "Your name, Hippolo… Hypolet…

"Hippolytus."

"Yes, that one. What does it mean? It's Greek isn't it?"

"Yes, it is. It means 'tamer of horses.' It was the name of Theseus' son by Hippolyta, Queen of the Amazons."

"Wasn't Theseus the Athenian who killed the Minotaur?" asked Gini.

"Yes, that's right," replied Hippolytus.

"I thought that he ended up with the daughter of the King of Crete?"

"Ariadne? No. The story is that she fell in love with him, helped him, and ran away with him, but he left her on the island of Naxos where she became the bride of Dionysus, God of wine."

"It's not very good that he left her behind," responded Gini.

"No," replied Hippolytus. "Heroes might be heroic with a sword in their hands, but they can be fairly shabby with those who love them. Theseus is no exception. But he did have this son, Hippolytus, whom he loved very much. That did not end well either."

"What happened?" asked Gordi, suddenly keen.

From across the courtyard, the lunch bell sounded.

"Ah, that is a story for another day. We are called to the table."

"Father Hippo…" asked Gordi, suddenly not quite sure how to pronounce the whole name. "Um, Hippos means 'horse' in Greek, doesn't it. That's the 'horses' part in your name."

"That's right," said the priest.

"Would it be very rude if I called you 'Father Horse'? I can't really say your proper name."

It was a moment when things might have changed. Hippolytus might have stood on his dignity and insisted on his proper name and title, but he understood this for what it was—a gentle, uncertain request, and a door into the world of a child he had come to teach. So instead, he smiled and said softly, "Father Horse it is. Come, children, shall we go to lunch?"

CHAPTER SIX

FATHER HORSE SOLVES A MYSTERY

The name stuck. Within a few days, everyone was calling him Father Horse, even Lydia. He was, truth be told, a bit proud of it. It was his point of connection with Gordi. What had begun with a little lesson about trousers had concluded with a new name, and he immediately saw the importance of this in developing the ease that the children were developing with him.

His teaching was not obvious. He remembered that when he had been a boy he had not much enjoyed learning the shapes and sounds of letters but he had loved the stories that they made. So he told stories. He told stories about heroes like Theseus, Hercules, Joshua and David; and about mighty women like Electra, Deborah, Judith and his own favorite, Hippolyta.

He also sensed that the classroom was the last place that these two wanted to be, especially as summer began to decline into autumn. Each day was that little bit shorter, the air that little bit cooler. There was an unspoken sense of urgency. Winter was on the way and with it, any real chance of exploring the world around Hightower. So he went out into the world with them—not to their secret places in the wood above the house—but he had them show him the farm and explain it to him.

He learned that the house was the center of a complex of buildings, each of which had been built or adapted to enable Glaucus to manufacture dyed woolen cloth. The wool came from the black-faced sheep that browsed in the fields around the house. Every year they were herded together and shorn in an open-sided shed near the house. Their fleeces were taken and stored flat in a brick barn close by; while another brick barn held the winter fodder for the sheep and a separate new building housed the dye works. This had been placed as distant from the house as possible, while still being convenient. The smell of the dye was truly horrible while that of the vats where the dyes were fixed into the wool was worse. A large timber building held the wheels and looms where the dyed fleeces were spun into yarn and woven into bolts of cloth. Set back from these was a long building where the rest of the farm slaves lived.

These buildings were all in a single field behind the house and enclosed by a waist-high dry-stone wall. Doors from both the kitchen and the bathhouse opened into this extended paddock, and near the kitchen door, there was a chicken run. To the immediate east of the house, there was a series of fruit trees. Hippolytus could not really call it an orchard because it was not well enough organized, but here, there were lemons, apples and plums to be had (at the right time). Hightower's gardens were cared for by Quintus, an old slave who had lived his life at the farm, and fought ongoing battles with bird and squirrel to keep the fruit on the trees until it was ripe enough for picking.

Father Horse had never seen anything like this before and so he was fascinated by the whole arrangement. It was like its own village, it was larger than many of the villages where he had ministered. There were slaves everywhere: slaves to run the house, slaves to run the farm, slaves to dye the wool, spin it, card it, weave it and store it. Gini and Gordi had lived in the midst of this, or something like it, all of their lives so it seemed completely normal and not at all strange.

What was not normal to them was the fund of stories that he seemed to have. To them, Hippolytus came as a complete surprise. They had expected another grey-voiced man who would sit them down with slate and chalk and make them learn all the letters from alpha to omega; a man whom they could ignore, defy and escape as they had done so often before. But, and perhaps even against their will, they found Father Horse to be rather interesting and they came to look forward to the time they spent with him.

Hippolytus was also learning their favorite and least favorite places. They disliked the bathhouse because that was where they were scrubbed pink whenever guests threatened to arrive, but they loved the kitchen where they could always count on Phormio to spoil them. He also came to enjoy sitting there, at the long table, nibbling bread and olives and telling stories. He did not mind the bustle of the kitchen and the fact that something was always happening around them. And he loved the smells of freshly-baked bread, the slow braising of meat in wine, the rich salt smell of the sausages hanging along the walls. He enjoyed the attention of Leo, the fat kitchen cat, who rubbed against his legs and looked up at him with pleading eyes, asking for scraps of food.

Most of all, he enjoyed the company of the chief cook, Phormio. Like Lydia, Phormio was a Christian. Unlike Lydia, he was a slave, having grown up as a slave in the Glaucus household. There he had married another slave and Simon, their son, was also born into their slavery. None of this seemed to bother him. His kingdom was the kitchen, and there he ruled with complete authority.

It was faith, and talk about it, that brought Hippolytus and Phormio together the first time that he visited the kitchen in the wake of his enthusiastic guides. When Phormio had settled the children (not just Gini and Gordi, but Simon as well) with some bread and ewes' milk, he sat down next to Hippolytus. "My son tells me that you are a man of God." He spoke softly, and looked down as he did so, so that he did not look directly at Hippolytus. It was a slave's way of speaking, and Hippolytus' heart lurched with sorrow that this proud and able man could not speak with him as an equal.

"Yes, Phormio, I am. I am the Lord's slave, as you are one in this house. We are both slaves together. Please, do not think of me in any other way."

Phormio looked up at him shyly and asked, "Would you like some ewes' milk too, or would you prefer a little watered wine? And perhaps some olives. They're very good. They came in the *Pegasus* with you. And some boar sausage. I make it myself."

"I would like that very much," said Hippolytus.

The schoolroom itself seemed to hold little joy for either of the children. For Hippolytus, it became his retreat where he could sit, read, and pray. Simon brought him snacks and made sure that his clothes were clean. Only on those dull days when the rain came was he forced to teach them indoors and even then he preferred the covered walkway beside the courtyard garden.

He was a natural storyteller and, as he spoke, the children listened to his tales. More importantly they asked questions and the questions led to conversations about good and bad, right and wrong, what might make things beautiful and what might make them ugly and even about the gods themselves. He was careful to mix up the stories he told: some from Greek history and mythology; some from the Bible.

Once Lydia had seen how things were going she had withdrawn from watching the children. They all came together at mealtimes and, after the children had gone to bed, she was eager to talk with Hippolytus about her own faith and the books that she had been reading. It was also likely that she valued the company of a peer. Glaucus had been absent on business for some weeks, travelling through the military posts north of Eboracum, selling scarlet cloth to the legions for cloaks and tunics. He wrote regularly on thin sheets of wood, a bit like long, square shavings, but Lydia did not enjoy the loneliness of her station, and so looked forward to mealtimes when she could discuss with Hippolytus the things that interested her.

If she was curious about Hippolytus himself, she did not show it. Her questions and thoughts were always about ideas and things that had happened, never about Hippolytus himself. Perhaps she sensed that there were things that he was unwilling to say, or perhaps she simply did not want to pry into his life.

The first Sunday came and Lydia asked Hippolytus to lead worship in the morning after breakfast. For once, she did not insist that the children join them ("they must come when they wish, not when I tell them," she had remarked to Hippolytus). Phormio came, and Simon, and Phormio's wife, Lois, who ran the laundry. A few of the other slaves joined them, all of them slaves of the house who had come with the family from Asia; none were the local British farm slaves. Lydia set up her room as a chapel. Simon helped move things around so that it looked more like a place of worship. The great table was set before the eastern window and chairs were brought in from other parts of the house. Lydia donated a silver goblet and plate while Phormio brought freshly baked bread and some of the better wine.

As he began to say familiar words, Hippolytus felt filled with the simple joy of the moment. The others seemed to feel it too, perhaps because they had not been able to worship like this for so long. The prayers became more intensely spoken, the psalm, more heartfelt, and the sharing of bread and wine became a glimpse of glory. After he had finished with the blessing, they all sat in silence, unwilling to break the moment. In the end, no one did.

Instead, Gordi and Gini burst into the room.

"We can't find Leo anywhere," cried Gordi. "He's disappeared!"

Lydia immediately took charge. "Tell me everything," she said gently.

Gordi was sobbing. He dearly loved the big cat who slept most of his days in the kitchen, dreaming of dropped morsels and slow mice.

Gini did the talking. "We went down after breakfast to give him a little bowl of ewes' milk. He loves that. But he wasn't there. We thought that he might have been waiting outside the backdoor into the yard, but he wasn't there. So we went out into the yard, and called him. We looked in all of the places that we thought that he might be—the ones that he likes—under the old cart, that sunny spot on top of the dry-stone wall, we even checked around the henhouse to see if he was eyeing any of the chickens. But no sign. He didn't come when we called, even when we had little pieces of bacon, which he always loves. We just don't know what to do. What if he's hurt? What if he went out hunting last night and was caught in a trap?"

Lydia was immediately calm, although she could sense her children's rising panic. "He must be somewhere," she declared. "Let us think about the likely places, look there and, if he is not there, then look in the unlikely ones."

"But what if we don't find him?" wailed Gordi.

"Well then, we don't find him. But I think that will be because he will not wish to be found," Lydia's voice was firm and gentle. "When cats are hurt or sick, they sometimes find a place to be by themselves until they are better or they…leave life." Her words were as careful as they could be, but they set Gordi sobbing again.

"Now children," Lydia was all business again. "You must calm yourselves. You are no good to Leo like this. We must search the house first and see if he has not been locked in one of the rooms. Father Horse, you must search this tower and the courtyard garden. Phormio, you take the kitchen and bathhouse. Simon, you must go with him, because we might have to look under the bathhouse. Children, you take the guest wing. I shall do the public rooms and family quarters. If we haven't found him, let's all meet back in the dining room in an hour."

The orders had been given. Everyone scattered to their tasks.

For Father Horse, there was rather less to do than for the others. Leo was obviously not in Lydia's room. He looked on the landing, and then in his own room, and finally on the ground floor, under the stairs and in the office there. He found not Leo, but Septimus, who was sitting at a table with a pile of broken pottery, a pen and a ledger.

"What is it?" Septimus asked a little gruffly.

"The children cannot find Leo. I have been sent to find if he is in here."

"I should know if he were. I have no great love for that cat, nor he for me. He's kept me awake more than once with his caterwauling and carry-on with his cat friends under my window."

"Very good, Septimus. I won't disturb you any further. Just one thing. Did you hear him last night?"

"No. It was quiet."

"Thank you for that. I didn't hear anything either. If by chance you do find him, please let the mistress know. The children are quite upset."

Septimus grunted his assent and Hippolytus showed himself out and went off to look in the garden.

Leo was clearly not there. He was under no bushes, on top of no walls, nestled into no nests. But while he searched, Father Horse had a think. That thinking led to an idea, and, since he had some time, he went off to see if it was the right one.

He was last back into the dining room where he found a group miserable with failure. The mood was as black as Simon, who had been crawling about in the heating space under the bathhouse and was covered in soot.

Every room in the house had been searched thoroughly and Leo stubbornly remained missing.

Softly, he broke the silence. "I think that I might have found the cat," he said.

Then everyone spoke at once, and only with difficulty was Lydia able to calm the storm of questions.

"We have not found Leo so far because we have been looking in all the wrong places. All of our searching has been based on our knowledge of Leo, has it not?"

"Oh, Father Horse, where is he then?" demanded Gordi, impatiently, nearly stamping his foot.

"Well," replied Hippolytus. "I was talking to Septimus and he gave me an idea. He told me that Leo had kept him awake at night yowling under his window. Now I know that noise. It's one that cats make when they fight other cats."

"Do you mean that he has been hurt in a fight?" Gini asked.

"No, no. Did anyone hear a catfight last night? I certainly didn't, and neither did Septimus. I asked."

There was silence.

"Gini, what can you tell me about Leo?"

"Well, he's our kitchen cat. He was here when we came. I suppose always in the kitchen," she responded.

"Good. So you did not know Leo until you came here?"

"That's right," she said. "He was everyone's friend, though, always looking for some food and a scratch behind the ears."

"So you made friends with Leo very quickly?"

"Yes," she said. "It was like he was always our cat."

"Who called him Leo?"

"I did," said Phormio. "He was in my kitchen, so I gave him his name."

"And why Leo?"

"It's a lion's name. It's a good name for a cat."

"Yes it is. But I think that this is where you might have led everyone astray without meaning to."

"What do you mean?" asked Phormio.

"Well, Leo is the name of a male cat, and I think that you will find that the cat that you have been calling Leo all this time is not a male. I think that you will find that Leo is actually Cleo (if I may) and that she—not he—has found a warm and cozy place for an altogether different reason."

"So our cat is…a lady cat?" asked Gini slowly.

"Oh, yes. And the sound that Septimus heard a while ago was not Leo fighting with another cat, but two different cats altogether fighting about who had the right to be the …ah….father of her kittens."

"KITTENS," said everyone at once.

"Oh, yes," said Father Horse, and if you would like to follow me, I will take you to them.

Hippolytus led them out of the house, through the yard and into the large stone barn where the fleeces were stored. It was a long, narrow building entered from one end, with occasional windows high up in the walls to let in the light. As the group came inside, silence fell upon them, and in that silence, they could just hear the unmistakable sounds of the squeaking mews of newborn kittens.

Hippolytus led the group to a little nest of wool that the cat had clearly made herself, for she lay within it, smaller than they remembered her (for the kittens which had been inside her were now outside her). Snuggled up to her belly were three little blind balls of fur, squeaking and seeking the milk of their mother. Cleo (as she had now become) looked up at the people who had suddenly invaded her little haven and hissed in alarm.

"Don't go too close yet," said Father Horse to the children. "It is enough to know where she is. She will want, more than anything, to protect her babies."

"Can't we bring her in to the house?" asked Gordi.

Lydia answered. "Not yet, children. Cleo is a mother now and she is looking after her kittens. She will be safe enough here. Of course, you may visit her and bring her milk and a little food, but for the next ten days or so, she must stay here with her babies. In fact, why don't you go off to the kitchen with Phormio now and find some things to tempt her. I think, Phormio, it might be time for some food. I don't know about the rest of you but all of this searching has made me hungry."

A little while later, the family gathered, along with Father Horse and Simon, in the dining room. There was a mood of relief and celebration. The lost cat had been found and the mystery solved. Gini and Gordi had already begun to meet the new cats, with gifts to their mother of pieces of bacon, cheese and a dish of ewes' milk. Simon's mother had washed and scrubbed him until he was pink and clean and Lydia was inwardly most happy, not so much at the finding of the cat, but because her choice of Father Horse for the children now seemed to have been the right one.

As they took their lunch together (the occasion seemed to demand that Phormio and his family join too), the mood was as light and jolly as it had been miserable only a couple of hours before.

"Seriously, Father," asked Lydia. "How did you know that Leo was Cleo, and that there were kittens involved?"

"Well, it's what I always tell the children. The way to wisdom is not thinking about new things in old ways, but about old things in new ways. I noticed that the cat was rather fat, but like the rest of you, I put it down to a generous family. But when Septimus told me about the yowling, I started to think and asked myself the basic question, how do we know that Leo is a male? What if this were not Leo fighting with another cat (something he otherwise seems rather too slow to do well), but two cats fighting about Leo? The only reason for that would be if Leo in fact were Cleo, and they were fighting over her. Once I had developed that line of thinking, then I wondered if Cleo were fat at all, or perhaps was carrying kittens, and that thought then took me to the woolshed. One thing that I have learned over the years is that a mother cat likes to have her babies in a quiet and warm place, both to be safe from other animals and to keep her kittens safe while they are too little to look after themselves. There seemed no better place than the woolshed!" And then he added, almost as an afterthought, "Oh, and I prayed of course."

Everyone laughed at the feeble joke.

Just then, there was a cough from the open door of the dining room. Standing there was Septimus, with a rolled up scroll.

"My Lady, a rider just brought this for you."

He gave her the letter, and she read it.

"Is there a reply?" he asked.

"No," she said. "There is no need. He may go on his way, but give him a good silver coin for his trouble."

"Yes, My Lady," said Septimus, and he bowed and left.

"Well," she said to everyone. "Glaucus is coming home, and he is bringing guests! This is what he says:

> *Septimius Glaucus to Aurelia Lydia, his wife, greetings.*
>
> *Things are well here with me as I trust they are with you. The business has gone well. I have been to a number of towns where there are tailors who make clothes for local men and women of distinction. They have been impressed with the cloth samples that I took with me, and I have been able to get a number of large orders. More importantly, I have also made contact with military authorities who order red cloth for the army. I have promised to supply as much as they need over time. The officers who oversee the ordering are impressed but, because it is such a large amount, they insist on coming to see the works before they commit to any*

order. I am in Eboracum now, and so I should be home the day after you receive this. I am bringing with me Tribune Herennius Maximinus, along with his wife, Sentia. Maximinus is the Head Quartermaster of the Sixth Legion, and the decision about the order is his to make. They will be accompanied by a small guard of six soldiers.

My heart flies to you more swiftly than my body. I shall be with you tomorrow, fortune being with us.

Farewell!

She rolled up the scroll, sat for a moment, and then took charge.

"Phormio, we must be ready for the best dinner party ever. You have a day to scour the house and your skill for the best recipes ever. Children, you must look your best but I do not insist that you come to the dinner. On the other hand, Father Horse, I rather think that you must. Now, the house must be spotless and guest rooms prepared for the tribune, his wife, and the escort. We've had a big morning this morning, so let's all have a bit of a lie down and a rest, and then get to it."

CHAPTER SEVEN

FATHER HORSE SHARES A SECRET

THE NEXT DAY WAS bright and clear with the promise of midday heat. Rules were laid down at breakfast. Lydia was quite clear.

"This is a working day for this house. We have important guests and they must be properly looked after. Children, I don't want to see you until late this afternoon when I expect your father. I'm sure that you and Father Horse can find places to be today that are not within these four walls. I have already told Phormio to make you up some food for your lunch. Go through the kitchen on the way out , but do not linger there. Father Horse, I entrust them to your care. Take Simon with you. You may have more need of him than his father. Now all of you, eat up and go! I have much to do and cannot stay and talk."

With that, Lydia was gone.

Father Horse thought for a moment, "Well, children, while we finish our breakfasts, we have an important decision to make. Where shall we spend our day? I have barely been outside so I have no ideas to offer here. Do you have a favorite place that you like to go when you escape from the house?"

"Our forest!" replied Gordi at once, and apparently without thinking. "That's where we go, don't we, Gini?"

Gini nodded and grinned.

"So, shall we finish here and meet in the courtyard in, say quarter of an hour?" suggested Father Horse.

Simon came in from the kitchen and a little more than fifteen minutes later, the four of them were gathered in the middle of the courtyard by the round plinth. The door in the side was open, as Quintus, the gardener kept the tools of this trade there. Quintus himself was already hard at work, searching for and plucking out tiny weeds and giving the rosemary hedge a very precise trim.

Hippolytus was rather glad to be getting out of the house. In the days that he had been at Hightower, he had rarely been outside the walls of the villa, and then, never out of its sight. He had been used to spending his days walking up and down the hills and valleys of his former parish, and he now felt eager for the opportunity to step outside and see a little of this new and strange countryside, especially that little forest that had always enchanted Gini and Gordi.

When they made their way to the kitchen, they found that Phormio was not going to let them go without generous supplies. He had packed a knapsack for each of them with bread, cheese, olives, dried and fresh fruit and some sliced sausage. He also gave Father Horse a goatskin flask of wine.

"There's plenty of water in the stream," he told him. "But you will, no doubt find this a better quencher of thirst. It's some of the good stuff from back home. You can't make wine like this here. It rains too much."

Father Horse accepted it with gratitude.

Once they were all loaded up, Hippolytus addressed his little party, "Let's go!" he cried with a real enthusiasm that surprised even him.

Out they went through the kitchen door and into the yard behind. This was just as busy. The chickens had been raided for their eggs and a pile of chopped wood was slowly growing by the kitchen and bathhouse doors.

They came to the gate in the stone fence, and it was here that Father Horse stopped. "All right," he said. "This is as far as I know. One of you will have to take the lead from here and take us somewhere terribly interesting. Who can do that?"

Gordi was immediately eager, bursting with excitement.

"Oh, may I Father Horse? I know the forest a little. Gini and I love to spend time there."

"Of course, young man," came the reply. "Lead on!"

Gordi led them through close-cropped sheep paddocks to the woodland that crowned the ridge above Hightower. At first, Hippolytus enjoyed the exercise. He had forgotten just how much he loved walking out in the open air. He had also forgotten his own limitations, and, just as importantly, he had forgotten his staff. At first, he had not minded, but as the climb became a little steeper, he felt the beginnings of a familiar cramp in the damaged muscles of his legs. Finally, at the gates of the forest, he called a halt and asked (between gasps), "What are the best things about this place? Tell me about the trees. What kinds are they?"

"Oh, I don't know," replied Gordi, a little nonchalantly. "Green ones with lots of leaves, at least in summer."

"Do you know, Gini?" inquired the priest.

"No. Well, I don't know much about the trees, except that there are rather a lot of them here."

By this time, Father Horse had his breath back, but his legs were still sore. He sat down instead on a downed tree trunk. The entire tree was out of the ground with one end broadening into the remains of its root system; the other into the wreckage of its branches.

Gini and Gordi wandered a little into the forest, but not too far, while Simon stood by Hippolytus, ready to assist him if he needed.

Hippolytus looked up at Simon. "Do you know what an ash tree looks like?"

Simon nodded.

"See if you can find me a sapling or a long branch that I can use as a staff. If you can't find an ash tree, then anything stout and solid will do. I will be using it a lot."

Gini turned round, puzzled.

"Why do you need a staff, Father Horse? You seem all right without one."

"Ah, child," came his reply. "You have only really seen me around the farm and at the house, walking short distances and on flat ground. If I have to go more than a little way, or up and down hills, than I need a staff. My legs are hurt, you see."

"Is that why you wear trousers?" asked Gordi, suddenly. "I knew there was a reason!"

"Indeed, it is. My legs are not good to look at, and so it is better that I found a way to cover them when I am with people so that it is me that they see, and not my legs."

As he finished, Simon came back with a stout piece of timber.

"I found this Father! It's an old oak sapling that must have been pushed over by some beast or maybe a boar. It should serve you well."

"So Simon, you know ash and oak. Do you know the other trees in this forest?"

"Oh yes, Father. I often come up with the farm slaves when they come up here to gather firewood, and with my dad when he is up here looking for mushrooms. He says that this forest is not too different from the ones back home."

"Well thanks to you, I can walk now. Simon, would you show us a little of what you know here. Show us oak, ash, beech and elm. Show us the best places for berries."

"Oh sir, I know the best place for wild raspberries!"

"Lead on, Simon. You shall be our guide."

"But this is our wood, Father," interrupted Gordi, crossly. "We don't need a slave to show it to us."

Silence fell in the forest. It was as if the wind paused in its rustling of leaves, the birds ceased for a moment to call one to the other. Even the flies forgot to buzz and the midges to hum.

"This is God's forest, Gordi," came Father Horse's soft murmur. "And Simon knows it better than you, or me, or even Gini."

Gini, who had been just as surprised by Gordi's outburst (although part of her secretly agreed), nodded without speaking.

They set off, going deeper into the woods, with Simon scampering eagerly ahead, keen to point out the trees and brambles that they passed by. After an hour or so, they came to a little clearing and, without saying as much, they all decided on a break. Father Horse sat on a log, while the children flung themselves face-up on the ground, looking up to the cloudless heavens, crowded as they were by treetops.

When they had caught their breath, Gini asked a question. "Father Horse, why did you call our cat 'Cleo' now that she is a girl? Have there been famous Cleos?"

"Well, I can think of two," responded Father Horse. "The first is the Muse of History. The Greeks believe that each of the Arts has its own goddess to inspire it what they call a 'Muse.' Since the Greeks think of the writing of History as an art, it has its own muse. Her name is Cleo. But all that's rather dull."

Gini and Gordi pricked up their ears. They had never heard a teacher call the gods of the Greeks dull before.

"There is a much more interesting Cleo or, in full, Cleopatra who was Queen of Egypt in the time of Julius Caesar. She was the last of a great family of rulers who had been Kings and Queens of Egypt since the time of Alexander the Great. By all accounts, Cleopatra was not especially beautiful, but Julius Caesar and Mark Antony both fell in love with her."

Gordi and Gini (and perhaps even Simon) suddenly were interested.

"What happened?" demanded Gordi. "Did they fight over her? Was there a big war over who could marry her?"

"Well yes, but not between Caesar and Antony. It was Julius Caesar who met her first when Caesar was fighting his civil war with Pompey. After he lost a big battle in Greece, Pompey fled to Egypt. There was a fierce struggle at the time in Egypt between Cleopatra and her brother, Ptolemy. When Pompey arrived by sea, he was greeted on the beach by two of Ptolemy's officials who immediately killed him. These men hoped by this killing to please Caesar. They could not have been more wrong. When Caesar turned up in Egypt, he was furious about the whole thing. That was when he met Cleopatra, and he fell in love with her at once.

"Caesar helped Cleopatra in her own fight with Ptolemy, and they spent almost a year trapped in the palace at Alexandria together before a Roman relief force could arrive. After Ptolemy had been defeated, Caesar made Cleopatra the unchallenged Queen of Egypt, and she bore him a son, Caesarion.

"After he left Egypt, she followed him to Rome. But then Caesar was killed, stabbed to death by a group of Roman senators at a meeting of the Senate. At that time, she left and went back to Egypt while Rome once again fell into a series of civil wars. That was when Caesar's family and friends fought those who had joined together to kill him. They were led by Caesar's old deputy, Mark Antony, and his adopted son, Octavian (what a lot of names!). In these wars Cleopatra always sought to help those who were on the side of Antony and Octavian. When the killers were defeated, Cleopatra went to meet Antony at Tarsus, your old city, and they fell in love.

"For ten years, Antony sought to rule the eastern half of the Roman world. Cleopatra was his main helper and support. This made Octavian angry. He thought that Antony should not be spending time with a foreigner, but be married to a proper Roman lady—in fact, his own sister Octavia. This led to another war, and another great battle. Octavian won and became the Emperor Augustus. Antony and Cleopatra both died, but their memory and glory live on."

"That's such a sad story!" Gini burst in.

"And it really happened. Come children. Simon is anxious to show us something."

"Raspberries, Father," called Simon. "They're just over the ridge here."

After some minutes, Simon stopped and peered carefully through the scrub.

"They're around here," he muttered, scanning the edge of the path on their left.

"There!" came his triumphant shout, and he pointed to a little break in the path where a track ran off. Simon bent low and plunged in. Gini and Gordi followed suit. Father Horse was too big to fit through, so instead he used his staff and his body to push his way through. It was hard work, but after thirty or so paces of forcing his way, and being scratched and tugged at by brambles, he broke through into a little clearing. There beneath the tree canopy were enormous raspberry bushes, each richly laden with fruit. The children were already thoroughly busy, filling their hands and mouths with raspberries.

Father Horse stood and watched as they picked and ate, picked and ate. Soon, their hands and faces (and clothes!) were red with the juice of their raspberry feast. After a while, Hippolytus gave a little cough and laughed.

"If only your mothers could see you now!"

Gini and Gordi looked at one another, faces smeared with red, and burst out laughing.

"We must look a fright!" Gini moaned, and then grinned, white teeth through scarlet skin.

"It looks like we have slain and drunk the blood of our enemies!" laughed Gordi.

"Ew, what a nasty thought," his sister replied. "Simon, is there somewhere that we can wash this off?"

"I know just the place," Simon spoke quickly. "There's a stream with a little pool not far ahead. It's where I go to see some of the forest animals when they come to drink."

Simon led them back to the path, the children bending and keeping low as before, and Father Horse pushing his way through. By the time they were back at the forest path, he was grateful for the cool shade cast by the trees. His progress through the bushes had been hard and hot work. They went further down the path and into a little gully. Soon they could hear the sound of running water; a gentle trickle at first, then growing into the bubbling, gurgling, rushing sound of a running stream.

The path through the trees led them down to a wide clearing. It was here that they at last found the stream. It had broken out of the forest, coursed over some rocks and fallen into a broad pool through which it flowed to an outlet at the other end. The children, Simon included, all ran to the water's edge and plunged their arms deep into the cool water, rinsing their hands and washing their faces. Then, almost without thinking, Gordi threw a handful of water at Gini; Gini splashed Gordi back; Simon was caught in the middle. Hippolytus called out to Simon, "Simon, be a good lad and fetch the sack with my food. I feel the need for a good, deep drink."

Simon scuttled away from the bank to where the bags lay under the trees. The other two stopped still, all thoughts of flinging water at one another now gone.

Father Horse looked up and around and sighed.

"What a blessed place. It is a relief on a hot day to have the cool of the water and the shade of the trees."

"Will you not cool your feet in the pool, Father"? Gini asked.

"No, child," he replied." There was a time when I should gladly have done so, but some years ago, my legs were hurt and they are not a proper sight for any but me and my God."

"What happened, Father Horse?" Gordi called to him.

"It is not a good story. You might not like to hear it."

"Oh Father, tell us, please!" Simon spoke up, a little hesitantly.

Father Horse thought for a moment. This was not going to be easy for him, but it would not hurt the children to know.

"Well, if you want to know, it was like this. Years ago, when I was a younger man, and studying in the city of Caesarea, a decree went out from the Emperor Decius that all the world should offer sacrifice to the gods. I was a young Christian then, a child in the faith and in the ways of the world. Many of the Christians in Caesarea fled the city, but one by one, so as not to draw attention to themselves. We could not offer sacrifice—none of us—since that would be giving honor to gods that many of us think are wicked devils, if they are there at all.

"I did not run. My teacher stayed and so I stayed with him. He said to me then, 'Let us take what the Lord sends.' I could have gone. There were places in the countryside where I could have hidden. Perhaps I thought that I was being faithful and noble. Perhaps I thought that I might be called upon to die for my faith. For whatever reason, I stayed with my teacher and, of course, the soldiers found us. In fact they came looking for him because he was famous as a Christian teacher and I imagine the governor thought that if he could be made to sacrifice then the rest of us would fall into line.

"We were taken to the steps of the town hall where there was a fire, burning in a brazier. The tribune commanding the soldiers told us to throw in a pinch of incense and swear by the divine spirits of the emperors. We refused. We each gave the response that we had rehearsed together: 'I am a loyal citizen but I cannot offer sacrifice because I am a Christian.' They took us and threw us in prison and left us there. They gave us neither food nor water save what we could scavenge, but my teacher was well respected in the city, and not just by Christians. Many pagans took pity on us and sent us food and drink in abundance. We spent weeks there, while they waited for our spirits to break. When they came back, we still refused and so they decided to torture us.

"Some forms of torture leave no marks except on the spirit. Our torturers were soldiers and good at their work. They knew just how much pain we could stand before we blacked out. That is how they began, hitting us again and again and again so that we bruised but did not break. This went on for weeks and weeks. They would beat us up, then wait for our cuts and bruises to heal and then do it all over again. It was cruel, but clever. But it didn't work. After some months of confinement and beatings, we were still defiant.

"Perhaps someone lost patience. For whatever reason, they decided to cut us. They began with our feet, hurting us enough that every step was agony for us. I won't go into details. You don't need to know what they did, only that they did it carefully, exactly and with great skill. They followed the same pattern as before: torture, pause for recovery, more torture. Sometimes they left us alone for days and days, for so long that we thought that they might have forgotten about us. Sometimes they brought us out in public and ordered us, again and again, to do the thing that we could not do.

"If we had given in, the enemies of God would have taken it as a great victory. They knew this, and we knew this. Then, unexpectedly, the emperor died. He was killed in a battle against the Goths. The order died with him. There was the usual chaos when an emperor dies suddenly. In that confusion, we were released. My teacher was exhausted and very badly hurt. He died soon afterwards. I survived because I was younger and stronger, but my legs and feet bear the terrible scars of that time."

The children had been listening to his story in complete silence. They even forgot to eat. As he finished, the only sound was the constant flowing of the water. Gordi and Gini still stood in the stream: Gordi, apparently unable to move as he came to understand just why Father Horse wore trousers and shoes constantly; and Gini with tears rolling down her cheeks. It was Simon who broke the silence. "But Master, that makes you a kind of martyr. They might not have killed you but they could have done. Your scars are not horrible to see. They are the marks of your devotion to God, honorably earned. Surely you should not be ashamed of them, but proud!"

Father Horse was surprised. Simon's words were not those of a child.

"You have taught me something, Simon!" Hippolytus finally responded. "I believe that I too shall cool my feet in the stream."

He kicked off his shoes, undid the drawstring of this trousers under his robe and, his scarred and twisted legs bare in a way that he could scarce remember, stepped into the water.

CHAPTER EIGHT

THE TRIBUNE COMES TO DINNER

A FEW HOURS LATER, the group tumbled back down the hill towards the house. It was neither the voice of Lydia that had summoned them, nor the growling of their bellies (Phormio had provided everyone with plenty to eat), by the eagerness of Gini and Gordi to see their father. Not only did they love him deeply, and miss him very much, but he also brought back presents for them every time he went on one of his long trips.

Father Horse knew that Lydia needed as much time as possible to organize the house but he also knew that the children would need to be prepared both to meet their father and to be presented to honored guests. He too felt somewhat bedraggled and tired and longed for a bath and a rest before the evening meal. For a time, he had sought to distract the children with more stories and questions of his own about the forest, but since Simon knew more about the place than Gini and Gordi together, that tended to embarrass them rather than engage them.

It was Gini who made the decision. They had been sitting under an oak tree and Father Horse had been telling the children about dryads when suddenly she stood up. "Look Father Horse, I suppose that this might be terribly interesting, but it's time to go home now. Our father might be there already and I have heard enough stories just for now."

Hippolytus smiled to himself as he caught Lydia's tone in Gini's voice. He also knew when not to fight a losing battle.

"Very well," he surrendered. "Off home it is."

The returned as they had left, through the yard behind the house. There, they found bustle and busyness. The woodpiles were being replenished, while the bathhouse slaves had the bronze boiler heated. Steam was already being pumped into the underfloor cavity. The fires of the kitchen ovens, lit that morning, were now reduced to the red hot coals that were best for cooking. The kitchen itself was the hottest place that Hippolytus had ever been. The children couldn't get out of there quickly enough. Instead, they soon found themselves in the courtyard by the plinth, where they had begun their morning. The garden was now more weeded, trimmed and prettied than the children had ever seen before. No leaf, nor blade of grass, nor petal was out of place.

"Don't you sit on anything!" came a voice from within the plinth. Rufus, the gardener, emerged from a little door set into the side. He looked tired and cross. When he saw the children, his face softened. "Beg pardon, young master, young mistress. Them kitchen slaves have been out here and I always have to clean up after 'em."

Hippolytus was curious.

"Is there a room in there, Quintus?"

"No, just a place to store my tools."

Still curious, Father Horse asked to look inside, and without waiting, poked his head through the door. There was a small space, four feet round and about the same high. The large gardening tools were leaned against the wall, the small ones, and a length of rope were stacked in shelves that were set into the wall opposite, and pegs hung from a ring set in the roof.

He grunted to himself, nodded, and then took charge, ushering the children out of the courtyard and into the covered walk.

"Children," he said. "You had better go and find your mother. She will want you scrubbed clean and in your best clothes. I must do the same. Simon, could you please bring me some water and oil, and I will do what I can to make myself presentable."

Father Horse trudged up to his room. He was tired after what had been a long day in the forest, and was not at all looking forward to the evening to come, although he was eager to meet Glaucus. He was pleased to find that a brazier had been lit in his room, and although the heat of the day still lingered, it meant that he could heat his washing water when it came. He sat down for a moment on his bed, then lay down. Within minutes, he was asleep.

He woke at Simon's urging. "Wake up, Father, they're here! We must get you ready!"

"Oh dear. How long have I been asleep?"

"Not quite an hour, but I did not have the heart to wake you until I heard the fuss from downstairs."

"Well then, let's get me clean and ready to meet the master and his guests."

The water was already hot, and Hippolytus gave himself a serious scrub, cleaning off the dirt of the forest floor, the smudges left by the brambles, and the green smears left by the trees.

When he thought himself sufficiently clean, he dried himself off, combed and oiled his hair, and turned to hunt out his best things.

Simon had already laid these out on the bed: a pure, white robe of woven wool, white linen trousers and a narrow sash of saffron yellow for his waist. Along with these went his pair of least worn shoes and his most worn staff. Hippolytus dressed swiftly took his staff and went downstairs as quickly as he could to join the family.

At the foot of the stairs, he met Gordi, who snatched at his hand.

"Come along, Father Horse. I've been sent to get you. We're all in the breakfast hall. Father and the others aren't there yet. They are still cleaning up after their journey."

When Hippolytus joined the rest of the family, he was impressed at what he saw. The hall itself had been cleared of furniture and the mosaic floor gleamed with recent washing. Both Gini and Gordi were surprisingly clean, their skins pink from scrubbing and the clothes they wore, their very best. Lydia simply looked magnificent. The ankle-length gown that she wore was pale blue, and she and her maids must have worked for much of the afternoon to create an elaborate hairstyle, complemented by artful makeup and a small amount of well-chosen jewelry.

She came forward and took his free hand. "Thank you so much Father, for the care that you have taken with the children today. They seem to have enjoyed themselves and, perhaps, even learned a thing or two." She smiled, and her eyes twinkled a little. Hippolytus wondered how much Gini and Gordi had said to their mother.

A new voice broke in from behind. "And is there none to greet me?"

They turned. Glaucus had come in, and was in the act of setting down a small wicker hamper.

"Father!" cried the children, and they both rushed to him together. He held them to him with real affection, only releasing them to say, "Now, perhaps you will let me greet your mother too."

This as a much more proper and formal affair. Not only was this more seemly in public, but it did not smudge Lydia's makeup.

The greeting gave Hippolytus a chance to see Glaucus properly. He was of average height, balding, and wore the short, clipped beard that was becoming fashionable. He wore formal dress for dinner, a tunic with a narrow purple stripe, short toga and the gold ring of his social rank. His was an open face, made more so by the broad smile when his children had grappled him. His eyes were blue, and there was both merriment and sadness there.

As if sensing Hippolytus' gaze, he turned around and addressed him directly, "So this is the man brave enough to take on my children! Let me look at you. Goodness me, but you walk with a stick. Have my children done that to you already?"

"No, Papa. He came with that!" Gordi interrupted.

"Just as well. I understand from what my wife has told me that the children like you, that they are learning, that they are far less horrible," (at this he grabbed Gordi and ruffled his hair) "and that you are fast becoming a valued member of the household. I trust that you will be with us for dinner."

It was not a request.

"And now, young man," he turned to Gordi. "I have something for you. Mind you use it carefully now."

Opening the basket, he took out a long object wrapped in cloth. Passing it over to Gordi, he nodded and smiled at the boy. Gordi eagerly pulled off the wrapping, and uncovered a wooden sword, about half the size of, and painted to resemble, a real one. He immediately grasped the hilt and mimed a series of thrusts and slashes.

"Oh, Father," he cried. "It's glorious!"

"Remember Gordi, it's not a toy. It is a training sword such as Roman soldiers start their sons with. We live in difficult times. Who knows when we might be called upon to use one for real?"

Then Glaucus turned to his daughter. "For you, my dear, something gentler, but I hope that you will love it just the same."

He took from the basket another cloth-wrapped parcel, this one the size and shape of a small box. Gini bowed her head to her father and took it with both hands.

"Thank you father, I know that I shall."

She hugged the package close to her for a moment and then, unable to resist any longer, unwrapped it. It was, indeed, a wooden box with a broad, sloping lid that hinged up. Within, there were (securely held) inkpots, pens, a penknife and, most wonderfully, a small sheaf of Egyptian papyrus paper.

"You spoil that girl," said Lydia. "I still have to use wood shavings to write on!"

It was not a bitter remark, nor badly meant, but Gini immediately turned to her mother.

"Would you like the papyrus, Mama? I shall do just as well with the shavings."

"

Lydia laughed. "No, my dear. I was teasing. You are not the only one to whom your father has brought rich gifts."

The new golden eardrops that she wore glinted in the lamplight.

A discreet cough sounded from the doorway.

They all looked over and Septimus stood there in his finest household livery.

"The tribune Herennius Maximinus and his wife, the lady Sentia are here, sir."

Glaucus' response was jovial. "Well, show them in, Septimus. Don't keep them hanging about in the entrance way."

Septimus made way for the guests who swept into the room, as if with the sound of trumpets.

The two made a sharp contrast. Maximinus was tall and large in the belly and Sentia was small and slight. Maximinus had a short-cropped beard, black, thinning hair shot with grey, and dark eyes; Sentia had fair hair and green eyes; Maximinus' features were fleshy, his cheeks red with broken veins; Sentia had high cheekbones, smooth skin, a sharp nose and sharp eyes. Maximinus wore the uniform of his station: a tunic and full toga marked with the broad stripe of the senatorial order. Sentia was more elaborately dressed. Her gown was of pale green silk—a frightful extravagance—her shoes were gilded, and her hair was gathered back in short braids that met at the crown of her head in what looked like a crest. Around her neck she wore a chain of gold that held a medallion bearing three emeralds, two smaller, each flanking a large stone in the center. From her ears there dangled matching earrings, each a small gold chain that held a single emerald.

It was more money than Hippolytus had ever seen in one place and to encounter it in a provincial dining room seemed to him to be rather overdoing it.

Glaucus bowed slightly to Maximinus.

"Most distinguished sir, allow me the honor of presenting my family to you."

Maximinus gave a short nod.

The family had clearly done this before. They lined up. Hippolytus, not quite certain of his own status, stayed in the background.

His left hand holding the fold of his toga, Glaucus gestured towards his family with his right. "My wife, the prominent lady Aurelia Lydia; my son, Aurelius Gordianus; and my daughter, Aurelia Verginia."

"And this?" Maximinus indicated Hippolytus with a flick of his head.

"My children's tutor, Aurelius Hippolytus."

"A philosopher? Out here?" The tribune sounded surprised. "Of which school? We are somewhat starved of proper conversation in the far provinces."

"I believe that he is a Christian, most distinguished sir."

Maximinus wrinkled his nose and grimaced as if he had eaten something nasty. Then he made an effort to be civil. "Well, I suppose that we cannot choose our company as much as we would like when we are so far from real civilization."

Hippolytus said nothing during this exchange. He knew that it was not his place to speak unless and until invited. In any event, he had endured more—and worse—before.

Now it was Maximinus' turn for introductions. "Prominent one, I Marcus Herennius Faustus Maximinus, tribune of soldiers and senator, present to you my wife, the most distinguished lady Sentia Sabina Aciliana."

As he listened to this little roll call of names, held by just two people, Hippolytus thought very carefully about what they told him. He now knew why Glaucus had gone to such pains. Maximinus was not simply some senior officer with the authority to send business Glaucus' way. Both Maximinus and his wife bore names that were ancient and distinguished. They were members of some of Rome's most famous families, families that had built and run the empire for hundreds of years.

In the midst of his thoughts, Father Horse heard the children being sent off to the kitchen for their suppers and he wordlessly followed the party down the covered way to the formal dining room. Three couches had been set up in a "U" formation, in the traditional Roman manner so that guests could recline as they ate. As hosts, Glaucus and Lydia took the central couch; to his right, in the place of honor were Maximinus and Sentia, to his left was Hippolytus so that he and Maximinus faced one another.

On the tables in front of them, there were bowls of boiled quail eggs, olives and nuts. These were just the forerunners of the great feast upon which Phormio had been working all day. The dishes came and went. Wine was poured. The point, of course, was not just the quality of the food. At a dinner party like this, what also mattered was the quality of the conversation.

This began badly enough. Glaucus, as host, had to lead the conversation. He was a businessman and had little talent for small talk. He talked a little about the house, and what he knew of its history, to try and get some chat going.

"I think that this house might have been originally built by the army when they came north," he ventured.

Maximinus' reply was dismissive. "I wouldn't know. It looks like an old fort except for that odd tower. It's well before my time. The army's been here for two hundred years."

Glaucus tried talking about the farm, but he did not know enough about the way that it worked to discuss grazing and growing with anyone who actually knew anything about it. And Maximinus did know. His family had run farms in Italy for generations and it turned out that he had grown up on a small mixed farm at the foot of the Sabine Hills near Rome. That led to some amusing stories from Maximinus about his ongoing struggle, as a boy, to keep the goats from the grapevines.

Then Glaucus asked a question that might have been disastrous if Maximinus had chosen to take offence. He did not. Instead, it became an opportunity for him to wrest the control of the conversation from the host and direct it in ways that he preferred.

What Glaucus had asked was, "So do you come from a very old family?"

Hippolytus, who already knew the answer to this, cringed inwardly. This could be a disaster.

But Maximinus, far from bristling took the opportunity for an expansive reply.

"My family have been supplying Rome with senators and consuls for hundreds of years. We were the patrons of Gaius Marius of Arpinum before he became a mighty general and saved Rome from the barbarians. Every generation, for over four hundred years, a Herennius has stepped forward to serve the state. So, yes, I come from an old family. It is our family and families like ours that has made Rome great. It was not that long ago that a Herennius was even emperor, if only for a little while."

Glaucus had no reply, and his silence was accepted as an invitation to go on. Maximinus took a long drink of his wine and continued. "You might wonder what a Roman noble of my pedigree and rank is doing here in a subordinate rank at the edge of the Empire. Sometimes I wonder it myself. Every time I salute my commander, the 'first spear,' the centurion who has grown beyond his station, I want to punch him instead. But at least that's as high as he can rise. The fool who calls himself emperor in Rome would have it different. He wants any mud-born peasant to have the right to command men like me. What right do they have to command me? Pannonian peasants? Sons of pig farmers who can't read or write. Vast men, all muscle and fight, with scars on their scars—all in front—and parade ground voices. They might look the part, our clever peasants, but they will fail, because such men do not have the right to command bred into them. But your most sacred emperor has decreed that senior military posts are no longer reserved for men who deserve to hold them, men of the right class and breeding, men whose ancestors built this empire, so that any Gaius or Marcus from the ranks can climb to command, and tell men like me what to do. A plague on Gallienus in Rome. Give me Postumus in Gaul any time. He knows real men."

He emptied his wine cup and held it out to be filled. Then he looked across at Hippolytus. "So, philosopher, or priest, or whatever you are, where did you study?"

Hippolytus, who had eaten lightly and drunk little, looked across and replied quietly, "Caesarea in Palestine, Lord."

"And who was your teacher?"

"Origen of Alexandria."

"Never heard of him. I suppose he was another one of your Christians. Who taught him?"

"He sat at the feet of Ammonius and Clement in Alexandria."

"Ammonius I know. My father's uncle studied with him. But not the other one." Maximinus was almost offhand, but then added, "I suppose he was a Christian too."

"Yes, Lord. We have a long tradition of learning."

"Long?" Maximinus scoffed. "You've only been in existence for two hundred years. Where was your Christ when Plato taught? Or Aristotle? Where was he when the Titans fought the gods, or when Hercules labored or the Trojans held off the Greeks for ten years at Ilium? Your God was not even born? How can that be learning? How can it be religion?"

Maximinus was probably more than a little drunk now. But his voice rose as he once again, found his favorite subject. "And that ass Gallienus, that lackwit, that half-brained deadhead has made you all legal. Best thing Nero ever did was to ban you people. You worship different gods—new gods. Actually, you're so new that you're making it up as you go along. There's no tradition that you don't ignore, no holy thing that you do not defile, no true god that you do not defame. I know this. This is what my cousin's husband, the emperor, died for. It's what his sons, died for. It's what she still weeps for. Watch this one, Glaucus. You've got a viper here. The next thing, your children and your wife will be lost to their crucified god, and the real gods of the empire will continue unrecognized and displeased and yet more good citizens will be lost to this creeping anti-Roman, anti-gods society that would bring down the anger of Olympus on us all."

He stopped to draw breath and take another drink.

As he did, Glaucus sought to recapture the conversation.

"Hippolytus, is a Christian education very different from traditional teaching?"

Hippolytus was now truly free to talk. He had been asked the kind of question that properly brought him into the conversation.

"It is the same, Lord. We begin with the same classics. We read Homer and Plato. We argue like Socrates. But we also read our own books. My master learned Hebrew, the language of the Jews, so that he could read the holy books. I was never quite so accomplished. Greek and Latin were enough for me.

"But from him I did learn philosophy and rhetoric. I learned literature and history and I learned the joy of faith."

As soon as he said it, Hippolytus realized that he might have provoked the tribune to another outburst. He ventured to look over to Maximinus, waiting for what might come. But nothing did. The tribune, overcome with good food, good wine, and the fatigue of the day, had gone to sleep.

Sentia looked down at her husband with a look that was almost fond, as his breathing became slow and regular; then she looked over at Hippolytus, gave a little smile and shrugged.

CHAPTER NINE

THE MISSING JEWELS

THE NEXT MORNING, FATHER Horse was a little late coming down to breakfast. His legs still ached from the exercise of the day before. *I will have to get back into the habit of long walks,* he thought to himself, and he had slept badly after the difficult conversation with the tribune over dinner. He worried that he had said something to put the business in danger and that together with the difficult memories the tribune had triggered, had kept him awake well into the night. He had even gone into the garden for a walk during the night, hoping that the peace and the silence of the ordered courtyard would ease his spirit. It did not. When he lay down again, the thoughts and the doubts came back.

It was only when he remembered the words of his teacher that his mind stopped racing and he could properly compose himself for sleep. On the evenings when they knew that torture was coming, Origen would say to him, "Give it to God, my boy. There is nothing that you can do. Worry built no buildings; fretting saved no souls. We cannot live in the day to come. It has not happened yet. So give it all to God. He has already endured more and worse for us. Empty your mind of cares and give your body to rest. Tomorrow will take care of itself."

Hippolytus had smiled at the memory, and his fondness for the great and good man who had taught him. Then he did as he was told, : he had emptied his mind and fallen into a deep sleep.

It was Simon who had woken him, with the sun well above the horizon. The boy was apologetic. He too had overslept, and had not even stopped to heat water before he came to wake his charge. Hippolytus shrugged. "I shall just have to wash in cold water, then."

Washed and dressed, Hippolytus hurried downstairs to the breakfast room where the day always began. As he expected, Lydia was already there, as were the children and, to his surprise, Sentia. The elaborate dress, hair and jewels of the night before had gone. Instead, she wore a simple off-white dress of good Egyptian linen. The women stood as he entered.

"Father Horse, you are late this morning," teased Lydia.

"Sleep did not come easily last night, Lady," he replied.

"Father Horse!" interrupted Sentia. "Is that what they call you?"

"Yes Lady. I think that we can blame young Gordi for that."

Gordi looked up from his full platter as Hippolytus spoke and grinned a mouthful of shattered pastry.

"It does not seem very respectful."

"Well, Lady, respect is as respect does. If the children listen to me and learn from me, then who am I to worry about what name they give me?"

"Well, I suppose it is your affair, and this family's. But if we are to talk of respect, we failed you a little last night. I regret the words that my husband spoke. He had eaten little and drunk a little too much. Do forgive him."

"It is gracious of you to say so, Lady. You do not owe me apologies, and if forgiveness is needed, I happily grant it."

"Good. Now do come and eat. You must be hungry. I saw that you did not eat much last night."

In truth, Hippolytus was ready for a good breakfast. As he filled his plate, he took the opportunity to look again at Sentia. She had not spoken the previous night, either when introductions were made or at dinner. She spoke as one who used words carefully and for the first time, Hippolytus saw a fierce intelligence dancing in her eyes.

Twenty minutes later, replete with bread, honey, boiled eggs, sheep's cheese and ham, he turned to the children.

"Well then, what shall we do today? I am too sore to walk again today. Do you think that we might sit for a while in the cool of the courtyard?"

"Why not here, Father," Lydia suggested. "The men are off looking over the property and the business operation, and I wouldn't mind sitting in for a while. Would you join us, Sentia?"

"Of course, but Fath … Hippolytus will have to forgive me. I was always slow with such elevated things as book learning."

"It seems I have a lot of forgiving to do this morning. But I am a Christian. It is my calling."

The joke was feeble enough but they all laughed anyway.

"Now I need an hour or so for my prayers and to gather my thoughts for the day. Shall we all be back here then?"

They all agreed, Gordi with less than good grace. He did not want to be at school with his mother watching.

The lesson turned out to be something quite different. Hippolytus knew that Lydia had a formidable mind. He suspected the same of Sentia, for all that she appeared otherwise. He knew that whatever he did, he had to do it with them in mind, and yet also ensure that the children were not left out. He used the break to have a bit of a think and to plan what he was going to do.

When everyone was back in the breakfast room, he had them sit in a circle. Then he turned to Gordi.

"Gordi, can you tell me the letters of the Greek alphabet?"

"Of course, Father Horse: alpha, beta, gamma—"

"Excellent, Gordi," Father Horse interrupted. "Now, choose one."

"Choose one?"

"Yes. Just pick a letter."

Gordi thought for a moment.

"How about 'tau'?"

"A very good choice, Gordi. What is it in Latin?"

"T"

"Right again. Now, can we think of any famous people, or things whose names start with 'tau' or 't'?"

There was a silence. Gordi looked blank. Gini was searching her memory.

Sentia broke in.

"Trajan," she suggested. "How about Trajan? Now there was a truly great man."

Gordi still looked blank. Gini looked intrigued.

"Was he an emperor?" she asked.

"Oh yes," replied Hippolytus. "Let me tell you a little about him."

For the next hour or so, Hippolytus told the story of how a senator from distant Spain had come to Rome and been thought of so highly that he had been made emperor. He told about his family, his loving and extraordinary wife, Plotina and his brilliant nephew Hadrian. He told of his military achievements, how he conquered the land of Dacia in the north, and the mysterious kingdom of the Arabs in the east. Then he had defeated the mighty realm of the Parthians beyond the Euphrates and added Mesopotamia and the whole land of Armenia to the Empire. He told of the group of talented soldiers that Trajan had gathered around him. Gordi wanted to know about all of the battles, but here, Hippolytus' knowledge fell short. Instead, Sentia continued, "Gordi, one day, you shall go to Rome, and in that wonderful and glorious city, you shall find a tall monument to Trajan. It is a huge column, mounted on a base a bit like your plinth here, but square.

Around the column, in a great spiral, there are a series of pictures that tell the story of Trajan's war in Dacia. I hope that one day you will see it."

"I hope so too," said Gordi, his eyes shining with excitement.

"But, do you know, children, what Trajan's greatest deed was?" asked Father Horse gently. "He provided money and other support for the orphans and poor children of Italy. He did not see all of the loot that he brought back from his wars as something for him personally to enjoy, but instead he shared it with the poorest people, those with no protectors."

Sentia sighed. "He was a truly great emperor. There has been none better. Certainly none of the men today who seek that power are worthy of it."

There was both sadness and bitterness in her voice. To her, this was not a conversation about the past. It was personal.

"Time for a break, I think," said Lydia, brightly.

Gordi immediately turned to his mother and asked with badly disguised eagerness. " Mother, do you know where Silvius might be? He promised to show me how to use my new sword."

"If he is not about the property with my husband, then you will probably find him in the kitchen trying to cadge food."

Gordi looked at his mother, she nodded and he scampered off.

Hippolytus was puzzled.

"Who is Silvius?" he asked.

"He is one of the military escort who came yesterday with the tribune and Sentia," Lydia answered.

"You don't think that we'd come without an escort, do you?" Sentia seemed surprised that Hippolytus had not considered that.

"Now that you say so, I suppose not. How many men in the escort?"

"Six, plus their commander makes seven. It is enough for protection without overdoing it, or creating too great a burden for our hosts," replied Sentia. "Silvius is one of the younger soldiers, in fact, I think, the youngest and little Gordi has taken a bit of a shine to him."

There was an awkward moment of silence, until Lydia abruptly stood up. "Shall we all go for a little walk in the garden. It is cool and pleasant there. I shall never quite get used to the summer heat here."

"It's the humidity," agreed Sentia. "I miss the clean, dry heat of the Italian summer."

The two women led the way, continuing in talk, while Father Horse and Gini trailed along behind.

"So how long have you been away from Italy?" Lydia asked Sentia.

"Too long," came the reply. "We came here when Maximinus gained his tribunate, twelve years ago. The emperor himself posted my husband here. That was Decius in those days. He was married to Maximinus' cousin (not his first cousin, maybe second, or third I think) and he sent us here with a view to giving Maximinus a legion of his own one day after he had learned the ways of command. But then Decius was killed in battle along with his son and everything changed. New emperors had their own friends and so we were left here. When Gallienus came along things did not get better. Maximinus and Gallienus grew up together and did not get along. It pleases the emperor to leave him here unrecalled, unrewarded, and unpromoted. My husband has put his energy into promoting the cause of Postumus who most here see as their emperor. It is a kind of exile, but it is honorable and we serve the state in our own way."

Lydia nodded. She had wondered much about Sentia since neither she nor her husband seemed to fit the roles they had been assigned. They were too big, too grand and too noble to be in Britain, and not in a more senior post. These words answered many of her questions. There was another questions that might be painful.

"Do you have children?"

"We have two boys and a girl. We left them in Italy with Maximinus' parents before we came north. It is one more reason that we would prefer to be home. The boys are almost old enough themselves for military service now. Our daughter is nearly of an age to marry. We write to them and they write to us, but that is no substitute."

Hippolytus, trailing behind, could feel the depth of her sadness, of her loss.

Sentia breathed in sharply, perhaps stifling a sob.

"Still, there is much for which to give thanks. The gods have blessed us with life, health, station, and family. It would not be right to be angry about the other things that they send us. I gain comfort in philosophy; my husband, in work."

Then she turned to Hippolytus. "And what of you? What is your philosophy, teacher, here at the edge of the world? Is your Christ enough for you?"

Hippolytus thought for a moment before responding.

"Lady, I follow Christ alone. I find there enough there for me."

"Christ!" Her tone was mocking. "What can you find in that crucified magician that is not there, and better, in good philosophy? What do you get from these children's stories that is better than Plato or Aristotle?"

"Lady, Aristotle is very good on the how of things. He takes his subjects apart, and breaks them down into all of their parts, and then sees how these parts fit together. This is a very good way of understanding how things work whether animal, or plant, or even human. Plato is less interested in the how of things than in the what of things. He is impatient with imperfection, although he sees it as our natural state. He tries to find a way of bringing the perfect and the imperfect together and, while I find much to like here, it never quite works because of the limits that he sets himself. It is Christ who brings it together for me. Indeed, he shows me more."

"What more?" Sentia snapped.

"He shows me that one can live a whole life in a world that is not perfect. He shows me that we have always been mistaken when we think to please the gods with sacrifices—by striking bargains with them, if you like—he shows me that we do not beat a path to heaven by negotiation or obedience, but that it is God who comes to us, who raises us up. When I understood that, much then fell into place."

"Shall we sit?" invited Lydia. They were in the shadiest part of the courtyard and all sat on the raised stone border of the garden bed on either side of the path, Lydia and Sentia on one side and Hippolytus and Gini on the other so that Hippolytus and Sentia faced one another.

It was not elegant, but it was a break from the long stroll they were otherwise taking around and through the garden.

Sentia had some time to formulate her response to Hippolytus, and her tone was kinder, almost as if she were explaining to a child.

"Don't you see that is just the kind of thing that causes communities to fall apart. For a thousand years, Rome has existed through the favor and approval of the gods. That favor was achieved by faithfulness in sacrifice and not just rams or goats or cattle. From time to time, Rome's greatest generals have offered themselves to death in battle so that Rome would succeed and grow. Now your new teaching comes along with your new rules, laws, and ways of doing things that ignores the gods altogether. No wonder things aren't going so well, with all of you people being lured into atheism, into denying the gods completely and into a different kind of society with no respect for laws and traditions."

"Lady, it is true that we are everywhere. You will find us in law courts, in the army, on local councils, in the market place, even in the Senate. We provide your food, your clothes, your shoes, your jewelry. We may be your slaves. We may be your friends. We are still few, but more than we were, and we are just as vulnerable as you are to disasters. When the plague came, Christians died too; when the barbarians attacked, Christians suffered death or slavery alongside everyone else. Your welfare is our welfare. Your prosperity is ours as well.

"What strengthens us in all of this is that the way of Christ is not just a teaching. It is not a philosophy. Socrates, Plato, Aristotle, and the rest all died. You called our Master a 'crucified magician.' So he was crucified. But he is also resurrected. We do not follow him. We believe in him, and not because he said good things or did marvelous things. We are his because he is still with us, leading us, inspiring us, filling us with power and hope and love."

When he finished, there was a little silence. Kindly, and a little hesitatingly, Sentia replied, "Hippolytus, I have spoken freely because I have little chance to say such things in an army town like Eboracum. Forgive me if I seem blunt, but I am grateful for the chance to speak my mind. But do not parade your faith too much in front of my husband. He feels much as I do, but his ways of expressing that are more—shall we say—direct."

Then she looked up and, as if noticing the plinth for the first time, asked, "What's that?"

"We call it 'the plinth,'" Lydia said. "We think that it was meant to be the base of a statue. It's hollow inside. The gardener uses it for storing his tools."

"How odd," mused Sentia. Then, turning to Gini, she said, "Forgive us, child, for talking such dull grown up talk and leaving you to sit in silence. Tell me something of your life out here. Is it much fun, or would you rather be in the city?"

Before Gini could respond, a soft cough sounded from behind them. Turning around, Hippolytus saw a large man with close-cropped hair and beard. His tunic bore the bull badge of the Sixth Victorious Legion on his shoulder, obviously one of Maximinus' escort but in plain clothes rather than armor.

"Lady," said the man, addressing Sentia. "There is a matter that needs your urgent attention. Will you come?"

"Of course," she replied to the soldier. "Do excuse me, everyone."

"I wonder what that was about," said Gini.

"I'm sure that we'll find out, if we need to know." Lydia was firm. "It must be coming on for lunchtime now," she continued. "Let us see if there is some food for us. All of this thinking has made me quite hungry."

"Then Father Horse must be hungry all the time. He never stops thinking!" laughed Gini, and they all went inside. The cool inside was a relief. While they had been talking, the day had darkened a little and the air had thickened with humidity. A storm was coming.

Gordi was waiting for them, rather impatiently, beside the table where their lunch was already set out.

His wooden sword was stuck through his belt, and his skin was rosy from exercise. They were barely in the room when he called out, "Can I please eat now mother? I waited but I'm really hungry."

Lydia smiled a little smile and nodded. Gordi filled his wooden bowl with food, and was deeply engaged in eating by the time that everyone else had their plates full.

As they sat eating, Gini suddenly looked up at Hippolytus and asked, "Father Horse, why are Maximinus and Sentia against Christians so much? Don't they know about—"

She was about to say "mother" when Father Horse interrupted.

"Best not say too much right now, but I think that we can say that for a long time Christians have not been trusted by the Roman government. That is because the government has never known very much about us, and when they have taken the trouble to find out (which is rare) they have found us to be, as we are, not a threat. But because most don't know much about us, and it is a general rule that people fear what they do not know, they are afraid of nothing much. So they make up stories about us and attack us when they can. Maximinus and Sentia have just inherited that tradition, that's all."

They ate in silence for a time until they were joined by Glaucus.

Holy, gods!" he exclaimed. "You all seem so glum!"

In the distance, there was a low grumbling of thunder.

"Not glum," Lydia replied. "Just talked out a bit. Tell me, how did you go this morning with Maximinus?"

"Well enough, I think," Glaucus was filling his own plate as he spoke. "I showed him all of the operations from the sheep farm to the shearing, spinning, carding, weaving and dyeing. He liked the idea that we could do the whole exercise here and so do it more cheaply than their usual contractors. We were talking money when one of his escort came and called him away. I hope that there is no urgent military problem from over the border. I've had enough of that for one lifetime."

Then he too began the serious business of eating.

A few moments later, both Maximinus and Sentia strode in. Neither looked happy.

Everyone rose and Glaucus motioned for them to join the lunch party.

"We're not here to eat. We will not stay in this house any longer, but we will not be leaving either. My escort are setting up a tent for us in the next field."

"Why, what has happened?" Glaucus was almost speechless.

"It is very simple. Someone in this house has stolen my wife's jewels. We are not leaving until we have found the thief and recovered our property. Until that time, you can all consider yourselves under my authority. Take what food you wish, go to your rooms and wait for my instructions. That is all."

As they both turned and swept out of the room, the first raindrops splashed into the courtyard.

CHAPTER TEN

THE SEARCH

THE FAMILY WAS STUNNED. No one spoke. They collected their food in silence and left the room. Waiting out in the covered way were the six members of Maximinus' escort. Gordi stopped, braced himself and then went up to one, the youngest, evidently Silvius.

The rain was now steady.

"I have to take you to your room, young master, and make sure that you stay there for a while. I'm sorry, but that's the tribune's order." Silvius was embarrassed, looking down at his boots as he spoke.

"And what about me?" asked Gini. "Is there another brave soldier of Rome to take me to my room?" There was a coldness in her voice.

"Steady now, miss," said another of the soldiers, who looked the oldest. "You should go with your ma."

"Then accompany us to my room," snapped Lydia. "There should be enough there to keep my daughter and me occupied until your commander sees fit to release us back into the rest of our home." Lydia's anger was apparent.

"Then I shall go to my office," declared Glaucus. "I can get some work done and pretend that this is not happening."

Hippolytus was less upset than the family. For them, their status as leading the owners of the farm and leading citizens of the district was being trampled upon by Maximinus. For Hippolytus the whole thing was less of a chore, since he did not think of himself as especially important. And besides, he had been locked up before by Roman soldiers in much less pleasant surroundings.

Glaucus broke in on Hippolytus' thoughts, addressing the soldiers. "If you are going to be wandering around our house while we are locked up, might we at least know your names?"

"Fair question," replied the oldest. "I'm the commander here, Optio Marcellus. I'll escort you, sir. Silvius, you know. He'll look after the little boy. This here is Aelian, and he will go with the ladies."

Aelian was a dark-haired young man with a missing front tooth and a nasty scar on his cheek.

"The teacher is to go with Germanus here."

Germanus did not look very German, He was a small man with dark hair and dark, intense eyes.

"And these two," he motioned towards two soldiers, leaning on either side of a column, "are Julianus and Victor. These fine soldiers, when they remember to stand up straight like Romans are going to commence the search."

"Search?" Glaucus was angry.

"Yes, sir. The tribune says that the jewels can't have gone far. The strong likelihood is that they are somewhere in this house. He means to search every inch until they are found."

Thunder exploded in the sky.

Glaucus knew when he was beaten. He couldn't very well threaten to complain to the governor when Maximinus had the governor's ear. He couldn't complain to the emperor because Maximinus grew up with him and didn't care too much what he said or did anyway. He couldn't complain to the Senate, because Maximinus was related to half of it. And besides, for Glaucus, there was the important matter of the army contract. A very big part of him wanted the matter resolved very quickly so that it did not get in the way of settling a contract to supply the legion at York with dyed cloth. That was not mere greed. It was the steady income by which he provided for himself and his family.

Germanus looked at Father Horse.

"Come with me now," he ordered softly. If he did not look German, he certainly sounded it.

As they went along the covered way, Father Horse asked companionably, "Where are you from?"

"I am Roman," was the clear answer.

"Yes, well I am too," responded the priest. "But we're all from somewhere. I came here from Lycia. My father had a big orchard outside Attaleia. He grew apricots and cherries. Come, what is your actual name? It's not Germanus. That's just what they call you."

"My name is Guntheric. They boys in the legion cannot say it, so to them, I am just 'the German.' My father was Sigismund, a warrior of the Alemanni. He was given land near Moguntiacum. For us, there is nothing but army."

"Well, you know how they call me Father Horse?" asked Hippolytus. "That's not my name either. 'Father' is my title, like optio or centurion or even tribune. And the children called me horse because the lad cannot say 'Hippolytus.'"

"Well, neither can I," said the soldier. "It is a hard name."

"Well, I quite like being called 'Father Horse.' Most of the family calls me that now. What do you like to be called: Germanus or Guntheric?"

The answer was clear. "Germanus. It is my army name, my Roman name. The other is, well, private. It is for my mother and my father, my brothers and sisters and my clan."

"Very well, then, Germanus. That is what I shall call you."

By now, they were on the landing outside Hippolytus' room.

"Would you like to come in and search it?" he asked. "I'm sure that your tribune will demand it sooner or later. If you need to make a mess, don't worry. Clearing it up will give me something to do while I wait."

Although his tone was light, Hippolytus knew that his room would be searched, alongside everyone else's, and so far as he was concerned, the sooner it were done, the better.

"No," replied Germanus. "We do this in pairs. Tribune's orders."

"Very well. You know that this room was not designed as a prison cell. It can't be locked from the outside. Or from the inside for that matter. Do you stand guard?"

"No. I will tie the door handle to the stair rail here. Then you cannot open the door."

It was a good solution and Father Horse had to admire it.

"Now please," gestured the soldier. Hippolytus went in and the door closed behind him.

It was late in the afternoon by the time Germanus returned. Father Horse had not been bothered by the wait at all. He read a little, prayed much, slept a little. He was waking from a doze when he heard the door open. Germanus was back and he did not look happy.

"Come now. You are to join the family in the eating room. Then we search your rooms."

The jewels had not been found. If Maximinus had hoped for a swift result, he was being disappointed, and his frustration had clearly crossed over to his soldiers.

"So, no luck yet," Hippolytus sighed.

"No talk, this time. Just get downstairs." Whatever goodwill there had been before seemed to have vanished.

Father Horse followed quietly, as he had been told, and found the family sitting glumly together downstairs in the breakfast room. Once he was in the room Germanus left him for his next task. They were all alone together.

The first fury of the storm had been spent. Now, there was just a steady rain.

Glaucus had been thinking while he had been shut in his office. Now he spoke to the family. "Maximinus is angry and frustrated and he is right to be. We must do everything in our power to help find these jewels. At the very least we must not get in the way when the soldiers are searching. I know that it offends our pride but our honor as a house, and our livelihood into the future, are both at stake. That man can destroy us with a word. Lydia, children, I want you to help where you can. Where you can't please let them go about their work. Father Horse you are new here and yet, it seems, already important in our lives together. I ask you to do the same. You are a clever man. Try and be more clever than our thief."

"Thank you, sir," replied Hippolytus. "I am honored by your confidence."

"Now then," said Glaucus, drawing in his breath suddenly. "I could do with something to drink. What has become of our slaves?"

The soldiers had gone, but there was not a slave to be seen either. The entire household staff seemed to have vanished.

"Gordi, you seem you be on good terms with the soldiers. Can you find out for us where our slaves are and when we might get them back. At the very least, we shall need our dinner tonight."

Gordi was gone for longer than expected, but when he returned, he had Simon with him. Simon had an angry mark on his cheek that was turning into a bruise.

"Simon," said Glaucus. "I'm very glad to see you. Where's everyone else?"

"The soldiers rounded us all up and took us out to the sheep shed, sir. They are questioning us one by one. They have already spoken to my parents, and to Septimus, and some of the house slaves."

Lydia saw the mark on his face.

"Did they hit you, Simon?"

"They had to," cut in Glaucus. "The evidence of a slave has no value in Roman law unless it is extracted through the use of torture."

"I think that they are doing their best," added Father Horse. "I have known soldiers to be far more cruel in the practice of torture."

"Simon, would you get some drinks for us?" asked Glaucus.

"Oh, that's hardly fair," said Gini, unexpectedly. "We've just been locked up. He's had a beating. We should get him a drink. I shall go to the kitchens and fetch some drinks. Come on Gordi, you can help."

As the children left, Glaucus looked after them. Father Horse could not quite read the look on his face. Was he annoyed? Was he proud? Or was it both?

"Well, Father Horse, what do you make of it? What do you think that they are up to?"

Glaucus was trying to sound light-hearted.

"Since you ask me, I think that Maximinus is making it up as he goes along. He doesn't have a military manual to tell him how to find the jewels, so he is trying to be careful. He knows, or can work out, a few things. He knows that the thief has to be in this house. It is too secure and busy a place for an unknown person to sneak in, go straight to the tribune's room, take the jewels and sneak back out again. So the first thing that he has to do is make sure that everyone is still here. That means that the jewels are too. The next thing that he has to do is to search the house. That's much harder because it is a very big house with a lot of hiding places. To make that easier, he is questioning everyone to see if he can get an admission. You should be with him while he does this, Glaucus, since the slaves are your property, but first he has to satisfy himself that you are not responsible for the theft."

"Me? Why on earth would I do such a thing?"

"Well," continued Father Horse. "Those jewels are worth a lot of money, probably more than you are hoping to make from selling dyed wool to the army. So you would be even richer, without all of that hard work."

"But he is our guest! How could he think that we would rob anyone under our own roof?"

"It is his job to think bad things like this. And being robbed, as you know, can make you very unlikely to trust anyone that you don't really know."

"So what can we do now?" asked Lydia.

"Well, I think that they will probably come to you soon. If they have not already found the jewels, and I hope that they have, then Maximinus himself will question each of us. I don't think that he really thinks that any of you did it. He is far less sure about me because I am an outsider."

There was an uncomfortable silence, only broken when the children came back. Gini was carrying a big jug of water, and Gordi had some cups in one hand and a stoppered wineskin in the other.

"You should see the kitchen!" said Gordi.

"It's a mess," Gini added hastily. "They have been through all of the storage bins. There's barley and wheat grain and peas and things all over the floor. There's broken pottery, but I don't think that they deliberately went about smashing things. It will take a while for the slaves to clean up."

"Why the slaves?" Hippolytus asked. "If they are all sitting in the sheep shed obediently waiting to be tortured, then why can't some of us do it? I'm sure that Simon knows where everything goes. How about it, children?"

Gordi and Gini looked for a moment like they would prefer to be tortured themselves.

"Oh, all right," said Gini, reluctantly.

"I suppose so," said Gordi, almost under his breath.

Lydia stood and said very firmly, "Well, if you are all going to do it, then I shall too."

Glaucus was doubtful. "What about Maximinus? His soldiers left us here. Surely this is where we are supposed to stay."

"Glaucus," Lydia was decisive. "This is your house and our home. You are lord here, and we should and can go where we wish. Right now, we have a job of work to do in the kitchen. You can stay here if you like. Come on, Father Horse, let's get started."

"Wait a moment," said Glaucus. "Let me think this through."

He paused, looked down for a moment at the floor mosaics, and then looked up again. "You are right. This is my home and I am master. I'm coming too. It is my kitchen, after all."

"Don't tell Phormio that," Lydia smiled at her own joke.

They all laughed a little, had that drink, and then trooped out of the room and into the kitchen.

It was, as Gordi had said, a disaster zone.

While the soldiers might have taken some care not to break things, they had not always been successful. There was a great deal of broken pottery scattered over the floor. What they had done was dig deep into the storage bins. As Gini had said, barley and wheat grains, chickpeas, split peas, lentils, and various varieties of dried fruit were spread over the floor. The table was covered in opened jars of honey, fish sauce and olive oil. Fortunately, they had left the obviously sealed jars and even the hanging socks of sheep cheese.

The family stood for a moment, taking it all in. Then Lydia took charge.

"Gordi, Simon, go and get a shovel and a big broom. Gini, we need baskets for the broken pottery. Keep the large pieces. We can reuse those for notes. Be careful on the floor. There's broken pottery all over. Father Horse, if you would begin to collect it, and put the pieces on the big table. And all that," she waved her arm at the mess on the table, "will have to go out."

"And me?" asked Glaucus.

"I'm not sure," replied Lydia. "I'm not used to telling you what to do."

"Well it is my kitchen," he responded.

Lydia was firm. "You might own it, but I run it."

That settled the matter.

"As you say," agreed Glaucus. "I place myself under your orders."

"Can you find some buckets, or something like them to put that mess on the floor in so that we can get it outside and into the rubbish pit?"

"How about cloth?" Glaucus suggested. "I'm sure that there are some old blankets around that we can use."

"Perfect," Lydia replied. "That's your job. There's no point in trying to rescue any of this food for eating. There's too many tiny crumbs of broken pottery in there for a start. If you can find the blankets, we can sweep or shovel the rubbish onto them. When they are full, take them outside and dump the contents."

Glaucus went off and soon he, Gini and the two boys were back with baskets, blankets and brooms. Gordi had found the big broom that Phormio used to scrub the kitchen floor but it was Lydia who used it to sweep up the mess on the floor. Father Horse collected the larger pieces of pottery and placed them in one of the baskets while Glaucus shoveled up the mess that Lydia had swept up and collected it all in the middle of a blanket. When the blanket was full, he simply folded in each of the corners to the middle, and then picked it up like a big bag, took it outside, and dumped the contents. The children were at work on the table. The mess there went into the middle of another old blanket, and much of the spilled oil and honey had to be cleaned up by hand. Gini and Gordi filled the blanket. Father Horse took it outside and dumped it every time it was full. Simon, since he knew where things were supposed to go in the big kitchen, put away the scattered pots, pans, and utensils.

Strangely, and despite the circumstances, everyone discovered that they were enjoying themselves. Working like this, they restored the kitchen to something like cleanliness and order. The floor and the table were clean. Things were put away where they went (they hoped). Within a couple of hours, they were all sitting around the table, hot, tired and red faced from the effort, but all strangely happy at the result.

"Now, I'm hungry," said Glaucus.

"Well," Lydia answered. "We are in the right place for that. We should know where everything is by now. I think that we can put together a supper very quickly."

But the moment was interrupted by one of the soldiers. It was Aelian, he who had taken Lydia and Gini away. He took one look at them, and then called behind him, "Sir, you were right. They're in here."

A moment later Maximinus walked in. His eyes widened as he took in the scene: the cleaned kitchen; the happy and tired family sitting at the table; the slave-boy Simon sitting with them.

"What have you been doing?" he demanded.

"Cleaning up," answered Glaucus, cheerily.

"That's slaves' work," Maximinus thundered.

"Well, you have all of our slaves for the moment. And someone must do this. I always thought that it was good leadership for a general never to demand anything of his troops that he wasn't prepared to do himself."

"I think that I'll be the judge of that." The thunder had gone and ice had taken its place. "I thought that I told you to wait for me in the meal room. Why do I find you here at all?"

"Because" Glaucus answered firmly. "While we are under your authority, as you say, we are not under your orders. This is my house and I am master here."

"For now," Maximinus was chilling. It was clear from his manner and tone that the jewels still had not been found.

"Wait here," he added unnecessarily. "My men will bring you some food. It's army food, so don't expect fine dining. I have finished with your slaves and I will release them back to you tonight. But for now, I need to talk to you!" Maximinus emphasized the last work as he stabbed his finger at Father Horse. "Come with me now."

Glaucus looked like he was about to protest, but the priest laid a hand on his arm.

"He is within his rights. Don't worry," he reassured Glaucus. Then he rose to his feet and followed the tribune out of the room.

Maximinus led him along the covered way out to the entrance hall of the house. At some point, as they went along, Father Horse became aware that two soldiers had fallen in behind him. The small party left the house and made for a group of army tents in the field next to the house. Four of them, were grouped around a little square. In the middle of the square was a fifth tent. Maximinus went ahead into this tent and the soldiers made sure that Father Horse followed. This tent was evidently intended as a working office. There were folding chairs and a writing table. Whilst it was still fully light outside, in the tent, the dimness inside was only relieved by the glow of oil lamps in each corner. There was a portable altar in one corner upon which coals glowed red. Maximinus went over to it and threw a pinch of incense upon them. Immediately, the still and musty air was sweetened by its fragrance.

Maximinus sat at the table.

"Sit," he said, pointing to a chair opposite.

"Well, teacher," Maximinus began. "You and I have a problem. Let me set this out for you. However kind and generous he may be to you, you are not a member of this family. In fact, you have only been here for a few days. They have been very good to you opening their home, entrusting their children to you, providing you with comfortable quarters and a good salary. They even seem to have gone along with your dangerous views about social order, doing work that is slaves' work rather than leaving it to those whose place it is to do it.

"Not only are you, in truth, not a member of this family, and dangerous to it, but you have also chosen to be an outsider. By embracing this foreign sect you have rejected civilized society with all of its rules and laws and instead have chosen to live by laws and rules of your own making which, so far as I can see, you are making up as you go along.

"None of this makes you guilty of stealing my wife's jewels, but it does make me very suspicious of you. What now makes me even more suspicious is evidence that I have that you were seen outside your room last night, long after everyone else had gone to bed. In a sleeping house, why is it that you alone were walking in the garden?"

"Because I could not sleep." Hippolytus said. "He had decided that he would answer all questions directly and not invite an argument with the tribune that he knew would end badly.

"Why could you not sleep?" The question was fired in swiftly and sharply.

"Because I had been upset by the disagreement between us at dinner. I kept going through it in my mind and wondering if I could have dealt with it better."

"Dinner party chat!" Maximinus was mocking.

"I set myself high standards. I have to. For me, every conversation might be a matter of life and death. I took the walk to clear my mind in the fresh night air."

"A neat answer. Well thought out. You involve me as the cause, as if to confirm your story. But, right now, I don't think that is what happened." The tribune was no longer asking.

"I don't know why you Christians do things, but then, no decent person does. I just know that you are different, that you play by different rules and that you see yourselves as apart from the rest of us. So, when you saw my wife's emeralds last night, you saw an opportunity to make your little sect richer. I think that you took the jewels when everyone was asleep, that you have hidden them somewhere in the house, and that you hope that we will all go away so that you can retrieve them and run off. Why are you smiling? What do you know?"

Hippolytus was, indeed, smiling.

"Because" he replied. "You have half of the story right. I think someone did take the jewels and has hidden them in the house. I think that person does intend to retrieve them when you have gone and then slip away. I think that all of that is quite right. It's just that the person who has done all of those things is not me."

"Can you prove that?" challenged the tribune.

"The only way that I can do that is by finding the person who actually did take the jewels," responded Hippolytus reasonably. "Of course, I should not have to do that. In law, you need to prove my guilt, not me, my innocence."

That was a mistake. It made Maximinus even angrier.

"Do not lecture me on law, Christian. Here, I am the law. And you are guilty."

He gestured to the two soldiers.

"Take him away and lock him up. We'll get the answers we need out of him tomorrow."

CHAPTER ELEVEN

THE TRIBUNE ASKS SOME QUESTIONS

FIRM HANDS TOOK HIPPOLYTUS by the shoulders from behind and guided his own hands together, with wrist over wrist.

"Steady now, don't fight me," came a strong voice. He recognized it as that of Marcellus, the optio.

Hippolytus needed little encouragement since he had decided not to resist some time before. He stood, passively, as he felt the rope go around his wrists and tighten. The rope was rough on his skin and his bonds were secure and uncomfortable, but not actually painful. Marcellus had clearly done this before. With his hands bound behind him, Marcellus led away Father Horse out of the tent and into the evening. The long summer twilight had begun, and the sky was carpeted with grey clouds. Drizzle moistened the air. He stopped for a moment to breathe in the fresh air, but then felt the unmistakable pressure in his back of a sword point.

He heard Marcellus say, "Put that away, boy. This one isn't going anywhere, are you now Christian?"

From that, he supposed that the other soldier was Silvius.

"Well are you?" Marcellus pressed.

"Hardly," replied Father Horse. "I couldn't really run, even if I wanted to. Where are you taking me?"

"All in good time. Then we'll be asking the questions. Enough talking for now. Get moving."

Marcellus led Father Horse back to the house but to a part that he did not really know. The guest rooms of the house were in the wing across the courtyard from the living quarters. These were generous in size and well appointed, but he was led past them to a set of stairs that led down under the ground. This was a part of the house that he did not know. The soldiers, who had searched the house, certainly did. Underneath was a long, cool corridor, lit by torches.

"These are normally for the slaves of any of the guests," explained Marcellus. "Septimus, the steward, told me about them. They seem like a good substitute for prison cells."

Marcellus stopped about halfway along.

"I think, this one," he declared.

The room was furnished simply with a bed, table, and a cupboard set into the wall, but it had a stout door with an external lock and a locking bar for extra security.

"In you go," said Marcellus, giving him a little push into the cell. "We'll all have a nice little chat tomorrow. I hope that you ate well today. I have no orders about food or water for you tonight."

"Aren't you going to untie me?" asked the priest.

"I don't have any orders for that either. You just stay as you are. Now Silvius here will be just outside. If you need anything, don't bother to ask. He has orders not to listen." Marcellus smiled a hard, nasty smile and closed the door.

Father Horse was alone in the little cell.

The only light came from four narrow skylights in the outer wall, now fading with the waning of the day. The floor was bare stone, the walls, plain brick, and the bed small and narrow.

He now saw all this for what it was. He was being softened up for torture. Not only was he being denied food and drink, but he was also being denied the use of his hands. This made both lying down and getting up very challenging and also meant that it would be very difficult to get into a good position to get off to sleep. The tribune clearly knew his business. It was going to be a long night.

This was nothing new for the priest. Hippolytus had already experienced many nights like this. He had experienced hunger, thirst, fatigue, loneliness, and torture and had a way of dealing with these things. He eased himself down onto the bed and sat, facing the door. He closed his eyes, cleared his mind and began to pray. It was not a wordy prayer. It was not a request to be spared pain or to be saved from his little prison. It was a prayer without words in which he sought to be still and find the place where God was, deep inside him. He kept his breathing deep and regular and in his mind's eye, he saw the feet of a man on a cross. He did not look up to see more. Instead, he concentrated on the feet, catching his conscious mind every time it tried to wander onto a different path or throw out a distraction. There, in that place, he was supremely happy, and deeply secure in the knowledge that, whatever tomorrow brought, he would conquer.

After a time, and as the sun dimmed and slid below the edge of the world, bringing Hippolytus' little room into full dark, he lay down on his side, wriggling a little to accommodate the arms still tied behind him, and fell asleep.

He woke in the morning from a deep and refreshing slumber. Dim light peered in through the skylights. He remembered snatches of an odd dream. He had dreamed of the house, but not as he knew it. He dreamed of it as he thought that it might once have been a small fort with a garrison of a hundred or so Roman soldiers. He knew that it had looked different in ways that played with the edges of his memory. Something bothered him, but try as he might, he could not pin it down.

He tried to stand and found, much to his surprise, that he could move his hands. Somehow, during the night, and he had no idea how, his bonds had come untied. The rope sat beside him on the bed, still tangled in its own knots. He stood, and faced where he thought east might be, then, wincing at the pain and stiffness, he knelt on the cold stone and prayed his morning prayers, giving thanks above all for the freedom of his arms, and asking for strength to bear the questioning that he knew was going to come.

As it grew lighter Father Horse looked about him. It was a small, plain room with space for the bed and table but not much more. The cupboard, set into the wall, saved a little space. It had a plain wooden board that hinged outwards as a door. A few shallow shelves were set inside and the back was timber slats. This surprised Father Horse a little. He had expected bare brick. The stones of the floor were stained with damp. Behind the bed, some bricks jutted out from the wall to form a little shelf for a lamp, but no lamp sat there.

He was about to get up and have a look at it when he heard the lock click in the door. Marcellus was back. This time he had Germanus with him.

"Up you get, then, Christian. Had a good sleep, then?" Marcellus' question was not kindly meant.

Then he saw that Father Horse's hands were free. "Well, aren't you the clever one? How did you do that? Is it some kind of Christian magic?"

"I really don't know. That's how it was when I woke up."

"More like Silvius didn't do his knots too well. I'll do it this time. Hands behind!"

Father Horse did as he was told. His wrists were bound again, this time more tightly.

Then he followed Marcellus back and out of the cell, out of the house and into the tent in the field next door.

Inside, it was as it had been the evening before. The tribune sat at his desk. Behind him was a lampstand and the portable altar. The fragrance of incense lingered in the air and a single curl of smoke spiraled up lazily from the coals on the altar.

Maximinus looked refreshed and relaxed. His confidence was plain. He had often done this. He had often confronted people who were tired, hungry, thirsty, unwashed and uncomfortable, and gained the answers he was seeking. Father Horse looked just that. His clothes were filthy; his hands were still tied behind him; he stood, looking down, as if ashamed; shifting from foot to foot to ease his pain.

The tribune waited. He knew that the best, and easiest, way to get Father Horse to talk was to say nothing. Instead he sat, quietly looking at the priest waiting for Hippolytus to break down, to fill the empty silence, to speak and to tell the whole story, to get the experience over and done with.

Father Horse said nothing. He knew exactly what was happening and was not going to be lured into speech. He had already resolved to answer all questions truthfully, and he had equally resolved not to give the tribune information that he had not asked for.

The minutes marched by, crawled by. Finally, it was the tribune who spoke. "Tell me about yourself, priest," he said.

"There is not much to say that you don't know already," replied Father Horse.

"Oh, I doubt that," said Maximinus. "I think that there is a great deal about you that I don't know and that I would like to know. Let's begin with the simple things. In what city were you born?"

"In Perge, in the province of Pamphylia."

"Your parents, were they wealthy?"

"By most standards, yes. My father owns a large orchard and grows fruit for market and for drying. It is a good business, and he does well. I remember growing up surrounded by the scent of lemons."

"How wealthy?" Maximinus forced the conversation away from lemons and back onto the path he wanted to take.

"My father is a member of the local Senate. He is a benefactor to the town with a named seat in the theatre and, whenever the governor visits, he goes to the official dinners."

"So your family has status, rank?"

"Oh, yes."

"And are they happy that you have become a Christian and a priest?"

"Not quite."

"What do you mean by that?"

"My parents gave up on me. They sent me to Caesarea to study. They did not want me as far away as Alexandria or Athens, so they sent me to Caesarea which is only a few days sail from Perge. At first it went very well for them, and they were happy with me. We wrote to one another regularly and my father seemed pleased with my progress in learning and philosophy. Then I found Origen and, through Origen, I found Christ. When I wrote to them and told them of that, my father wrote me one more letter, and then none since. In that letter, he formally disowned me, cut me out of my family and my inheritance and stated that he regarded me as dead. Since then, we have had no contact."

It was a longer answer than he intended and gave away more than he meant to say. He mentally chided himself for saying too much and complimented Maximinus for getting him to do it. *I must not underestimate this man*, he thought to himself.

"I suppose that's when the money stopped coming," the tribune suggested swiftly.

"I had some savings. Then I found work as a grammar teacher such as I am now. It was enough. My needs are simple and easily met." Hippolytus was firm.

"So why did you take the jewels?" shot Maximinus. "Was it out of some loyalty to your Christ?" So there it was.

"I did not take them," Father Horse replied quietly and clearly.

"I think that you did. You are the only person who was seen that night, and you admit that you were up and about. You had no real reason to be out there and your own explanation was feeble. Besides, who else had such reason?"

"What reason do I have?" asked Hippolytus.

"That's clear. You Christians hate everyone else. To you, we are not your betters, or your neighbors, or your servants. We are simply fodder for you to steal from, sheep to fleece or devour." Maximinus seemed to be getting quite angry now.

"The good shepherd lays down his life for his sheep," murmured Hippolytus.

"What's that?" demanded Maximinus, and then thought better of it. "Never mind. It's one of your Christian things. So let me tell you what I think. You are not here to care for these children. You are here because you have been sent here to make them like you. You have wormed your way into the affections of this noble family, but all the time, you have been meaning to use them—to take their money and send it to your masters in the east, and to turn these children into Christians and to take them away from their family as you were, rightly, thrown out of yours.

"Then you met me and saw Sentia's jewels. What an opportunity! You must have thought that your god had sent us to you. Take the jewels and enrich your little group beyond your dreams. Take the jewels and have revenge on the Romans whom you hate so very much. That is what I think happened, and somewhere in that house are the jewels that you stole. You know where they are. If you tell me now, the worst that will happen to you is that I will send you away from this province with your life. The longer that your silence on this continues, the more severe the penalty will be in the end."

Throughout this long speech, Maximinus had spoken quietly, but precisely and matter-of-factly. He was in no doubt. That absence of doubt, Hippolytus saw, came from the tribune's complete confidence in himself and his own strong inner sense of his own importance. A social inferior had never said 'no' to him. He did not even imagine that Father Horse might be the first.

Hippolytus decided to be bold.

"Who saw me in the garden?"

"What?" said the tribune.

"Who saw me? If there was someone to see me walking in the garden, then I wasn't the only one awake and about at that hour."

"None of that is your concern. The one who saw you had good reason to be there. I have heard his explanation and I accept it. Now, let me remind you of something. I ask the questions!"

Maximinus nodded to Marcellus who kicked Father Horse's legs out from underneath him. Without his hands to break his fall, he landed heavily on the ground.

"Now, get up!" The tribune's voice was ice.

Without his hands to give him purchase on the ground, all Father Horse could do was wriggle around until, using one knee and his chin, his could bring up one knee underneath him. Then he struggled to bring up the second knee. It took him a long time until he was on his feet again, but he did it, Maximinus watching him all the while. Finally he stood up straight, filthy, grazed and grass-stained from the effort.

Maximus nodded at Marcellus again, and again the soldier lashed out tripping up the priest and landing him heavily on the ground.

"Do it again," ordered Maximinus. "Let's see you get on your feet again."

As father Horse wriggled around on the ground, Maximinus turned to Germanus.

"Time for breakfast. I'll have mine right here."

By the time that Father Horse had struggled back to his feet, the tribune had a platter of food in front of him and a jug of water. \Maximinus evidently liked his breakfast. The platter was heaped with smoked pork, cheese, olives, roast chickpeas, boiled eggs and bread. Maximinus picked up one of the eggs, carefully shelled it, sprinkled a little salt on it and took a big bite.

With his mouth full of egg, he looked over at Hippolytus, lifted an eyebrow and said,

"Hungry?"

Here was the next stage of the questioning. Maximinus was showing his power and, in turn, making it clear to Father Horse just how little power he had.

Hippolytus was less hungry than he was thirsty. He was used to not eating. Going for days at a time without food had long been an important part of his life. He had drunk no water, however, since the day before and that was beginning to have an effect. He knew, though, that he could still bear it, so he stood saying nothing, watching the tribune eat.

Maximinus ate slowly and with deliberate wastefulness. Chickpeas and olives fell on the ground, along with the eggshells. After a while, he looked up from his plate, belched, took a long drink, and signaled to Germanus, who brought him a cloth on which he wiped his hands and face. Then he sat there, surrounded by the wreckage of his meal, looking right at Hippolytus.

"It would not be difficult to arrange a similar meal for you," he said. "All you have to do is to tell me where the jewels are. Just that. Just the jewels, and there will be bread and oil and honey; there will be eggs and meat and fruit. Wine to wash it down. Water to cool your mouth and kill your thirst. Would you not like that?" As he spoke, Maximinus placed special stress on each of the items of food and drink he was mentioning as if to make his point even clearer.

"I would like that very much," admitted Father Horse.

"So where are the jewels?" The tribune asked quickly.

"I cannot tell you what I do not know."

Maximinus nodded to Marcellus. Again, he kicked Hippolytus' legs out from underneath him. This time, the priest landed heavily. He could feel the blood leaking from his nose.

"I think that the time for talking is done," Maximinus conceded. "It is time for more direct measures. Get him to his feet!" he ordered Marcellus. The soldier hauled Father Horse up, but then priest was not steady at first and need to be held for a moment before he could find his balance."

"I am going to free your hands in a moment. Don't get your hopes up. It's for Germanus here. He has some skill in hurting people simply by doing things to their fingers. If you wish to have the use of your hands again, I suggest that you tell the tribune what he wants to know."

Father Horse felt the knife as it cut through his bonds. He brought his hands around in front, wiped his nose with his sleeve and then rubbed his wrists where they had been chafed by the rope.

"That's enough," said Maximinus, impatiently. "Let's get started."

"A moment before you do," said Father Horse. "You need to see something."

Before they could react, he had shucked off his shoes, reached under his robes and undone the drawstring of his trousers and kicked them off, so that he stood there with the full horror of his scarred legs and feet revealed to the tribune, Marcellus and Germanus.

"I told you I was in Caesarea. What I had not told you was that it was there that I was in prison for nearly two years for the crime of being a Christian. I was there for so long because I refused to do what was asked of me, to deny my faith. They would have been easy words to say, but I refused to do that because it was not true. I bore all of the tortures that the soldiers of Rome could inflict on me. I was young and strong. I survived. But if I could endure all of that for the sake of saying something that I could easily say and do, how much more do you think that I can bear the tortures you will inflict today to make me tell you what I do not know. I do not know where the jewels are. I do not know now and I will not know after you finish all of the terrible things that you are planning."

There was a stillness when he had finished. The sight of Hippolytus' scars and the power of his words stopped the tribune's breath. He knew that he was looking at the remains of terrible pain. He knew that he was facing a survivor who could not be forced or tempted to speak. Even the soldiers looked at the priest with something like respect.

Finally Maximinus said, "In this he is right. Take him away. Take him back to his little room. Maybe some more time without food and water will persuade him if pain will not."

This time, they did not bind his hands.

CHAPTER TWELVE

FATHER HORSE HAS AN IDEA

His body ached, his face hurt and his legs were pillars of pain. He could barely make it back to the cell without falling and, once inside, fell on the bed and just lay there trying to still the fire in his muscles and the rapid beating of his heart. After a time, he calmed.

Even with the pain, he was rather glad to back in the bare little room that was his cell. It was not so much relief at the end of the session with the tribune as it was an opportunity to think clearly and without interruptions. There was a puzzle here to solve. Like the tribune, he was certain that the jewels were still in the house. Unlike the tribune, he had no theory yet to tell him where. All he knew was where they were not and that was little help either to him or to Maximinus.

He sat up after a time and tried to clear his mind. So many things kept crowding in and his focus was nearly lost in the swirl of thoughts and images. He knew that somewhere in that chaos of memories and impressions there was something that would lead him to the answer. He had already felt something niggling at his mind when he was in the tribune's tent. Rather than seek the idea, rather than hunt and fossick through his own jumble of thoughts, he determined to try and empty his consciousness and let the answer come to him.

As he sat there on the bed, back against the wall and knees drawn up under his chin, he began with his breathing, slowing it down to long, deep breaths. He sought to still his mind by concentrating only on the sound of his breath. Images in his mind came and went; thoughts and stray memories were summoned up and dismissed as he sank deeper and deeper into his meditation.

As he breathed, he became aware of a sound like wood being stacked, a scraping and a muffled thudding. He could not wish this away. He tried to ignore it, but it asserted itself in his mind such that he found himself swimming up and out of the stillness and towards the world.

When he opened his eyes, he blinked with surprise. The door to the cupboard in the wall of his cell had swung open and there, standing in front of him, was Simon! Father Horse almost spoke, but as he opened his mouth, Simon put his finger to his lips, signaling for silence. Then he went back to the cupboard and beckoned Father Horse over. The priest stood up, fresh pain stabbing through his legs, and shuffled over to look. The back of the cupboard had been removed, revealing the same cupboard set into the same wall of the cell next door. The back of each cupboard formed a thin, wooden barrier between the cells. With it removed, there was a neat way in and out of Father Horse's cell, even if it was set hallway up the wall.

Simon signaled to him, pointing at the cell door and miming a soldier walking up and down. Father Horse understood. He was under guard. They would have to speak very quietly.

"Did you come in last night and undo my bonds?" he whispered.

Simon enthusiastically nodded back, his mouth spreading into a grin.

"That was a good trick and it really upset them, I can tell you," said Father Horse. "Now tell me, how are the family? And the household?"

"The slaves have all been questioned, even the farm slaves who don't come into the house. The soldiers never ask a question without hurting us, so everyone has bruises. The family are very confused. Glaucus is angry with everyone so Lydia sits reading in her room. Gini can't stop crying and Gordi won't talk to that young soldier who was teaching him swordplay. They all sit in silence at mealtimes and barely eat. Maximinus and Sentia don't come into the house but stay in the camp next door, so it's just the soldiers who seem to be tramping up and down the all the time."

"Can you get me some water? There's none here and I haven't had anything to drink since yesterday," Father Horse asked.

"Just a minute," said Simon and scrambled through the cupboard and into the room next door. Then, as if the cupboard were a serving hatch, a pottery jug of water and a cup appeared from the other side, along with a platter of bread. Father Horse poured himself a cup, and sipped at it gently.

"That was thoughtful," he said.

"My father told me to me bring some food and water, and to keep it simple. I hope you don't mind. It's slaves' food. Do you want me to bring more water so you can wash? You really need one!"

"Your father knows about this?"

"Yes, I told him about my trick with the rope this morning. He thought that it was a bit funny but then he told me to come back this morning to give you some food and water."

"Does he know about the cupboard?"

"Oh, we all know about those."

"Those?"

"Yes, all of these rooms have them. If you take the backs out, you can go all the way through to the end. Everyone knows, everyone who's grown up here, at any rate. We think that they were barracks when this was a fort and then they were converted to slave quarters when it became a private house."

"Do Gini and Gordi know?" Father Horse asked.

"I don't think so."

"Then bring them here when you can. You can't talk to Glaucus and Lydia like they can. Simon I'm very grateful to you and to your father for this. You have put yourselves at risk to do it."

"Father says that we are to feed those in prison. I'll go now and tell the others. Do you want some water for a wash? You look terrible."

"No," replied Father Horse, through a mouthful of bread. "I don't want the soldiers to move me, which they will if they find out that I can somehow get water for drinking and washing. Besides, I want Glaucus and Lydia to see me as I am. It's not to punish them, but to persuade them of my innocence. Glaucus, at least, must be suspicious of me, even a little bit. I'm one person in this house that he does not know well."

Father Horse poured himself some more water and drank it down.

"Simon, I cannot thank you enough for all of this. Now you must put everything back, go and fetch Gini and Gordi, and leave me to think for a little while."

Simon took the cup, jug and platter, and disappeared through the cupboard to the next room. Father Horse put the shelves back and closed the door. Soon he could hear the sounds of the partition at the back of the cupboard being put back into place. Satisfied that Simon had gone, he went back to his bed, and again sat and set his mind to the problem.

Simon had said something that again caused him to pause. He had referred to what the house had once been. Perhaps that was his clue and the line of thinking that he needed to follow. He settled back on the bed and this time, instead of trying to discipline his mind, he allowed it to wander. He thought of Maximinus and his soldiers and just how much they reminded him of the soldiers who had tortured him at Caesarea. Maximinus showed the same certainty as those officers; his men, the same ordered obedience as the legionaries in Caesarea. It led him to think about the discipline of Roman soldiers, and a culture that had not varied for centuries. He thought of the camp in the field next door, and how the tents had been arranged in the same shape as had been done for hundreds of years with the command tent in the center and the others in ordered array around it and two little streets between the tents, one running north-south, the other, east-west.

He remembered the permanent military camp of the Sixth Legion, a day from Caesarea, with row after row of barrack buildings and storehouses, quarters for officers' families, armories, granaries, cookhouses, and mess halls. At the heart of it all was the vast headquarters building, where the legate had his office and the clerks and paymasters all sat in cubicles counting the legion's money, making sure none of it went astray. It was the same design as the little garrison camp that he had passed through in Petuaria. From Britannia to Persia, across the whole huge mass that was the Empire of Rome, military camps all looked and worked in the same way.

Now he knew that he was onto a train of thought that might yield something. Now he could concentrate and let his mind follow the scent that he had identified. Origen had been right all along. The secret to this little mystery was not to torture and bludgeon an answer. That was the old, blunt, brutal, Roman way. No, the way to the truth was to use this insight as the key to unlock the truth.

Someone looking at Hippolytus, say a soldier looking through a door to check on him would have seen a man, sitting on a bed with his back to the wall and his knees drawn up under his chin. His closed eyes, and shallow breathing might have led a watcher to think that he was asleep. Part of him was. But another part of him, his fiery and questing spirit, was tracking an idea, like a dog following a scent.

Time passed. He did not know how much. He was jerked back to awareness of the world by the voice of Marcellus.

"Sleeping, Christian?"

Marcellus was standing just inside the door, which he had opened quietly enough not to disturb Father Horse. The soldier had been intending to surprise him.

He was carrying a large pottery jug.

"Some water, Christian? The tribune did say no, but I could be kind."

Marcellus raised the jug to his lips and took a very long drink, the water sloshing over the sides, dribbling down his short beard and onto his chest.

He finished, wiped his face with his sleeve, and sighed a theatrical sigh of contentment.

"Or not. Nothing like a long cool drink on a hot day, Christian. Well, I'm off to lunch now. Pork and peas. Good soldiers' food. Silvius will take over. A double shift, I think. The boy has to learn to tie his knots better."

He smiled a cold, cruel smile. Then he was gone, locking the door behind him.

All was quiet again.

Father Horse had not moved during this performance. With Marcellus gone, he again bowed his head to return to his thoughts. This time, the interruption had been upsetting. They did not return to him so easily. Instead, he compiled the questions that would help him develop the idea that had begun to form in his mind. He just needed a little more information to be certain. Then he could talk to Glaucus.

Then he heard something odd. It was the clatter of wood on wood, not, as before, the sound of the partition being dismantled. This was less regular, and seemed to come from outside his cell door. Voices, too. He could hear voices. One was Silvius and the other was Gordi. He went to the door and listened for a while. Gordi had gone to Silvius to get another lesson in swordplay, and Silvius probably bored with guarding a man who had not shown the slightest desire either to disobey or to escape was showing him parry and thrust.

When he heard the familiar noises in the wall cupboard, he understood. Gordi was distracting Silvius so that Father Horse could have a proper chat to whomever was coming through the cupboard door. A moment later, the door popped open and Simon slid into the room, followed by Gini.

When Gini saw him, she gave a little gasp, and put her hand to her mouth.

"Oh, poor Father Horse," she said. "What have they done to you?"

"They have been trying to get me to give them information which I do not know and that they think that I do know. Or at least I didn't know, but I think that I might have worked something out. I need to ask you both some questions.

"Before you ask, we've brought you some lunch," answered Gini.

She went back into the next room and brought out a basket, which she put on the floor of the cupboard like it was a serving hatch. There was some cold chicken, some boiled eggs (shelled), some olives, bread, a little jar of oil, and a jug of water. Gini also had the forethought to cover it all with a cloth, which she then spread out to catch any crumbs of food. Before he ate, Father Horse spread his hands above the food and softly said the familiar words of blessing. Then he took the bread, tore it into pieces, offered it to Gini and Simon and ate. He ate carefully, and not too much, and when he had done, he wiped his face and hands and cleaned everything away so that there was no sign of his meal.

"Thank you very much," he said to the children once he had done. "I am most grateful for all that you have done."

"We've had help from my father too," answered Simon.

"Oh, I thank him too," replied Father Horse. "And the one who is Father of us all. Simon, before we go on, I think it best that you go through the cupboard so that both of you are in the next room so that, if anyone comes to look in on me, you don't get caught."

Simon nodded and scrambled back through the hatch.

Now," continued Father Horse, talking to them through the hole in the wall. " I have some questions. Both of you many know the answers, or only one of you, or maybe neither of you, so let's go."

"Do you go into the courtyard garden often?" he began.

"Almost every day for me," said Gini.

"Me too," agreed Simon.

"Can you describe it for me," Father Horse continued.

Gini was first to respond. "The whole courtyard is a big square, and there are four garden beds, one in each corner. The two garden beds at the kitchen end have herbs and vegetables. The other two have flowers, different ones for each season, although I know that Quintus is very proud of his roses. Each of the beds has a little wall, about the height of my knee running around it and between each of the beds there is a pathway wide enough for four people to walk abreast. The two vegetable beds have little hedges of rosemary as well, but not all the way around. In the middle there is a bit of a clear space and right in the middle of the middle is the plinth."

"Now can you describe the plinth," Father Horse asked.

"But you know it well. You've even been inside it, which is more than any of the rest of us have done," replied Gini.

"Really? Why is that?"

"Well, isn't it where Quintus keeps his tools and garden things?" she replied.

Father Horse grunted.

"What about you, Simon?" he asked.

"Oh, lots of times," he said. "Father often sends me into the garden after something or other. Father sometimes sends me to Quintus to give him dishes that he has made from vegetables, herbs or fruit that Quintus has grown. If he's not around the plinth, I leave whatever it is inside so that he can get it when he comes back. It's only a little shed."

"Very good," said Father Horse. "Now, I think we are getting somewhere."

"What do you mean?" Gini asked.

"Well, when you go walking on the pathways on the garden, what do you walk on?"

"Well, the ground."

"No, Gini. I mean, are they dirt paths or are they paved?"

"Well, paved, but I don't see what difference it makes."

"Simon, when you were inside the plinth, was the floor paved?"

"No. I think that it is wooden planks."

"That's right," said Father Horse. "I stuck my head inside there once because I thought it such an odd little building, and I remember a wooden floor too."

"But so," said Gini, a bit crossly. "I don't see what difference that makes. What has all that to do with the missing jewels?"

"Gini, do you remember what I said the true key to wisdom is?"

"I think that I do. You said that the surest way to wisdom was not to look at new things in old ways, but old things in new ways."

"Quite right," he said. "And that is what we have been doing."

"So have you worked it out, Father?" Simon asked.

"Maybe," he answered. "I have an idea, but one can never be quite sure until it is tested."

"How will you do that?" Simon persisted.

"Well," said Father Horse. "That is where I am going to need Gini and Gordi to persuade Glaucus to come down here to see me."

"Why can't you just tell the answer to the tribune?" Gini asked.

"Because if I do that, he will believe that I have been guilty all along and that I am just pretending to have solved the mystery so that he will let me go. That means that, while I could give him the answer to the mystery, it couldn't save me. He has to be led to the answer another way."

"What way?" asked Gini.

Outside, the clatter of wooden swords had stopped and there was just the low hum of voices. Now they had to whisper.

"Simon, I am going to ask you to do something that might not be easy and might be a bit dangerous, but you are best placed to do it."

"What's that, Father Horse?" he asked.

"I want you to look in the plinth and see if the floor is really a trapdoor. You see, I think that there is a room underneath which only a few people know about."

"How do you know?" Gini asked.

"All army forts follow the same pattern and in the middle there is a headquarters. The headquarters also houses the shrine of the unit and a place where valuables are kept, sometimes in an underground room. I think that there is an underground room beneath the courtyard and the entrance is through the plinth. That is what I want you to check for me, Simon. If there is, that's where Gini comes in.

"Gini, we are going to need the help of your parents. I know that your father is very cross with me, because he can't quite bring himself to believe that I had nothing to do with this. But if you can persuade your mother, then she can persuade him to come and see me. He could tell Maximinus that he wants to see me and to tell me what an ungrateful dog I have been to do this terrible thing under his roof. Something like that."

Then Father Horse heard the rattling sound of the key in the lock.

"Go now, quickly," he whispered and he shut up the cupboard just as the cell door opened. Silvius came in a little uncertainly. He was red in the face and his forehead was sweaty with exercise. He carried a jug and a cup.

"Forgive me, Father, but I have been told to do this." He poured water from the jug into the cup and drank it down: once, twice, three times.

Wiping his lips with his sleeve, he said, "Sword practice is thirsty work."

Behind him, Father Horse could see Gordi—unable to contain his curiosity—poking his face into the cell. When Gordi saw him, the boy was unable to stifle a gasp. "Father Horse, what have they done to you?"

Quick as anything, Silvius turned around and with his free hand, bundled the boy out of the cell.

Clearly angry, Silvius scolded Gordi, "You should not have done that! He is not allowed to see you! I'll catch it if the tribune finds out."

"Well, I won't tell him," said Gordi.

"You'd better get going now, little one, before my commander gets back. Let's not do this again down here, it's better up in the courtyard where there's more natural light."

With that, Silvius closed the door and locked it.

Father Horse turned back to the closed cupboard, and carefully and quietly, opened it up. The shelves and wooden backing of the cupboard stared back at him. Simon had, ever so silently, replaced it all.

Then he went back and sat on the bed. He had a plan. All he could do for the moment was wait. And pray.

CHAPTER THIRTEEN

LYDIA, SENTIA, AND GINI

Elsewhere in the house, it was much as Simon had described. Lunch had come and gone, with not much eaten and some quietly set aside for the benefit of Father Horse. Glaucus had withdrawn to his business office where he sat in gloom. He was angry. He was angry with Lydia for bringing Father Horse to the house; he was angry with himself for liking the man. He was angry with Maximinus for acting so high-handedly, for taking over as the head of the house, for taking his tutor from him; he was angry with Sentia for bringing the jewels in the first place; he was angry with Father Horse for being the sort of person who could take the blame. He did not know whether Father Horse had done it or not, indeed by now, to his mind, that mattered less than the fact that the tribune thought that he had. He sat, and sulked, and drank too much wine.

If Lydia was angry, it was a cold and quiet anger at the tribune that she buried deep beneath her surface appearance. She knew that she had to keep Hightower ticking over, and so all morning she had kept busy, ensuring that things were put back in their places after the soldiers had been through the house.

After lunch, she sat in her wicker chair in her room with a cup of flower tea. She needed time to think. Had she had done a terrible thing to bring Father Horse among them? Lydia had loved him, as the children had, and enjoyed the fact that there was one who was both an educated Christian to talk to and a priest who might share worship with them. She went through in her mind all of the reasons that she could find for having Father Horse around; while across her heart lay the chill of dread that the tribune would take him away. She found it really difficult to believe that Father Horse was a thief, but then she had to ask herself, if he had not taken the jewels, who had? Someone had done it.

It was while she was pondering this that she received an unexpected visitor. As she sat, sipping her tea and pretending to read a book, she heard a knock at her door. It was Septimus.

"My lady," he said. "The Lady Sentia is outside and wishes to see you."

"Please allow her to come in, see that she has everything that she needs, and then leave us for a while."

"As you wish, my Lady."

Septimus showed Sentia in, and Lydia rose to greet her.

"Lady Sentia," she offered. "Would you care for some refreshment?"

"That is most kind, but no thank you."

Septimus bowed and withdrew from the room, closing the door behind him.

"Dear Lydia," Sentia began. "I am here really to appeal to you. You know this man better than anyone. He has been most stubborn. He refuses to tell Maximinus where the jewels are, and while my husband has been most patient with him, that is a patience that will not last long."

"My dear Sentia, what makes you think that he knows where they are? Why do you think that he is guilty at all? Your husband does seem certain; but, so far as I know, there is no real evidence."

"Well, he's a Christian, isn't he? Isn't that enough?" Sentia insisted.

"Five years ago, perhaps," responded Lydia. "Things have changed. The state is changing. It's not illegal any more. You'd be surprised at where you might find Christians. I'm told that there are even Christians in the army."

"No!" Sentia was shocked.

"For all we know, one of those fine young boys out there who guards your husband might be a Christian. Or some of your household slaves, or some of mine, or even me!"

"Oh, surely not!" Sentia was scandalized.

"Actually, my dear, I am a Christian. I have been since I was a child. Not Glaucus, or the children. Just me. My brother is a bishop and it was him who sent us Hippolytus at my request. It is not an accident that my children have a Christian tutor. I wanted one. I asked my brother to send me one, and he did," Lydia replied evenly.

Sentia rose preparing to leave. "I don't see much point in continuing this," she said curtly, anger rising in her voice.

"Please my dear, sit down. Let us talk about this like sensible women. I know that you are no fool. Perhaps between us, we can solve this." Lydia said, reasonably.

"How can I trust you?" Sentia snapped, but then stopped, thought for a moment and settled back into her seat. "Convince me!" she demanded.

"Your husband has a soldier called Germanus, doesn't he?" asked Lydia.

"Yes, but I'm sure that he's no Christian."

"As am I Sentia," assured Lydia. "But it is not that long ago that he, or his family, were fighting against Rome on the battlefield. He is a Roman now. If that is so for one who was born outside the bounds of the empire, how much more is it so for us who are children of Rome? We are Christians, and loyal Romans too. That is what our teachings tell us."

Sentia sat for a moment, thinking through what Lydia had said. She might have walked out at that moment, and nearly did, but something held her back; something about what she had been told and what she had heard. After a while, she said, almost unwillingly, "My husband does trust Germanus. He must. He only brings the men that he most trusts on visits like this."

"Am I not worthy of the same trust?"

"But my dear, we only just met!"

"And yet," responded Lydia, "I have just trusted you with something about me that, a few years ago, could have cost me my head."

Sentia saw the point at once.

"So what do you want me to do about it?" she asked.

"Nothing. There is nothing that either of us can do. The decisions are with your husband. But we can, at least, talk. I am curious about one thing, although you may think it forward of me to ask."

"We are this far in. A little more boldness can't hurt," smiled Sentia.

"Well then, tell me, why did you bring the jewels at all? You didn't know us. Surely there was no reason to try to impress us."

"But there was. The jewels themselves have been in my family for some generations. They come from the Emerald Mountain in Egypt. Before he was old enough to enter the Senate, great-grandfather was on the staff of the governor of Egypt. The family story is that he bought the jewels for his mother, and she never liked them. I have always loved them, and so when I married, my father had them set and gave the jewels to me. They are quite important to me, and I never travel without them. They are a link, you see, to my ancestors who have been Roman and their long history of service to the state. Whenever I lament being here in Britain, so far from all that I love, I look at the jewels and realize that these things are the price of being a member of my class.

"It's never about the money. There is no point in wearing them in a house like this where there may be just as much wealth as I will ever hold. It's about station. When I wore them, it was not to say how rich we are, but that to stress to you in an unspoken way that however much you may live amongst us and become Roman, we have always been Roman."

"Well, let's hope that we can find your emeralds, then." Lydia replied. "One thing about you old nobility you do know beauty when you see it!"

The two women smiled in unison, and the air in the room became a little easier to breathe.

"I find that my tea has gone cold. Would you share a fresh cup with me?" asked Lydia.

"I would be delighted," Sentia answered. "What flowers do you use for flavor?"

"I have dried Egyptian hibiscus brought here on our boat every few months. It is very much my favorite."

"Mine too," said Sentia. "It is another one of those things that great-grandfather brought back from Egypt all those years ago. His mother liked that far more than the emeralds"

Lydia had a little bell that she rang and a moment later, Lois, her personal maid came in. Lois was much the same age as Lydia and the two had become as close as slave and mistress could be over the years that Lydia had been in the household. They had even had their sons within months of one another.

"Lois, may we have some more tea?"

"Of course, Lady."

"And I don't suppose you know what our boys are getting up to?"

Lois had to stop herself from looking at Sentia as she answered:

"I'm sure that they are about and up to no good, Lady."

In fact, Lois knew perfectly well, having provided Simon with the lunch basket for Father Horse, but she could not let Sentia know that.

"Well," reflected Lydia. "So long as they turn up clean for their dinners."

"That might be asking too much of boys, Lady" smiled Lois.

Lydia turned to Sentia.

"It must be so hard on you, to be separated from your boys. Mine is a terror, but he is a wonderful one."

"It is the price of politics."

Lois was lingering, but Lydia looked at her with meaning. "Tea," she said, and Lois hurried off.

When Lois had left the room, Sentia turned to Lydia and said, "You seem very familiar with your maid, and you allow her boy to play with your children? Is this some Christian thing?"

"The boys actually don't play together much, but I would be happy if they did. As to your question about my religion, I am not entirely sure. I know some Christians who treat their slaves much as everyone else does. Our teacher, the Holy Paul, says that there is no difference between slave and free before God, but I do not know if that is what makes me as I am. I do know that most slaves are slaves through no fault of their own. I think that you met Glaucus' personal slave, Philip, when you were travelling?"

Sentia nodded. "He was very quiet, but he was always there."

"Philip comes from a farming family in Asia, not far from Ephesus. For some reason, his father had serious financial problems. I don't know what they were—perhaps taxes, or bad seasons, or even careless spending—but the family might have lost the farm. So, to meet his debts. Philip's father sold his youngest son into slavery, and that was that. It's not Philip's fault that he is a slave, nor does it mean that he is a lesser person—"

"I think that is your Christianity speaking," Sentia broke in.

Lydia was going to continue, but just then Lois came back with the hot drinks, and Gini.

"Look who I found moping around the garden," she said to Lydia.

"Verginia," Lydia addressed her daughter with her proper name. "You recall meeting the Lady Sentia." It was not a question.

"Yes mother."

"Come girl, sit with us and have some tea," invited Sentia. It was not a request.

As the three settled over the warm, sweet hibiscus tea, Sentia tried to make conversation with Gini. "How do you spend your days here, Verginia?"

Gini decided to be both truthful and more than a little cheeky, "My brother and I used to spend them dodging our tutors, but since Father Horse came, we cannot wait to be with him and learn what it is that he has to teach."

"Oh," said Sentia. There was one of those awkward moments of silence when everything seemed to stop for a little too long.

Sentia might have given in to anger, stood on her dignity as a Roman noblewomen, and scolded Gini, telling her that the arrest of a thief was none of her business. She did not. Instead, she used the moment to give in to wonder. How was it that Father Horse had so captured the affection of these children? She even allowed herself to ponder the possibility that Maximinus might have been wrong about the priest after all.

"You must miss him very much. I am sorry about this business," she said kindly. "I think that I'll go now and walk in the garden. It is very lovely. Your Quintus knows his plants."

She rose to her feet, as did Lydia and Gini. Mother and daughter bowed slightly to their visitor; Sentia nodded her head by way of reply and left the room.

For a moment they listened as Sentia went down the stairs and, once she was satisfied that Sentia was far enough away, Gini spoke, "Mother, we've seen Father Horse. We know where they are keeping him. He looks terrible, like he's been in a fight or something."

"Where is he?" Lydia was urgent and insistent.

"The soldiers have him locked up in one of the old cells in the basement underneath the guest wing."

"Here in the house?" Lydia was surprised.

"Yes. Simon knows them well, and also that there is a way into his room from the room next door that the soldiers don't know about."

"What have you been doing?" Lydia demanded.

"Well, the soldiers weren't allowing him to eat or drink, so we gave him lunch, and a big drink of water. And they tied his hands behind his back last night so that he couldn't use them or even lie down properly. Simon waited until everyone was asleep last night, crept into the room and untied them. Even Father Horse didn't know what had happened until late this morning. The soldiers were rather cross with each other; it was very funny."

Lydia didn't know whether to be angry or amused. She settled for both at the same time.

Smiling, she said sternly, "Tell me everything."

Gini told Lydia the whole story, from the feeding of Father Horse to the hatching of his plan. As she spoke, Lydia could feel her heart burst with pride. Her daughter had defied soldiers and their commander to do what she saw as the right thing. Even if she could not formally approve, she was impressed.

When Gini had finished, Lydia thought for a moment, "Come on my girl. Let's find your father. We need him to make this plan work."

Glaucus was not hard to find. He was stretched out on the couch in his office, fast asleep, the remains of a jug of wine on the table beside him. Lydia's heart gave a lurch. She was not used to seeing him like this. She turned to Gini.

"Find Philip. He can't be far, and get him to bring a jug of cold water."

Gini bobbed her head and left, and Lydia set to work on waking Glaucus.

"Come, my dear," she said loudly. "You have slept enough. We have work to do, and must do it quickly."

Glaucus stirred and grunted.

"Glaucus, come on, wake up! The master of this house is needed!"

He struggled to open his eyes and focus. Then, slowly, he rubbed his face, yawned, looked up noticed Lydia. "This is unlike you. What brings you here in the middle of the day?"

Almost on cue, Philip walked in carrying a jug and a plain cup. Philip was a little older than Glaucus, a tall, spare man with thinning hair and a beaky nose. He poured out some water and, wordlessly, Glaucus took the cup, drank it down and held it out for a refill. When he had drunk the second cup, he turned again to Lydia.

"So my dear," he said. "Suppose that you tell me all that this is about."

"You know as well as I do that this is about Father Horse," she replied.

"What can we do? The tribune is convinced that he is the thief."

"What do you think?" Lydia asked sharply.

"I don't know what to think," replied Glaucus forlornly. "On the one hand, I like your Father Horse very much and I can see that he has done the children a lot of good. On the other, I don't see how the tribune could be wrong. Someone took those jewels. Why not someone who is both a newcomer and, to all intents and purposes, a foreigner?"

He regretted the words as soon as he had said them.

"So what does that make me, husband?" she replied heatedly.

Glaucus knew that he had ground to make up, as Lydia continued, "You know, of course, that the tribune has taken over the house?"

"What do you mean?" Glaucus replied, although weakly.

"I mean that he has Father Horse locked up in the old rooms underneath the guest wing. I mean that he has a guard set in that corridor with instructions to admit no one. Did he even ask? Whose house is this, Glaucus? Is it ours, or is it Maximinus'?"

"He did ask. And I did suggest those rooms because I knew them to be secure. How else do you think that he found them?" replied Glaucus, the meekness falling away a little as he found himself having to justify himself to Lydia.

"So you are happy that there is a guard there?"

"No. I am not happy at all. I am not happy that Father Horse is locked up there. I am not happy that there is a guard and I am not happy at all about any aspect of this business."

"Well, let me put another question to you, husband. What if Father Horse is as innocent as he says he is?"

That stopped Glaucus. He had only thought in terms of meeting the needs of the tribune. He had not considered at all that he might be being a party to an injustice.

"How will I know that?" he asked.

"Why don't you ask him yourself," replied Lydia evenly.

"But the tribune has forbidden anyone to speak with him."

"Oh, this for the tribune!" exclaimed Lydia, snapping her fingers, crossly. "Whose house is this, his or yours? If he is under your roof, you have the authority here."

"Very well. I shall talk to your priest. But first, Philip, I shall need another cup or three of water. My mouth is quite dry from all this talking."

Half an hour later a small party, with Glaucus at its head, made its way down the stairs to the dank corridor outside the old slave rooms. They found Aelian, the soldier with the missing front tooth, outside the door standing sentry and looking bored. He brightened up when he saw them. Here, at least, was something to do.

Glaucus went right up to him and said, very clearly, "I want to see your prisoner."

Aelian was equally clear.

"I have orders to admit no one. He sees no one. My commander was quite clear."

"This is my house," replied Glaucus. "I go where I please."

"My orders are clear. You cannot see him."

"In this house, my wishes override your orders," insisted Glaucus.

"Not while I have this," said Aelian lightly, as he stroked the hilt of his sword.

"Then you shall have to kill me. I have my own key and I will not be denied in my own house," Glaucus was bluffing. He did not feel half as brave as he sounded. "Are you going to tell your commander that you killed the master of the house because he wanted to go into one of his own rooms?"

"Nobody said anything about killing, sir. I just have my orders." Aelian was adamant.

As Glaucus reached for his key and Aelian began to slide his sword out of its scabbard, the voice of Marcellus cut in.

"There's no need for any of this unpleasantness. Aelian, you're a good soldier and you know how to follow orders, but you'll never be a diplomat. It's this man's house. He is master here and the tribune knows it. Let him into the room. I'll take responsibility for it."

Aelian stiffened to attention and slammed the sword back down into the scabbard.

"Yes sir!" he said.

"Just the master here, mind," continued Marcellus from the shadows. "The rest of his little party will have to wait outside. Can't say fairer than that, can we?"

Aelian took his key, opened the door and allowed Glaucus to enter. Then he closed the door behind him and waited.

CHAPTER FOURTEEN

GLAUCUS TAKES CHARGE

The room was gloomier, if possible, than the corridor outside. Glaucus blinked a few times to accustom his eyes to the dimness. Father Horse was standing with his back to the door, and in the act of turning to face Glaucus. When he saw who it was, he gave a lop-sided grin and said, "Thank-you for coming to see me."

Glaucus did a double take. Father Horse looked like he had been in a serious fight. His forearms and face were mottled with bruises. He had a split lip and a cut above his left eye. There was dried blood around his nose. His clothes were smeared with dirt and grass stains and something darker that might also have been blood.

He had not given permission for the priest to be tortured under his roof, and he doubted that it was even legal. He asked the obvious question, "Have they been torturing you?"

Father Horse shrugged and said, "I am as you see me. They will, no doubt, say that I tripped down the stairs when they were bringing me back here."

Glaucus was suddenly angry.

"It doesn't matter what you are accused of. If you are under my roof, you are under my protection until I, not the tribune choose to withdraw it. Why have they done this?"

"Because I do not know where the jewels are. They think I do, and they believe that by starving me and depriving me of rest and water, and by subjecting me to pain, that I can suddenly tell them what I do not know."

"Torture of citizens is illegal," Glaucus protested.

"Maximinus was quick to remind me that here at Rome's farthest frontier, he is Roman law," replied Father Horse.

"Well then," responded Glaucus. "What can we do? How can we get you out of this?"

"Do you not still think that I might have taken the jewels? That I might deserve this?"

"Nobody deserves this," said Glaucus, more forcefully than he had intended. "I saw enough blood and pain under my roof when we left Tarsus to last me the rest of my life. I hoped never to see it again."

Glaucus was also beginning to think, too, that Father Horse might be innocent after all. No one could take all that punishment and still not tell what they knew, particularly if it concerned a few (admittedly very valuable) rocks.

"Hippolytus, I will ask you once," he said. "And I expect you to answer truthfully. Did you take the jewels?"

"I did not," his answer was clear.

"So how do we get you out of this?"

"I do have a plan," said Father Horse.

"Go on," Glaucus prompted, fascinated with what this ingenious tutor might come up with.

"In order to prove me innocent to the satisfaction of the tribune, we have to find the one who is guilty, and lead the tribune to catch them with the jewels in their possession."

"How do we do that?" Glaucus asked.

"What helps here is that I think that I know where the jewels are."

"What!" said Glaucus, sharply. "So why not just tell the tribune and be done?"

"Because unless we show him who took them, he will still think that it was me, and that I cracked under all of the pressure he was putting me under. That puts me back in chains in a cart for Eboracum and a trial.

"I can give him his jewels back, but I have to prove to him who took them in the first place as well. Otherwise it will not help me, nor will it help your contract."

"That contract!" exclaimed Glaucus. "In all this fuss, I'd forgotten about it entirely!"

"That makes you a good and decent man," said Father Horse. "But we have two situations to rescue here; my freedom and your livelihood!"

"Surely I won't get the contract with all of this bother? How can Maximinus trust me to honor a business arrangement when he cannot sleep a night safely under my roof?"

"Well then, let's give him a good reason to trust you again."

"How do we do that?"

"Maximinus is a proud Roman, isn't he?" This wasn't really a question. Father Horse was beginning to lecture. "From whom do the Romans claim descent?"

"Romulus," answered Glaucus, puzzled as to where this was going.

"Before Romulus," Father Horse persisted. "Come on, what books did you read when you were young?"

"You mean Aeneas?" asked Glaucus.

"I mean Aeneas, the Trojan prince who escaped from burning Troy as it was being looted by the conquering Greeks."

"What of him?" asked Glaucus, intrigued.

"Your name is Glaucus. You are named for the leader of the soldiers of Lycia who fought on the Trojan side in that war. Your ancestors and his were ancient allies, against the Greeks who destroyed your city and shattered your alliance."

"How does that help?"

"It helps you persuade Maximinus, who cares about such things, that you are both on the same side. You are both fighting a war against a mysterious and dangerous enemy who is seeking to tear you apart."

"But Father Horse, Maximinus thinks that enemy is you."

"Then we have to persuade him otherwise, using both of the weapons that the great war for Troy left us with—those two great poems, the *Iliad* and the *Aeneid*."

"I don't understand!" said Glaucus, still puzzled. "How will those old books help us?"

"I think that I am going on too fast, and we do not have much time," Father Horse spoke quickly. "The guard will want you out of here in a minute. You have already been here long enough. Listen," his voice now became urgent. "There is more to this house than you know. I believe that underneath the garden, there is a secret chamber that used to be the strongroom when this was a legionary fort. That is where I think that the jewels are. The rest of my plan, I will tell you through the children. If you can get me a writing tablet and stylus, they can pass it back to you. They have a way of getting in here that the guards do not know. But remember this. We cannot go straight to Maximinus with this, or all will be lost. We have to let the thief, or thieves, incriminate themselves. Now, please go. We have lingered long enough. No doubt the guard will report just how much time you spent in here."

Glaucus nodded, turned and banged on the door.

"I will await word," he said and, as Aelian opened up, he slipped through and was gone. The door banged shut and Father Horse was alone, again, with his prayers.

While Glaucus had been in the cell with Father Horse, a conversation of a different kind was taking place in the corridor outside. Glaucus had brought the two boys with him for exactly this reason. He needed Aelian distracted so that he could talk to Father Horse properly, and who better than two boys fascinated by big, armored men with swords?

It was Gordi who began with an innocent enough question. "What's it like, being in the army?"

"Well, what do you mean? Like what?" Aelian was puzzled.

"I don't know. Is it all battles and fighting, and rescuing noble citizens from bands of barbarians?"

"Oh, I see. Well we don't do a lot of rescuing as a rule. Mostly it's marching. We marched here from Eboracum. We'll march back again when the tribune's ready. Then we'll march somewhere else. Sometimes we don't have to march, and that's when we ride, but we don't ride into a fight. That's for the cavalry. We do our fighting on our feet."

"So have you fought in a battle? Is that where you got that scar? Did you get that fighting a thundering horde of barbarians?"

"Hardly," laughed Aelian. "I wish I had. This I had in a fight in a tavern over a girl and some spilled beer. This, and the tooth."

"Oh" said Gordi, sounding just a little disappointed. "But then you could still have been in a battle."

"Well, I suppose that I've been in a couple. Up in this part of the world, we don't get big battles. The tribes across the wall are pretty quiet. We don't get much trouble from them. No, if we do any fighting at all, it's chasing bandits or catching outlaws, that sort of thing."

Then it was Simon's turn. Sitting cross-legged at Aelian's feet and looking up at him with eyes wide in wonder, he asked, "So why did you become a soldier? Was it for the fighting and the rescuing, or for the glory of Rome?'

"Well, not any of those things really," Aelian replied. "I joined up because it's a living. I get a steady wage, regular food—even if it's not always the finest, a place to sleep and a chance for a family. It's a family thing. My dad was a soldier. His dad was a soldier. I'm a soldier."

All through the conversation, the boys had been careful to stay away from the door and, if anything, to keep Aelian's back to it. It was a trick that Glaucus had taught them to keep Aelian distracted. If he did not look at the door, then maybe he could be distracted long enough for Glaucus to have the discussion that he needed with Father Horse.

"Is this a long way from your home, then?" asked Gordi.

"That's not quite so simple. I was born in a town called Bremetannacum that's not so far from here, a few days march or a couple of days hard riding. It's a town full of old soldiers and their families and we all come from the same place. Many years ago, my people were enemies of Rome. We were defeated by the wise emperor Marcus Aurelius, and thousands of men were sent to Britain to serve as horse soldiers on the frontier."

"Horse soldiers?" Simon was curious.

"My people were—still are, I suppose—Sarmatians. We are an old people and hundreds of years ago, we came on horses from the distant east across the grass plains until we arrived at the gates of the Roman Empire. We were horse people. We rode horses from childhood and fought on horseback. The land we settled in kept us poor. It was too wet to farm, so all we could do was graze our horses, cattle, and sheep. Sometimes we raided the Romans across the great river; sometimes they raided us. But then our ancestors decided to try and take some of Rome's riches for themselves and lost the war. But the wise Aurelius liked the way that we fought. He saw that we could help keep a narrow frontier like this one secure by being able to get to trouble spots quickly, so he sent my ancestors here. Here we have stayed, forgetting the ways of the horse, and learning how to be Romans. I can ride, but not like my father's father could ride, and while I am good with a sword, he could charge into battle, both hands gripping his lance, and riding his horse with his knees. Forgetting these things is the price of being a Roman."

"Is your old country far? Would you like to go back?"

For a moment, Aelian looked down. "I suppose it is far. I don't know. This is my world now. How could I go back? What would I go back to? Britain is my home now, and Rome is my master. I have nothing in the other place."

There was a sad silence, and then Aelian remembered what he was supposed to be doing, there in that corridor, in the late afternoon. He turned and reached for the door handle, but as he did so, they heard Glaucus banging on the door from within. The plan had worked.

Later, in the kitchen, the family sat around the big table as Phormio served up the kind of food the family loved. There was cold ham, boar sausages, lettuce salad, cucumbers in sweet dressing, roast chickpeas and plates of sheep's cheese, and fruit. There was lemon water, mint tea and wine, the fresh, coarse spelt bread that everyone loved and dishes of peppery olive oil for dipping. The only one not there was Simon. He had his own errand. As the family ate and talked, often over each other, Simon quietly slipped in and handed Glaucus a writing tablet. He took it, opened it, read it and gave it, wordlessly, to Lydia. There was a little bit of quiet at the table as she, too, read it, until Gordi, impatiently, burst out, "What does it say? What does it say?"

"Hush, my dear," replied his mother. "All in good time." She motioned to Simon who took a place at the table beside his father, filled a plate with food, and set about eating it, as only a hungry boy can.

After everyone had eaten, Glaucus turned to Gordi. "Gordianus, I have an important task this evening for which I need your help. Out of all of the people in this household, you are the one best fitted for the job that I have in mind. Come with me now to my office. I have a letter to write and you must take it and give it directly into the hand of Maximinus himself. Do you understand?"

"Yes, sir!" Gordi was enthusiastic. This was twice in a day that his father had given him an important and difficult job to do. First with Simon, to distract the soldier in the corridor, and now this. He basked in his father's sudden confidence and felt very grown up indeed.

In Glaucus' office, he waited while his father wrote the letter. It was not easy. There were some false starts and a lot of crossing out, but after an hour or so, Glaucus had composed a text that he felt pleased with and written out a fair copy on a square of good papyrus that he generally reserved for correspondence with his best customers. It was not a long letter, although very formal.

> *To the most distinguished tribune Marcus Herennius Faustus Maximinus, from the prominent man Marcus Aurelius Glaucus of Hightower, greeting.*
>
> *I hope that things are well with you.*
>
> *I believe, my Lord, that we have a common interest and common concern in the fate of the Christian, Aurelius Hippolytus, who is a member of my household and, as such, under my protection. You have cause to believe that he is guilty of the theft of your wife's jewels. While I would be angered beyond measure if this were to be true, I am not yet certain of his guilt and until I am, I will not release him to you.*
>
> *I believe that there is a way to resolve this in a way that will be satisfactory to both of us. I have a plan that should enable us both to be certain of the identity of the thief, and to secure the return of the jewels. This is a time, my Lord, when men must work together, as our ancestors did on the battle for Troy. There, your great ancestor Aeneas, and mine, also named Glaucus, threw back the assaults of the Greeks again and again by standing, shield to shield. If you recall, it was cleverness and not force of arms that brought down the walls of Troy, and sent our forefathers away in defeat. I believe that we can learn from our ancient enemies. My plan, I think, is worthy of the cunning Odysseus, whose idea it was*

to pretend to leave while leaving behind great warriors in the belly of a wooden horse to open the gates of Troy from within.

I will outline my idea to you tomorrow, over breakfast, if you are willing. I will have food prepared and tables set up in the field between the house and your camp so that none may hear our plan. You may choose not to come. There is no shame in that, but there would be little progress in resolving this matter either. Farewell!

Glaucus sealed up the letter and handed it to Gordi. It was now late in the long British twilight and the pink rays of the setting sun lit Gordi's way as he ran along the little track that was being worn in the grass between the soldier's camp and the house.

The soldiers had been at work during the afternoon, transforming a group of tents into a proper Roman camp. They had dug a ditch about four feet deep most of the way around and piled up the dirt into a kind of wall between the tents and the ditch. All that they had left was a causeway just wide enough for a wheeled cart and a gateway in the makeshift wall. There was a soldier there on guard duty. It was not one of those to whom Gordi had talked before. It was, instead, the one called Julianus.

He went straight up to him.

"What do you want, boy?" Julianus spoke roughly.

"I have a letter for the tribune from my father," replied Gordi, reminding Julianus (although unintentionally) of the difference in their status.

"I'll take that then and make sure that he gets it," responded Julianus, a little less gruffly.

"No," said Gordi. "My father was very clear. I must take it to tribune Maximinus and give it to no one else."

"Well, I can't leave here," replied the soldier. "And I can't just let you go wandering about the camp."

" I can wait here if you like, but I must do as my father has told me." Gordi was determined to do exactly what his father had asked of him.

"Very well," said Julianus gruffly. "But no more talking. I need to be alert."

Gordi did not have to wait all that long. After a time, one of the tent flaps opened and Silvius emerged. Catching sight of Gordi in the deepening twilight, he strolled over. "What are you doing here?"

"I have a letter from my father to the tribune. My father says that I must give it to the tribune directly," said Gordi.

"Well, you'd better come with me then. The tribune will turn in when the sun is gone so there is not much time. But he is still at supper with his lady. Follow me."

With a nod to Julianus, Gordi turned and followed Silvius into the camp.

As they approached the tribune's tent, Silvius turned to Gordi and told him to wait where he was. Then the soldier marched to the open tent flap and stood at attention, waiting to be noticed.

The sun had now gone, and the only light was from the braziers. Insects clustered around them, drawn to the flames. The night was still, and in that stillness Gordi heard the soft rumble of voices from the tribune's tent. They stopped briefly and Silvius went in. A few moments later, Maximinus came out, leaning on Silvius.

"So you have a letter for me, boy?" he said to Gordi, his voice slurred with wine.

"Yes sir. My father told me to give it to you and to no one else. He also said that I needn't wait for an answer."

"Well, give it to me, then," Maximinus ordered roughly.

Gordi handed over the little papyrus package to the soldier, who remembered—perhaps too late—that he was only a boy.

"There you are, lad," he murmured, more softly now. "You can tell your pa that you've done your job. Now off you go to bed. I'll read this presently."

Gordi turned and watched by the soldiers, ran back through the camp and into the night.

In his silent cell, Father Horse had gone to sleep. Since Glaucus' visit in the afternoon, the priest had been left alone except for Simon's stealthy visit to the next-door cell. He had placed bread, water, and the writing pad that was needed into the cupboard between the rooms. The soldiers on guard had come and gone outside, but had not so much as opened the door and looked in, confident that their prisoner was not going anywhere.

Undisturbed, Father Horse had eaten and drunk, and written his letter for Glaucus. He had taken nothing out of the cupboard, preferring instead to stand at the open door and use its floor as his table. Then when he closed it up, there was no trace of what he had been doing: no crumb of bread, no drop of water, no telltale scrap of wax. When full night had come and the dim light in the room had waned to blackness, Father Horse had groped his way to the bed, composed his thoughts and gone to sleep.

Two hours later, he woke sharply from a deep sleep, dripping with water. He shook his head and cleared his eyes. Pale light spilled in from the corridor through the open door. Marcellus stood at the foot of his bed, holding an empty bucket, and with an evil grin on his face.

"I thought you'd like that drink now," he said leering at him, and left.

Father Horse licked at the water that ran down his face. It was salty.

CHAPTER FIFTEEN

THE TRIBUNE COMES TO BREAKFAST

In the dim predawn light Germanus, whose turn it was to stand guard on the camp, was startled by the approach of a group of Glaucus' slaves.

On a flat patch of grass between the palisade and the house, they paced out a square of ground and hammered four long poles into the earth, one in each corner. On top of each of the poles was a little spike. Once the poles were firmly fixed into the earth, a large cloth was produced with a loop in each corner that fastened over the spike so that what emerged in a matter of minutes was a makeshift shelter. They finished off the process by securing each of the poles with guy ropes that were, in turn, fastened into pegs driven into the ground. Once this structure was completed, they went back into the house and fetched out a long, low table and two dining couches. These, they set up under the shelter with the couches facing one another over the table.

Finally there came a small procession of kitchen slaves bearing fresh-baked bread, bowls of olive oil, dipping sauce and salt, platters of fruit and cheese and sausages of various kinds, boiled eggs, nuts, and dried fruit. Then came two wooden plates, two bowls of water, and two of Glaucus' napkins of finest Egyptian linen. Finally, and with a sense of ceremony, and accompanied by Simon, came Phormio himself, bearing two silver goblets and a jug of watered wine.

It was a breakfast feast, a grazing table for the very hungry. Phormio stood and looked over the table and the layout of the various dishes, adjusted one or two, considered himself sufficiently satisfied, and then gestured to Simon who produced a fine linen cloth and handed it to his father. With a grand sweep of his arm, Phormio flicked the cloth out and let it settle over the food. With a final twitch or two to ensure that the cloth sat straight,

Phormio nodded to Simon, and both turned and returned to the house, followed by all of the slaves in the field.

All was quiet. By now the eastern sky was ablaze with the dawn and the sun's rays were beginning to bathe the walls of Hightower with the growing light of day. As the day's splendor began fully to announce itself, Glaucus emerged from the main door of Hightower. He had taken the time to bathe, shave, and dress in his formal toga. He was unaccompanied. Alone, he strolled to the little breakfast pavilion, lay down on one of the couches and waited.

This was the moment of risk. Maximinus had not been asked to reply to the invitation so he was free to ignore it and get on with his business. Glaucus might find himself left out in the middle of a field surrounded by a vast breakfast and no one with whom to share it. He might end up with more egg on his face than was on the table.

As time went by and the warmth of the morning grew, the camp woke to life. Glaucus could hear the soldiers talking and laughing as their breakfast fire was kindled. Soon, he could smell frying bacon and his empty stomach rumbled. Although he had a feast before him, he had determined not to touch it until and unless Maximinus joined him. He waited.

Minute built on minute with no sign of the tribune. Glaucus felt a crawling dread slide into his heart. Perhaps Maximinus would ignore him, snub his invitation and go his own way. He was tempted, for more than a moment to stand up and leave, to give up on the whole business and hand Maximinus his victory. He could feel that seed of anger growing again within himself, a dark worm of resentment at all that had happened since Hippolytus had arrived. The tribune's visit should have been a triumph: a tour of the farm, a memorable dinner, happy farewells the next day with a contract for new business in his hand. Instead, the family had been disturbed; the contract was at risk; and powerful people had been offended. Was this troublesome priest really worth all of this effort and worry? Hadn't this Christian upended his household, suggested that they all do slaves' work, plotted with him to deceive the Roman army, moved the family to eating in the great kitchen rather than its proper place in the dining room? True, Glaucus' children liked him; true, he was the first tutor that they had ever had who engaged their interest and taught them the things that they needed to learn; true, Lydia found his presence a comfort. But none of that mattered if he, the master of the house, had been wronged, if the Christian had betrayed his trust to turn his household into this strange place where his authority was less than that of this interfering priest. Glaucus had almost convinced himself. He had almost begun to move, to get up from his couch and march angrily back to the house and toss the Christian to the soldiers. But he didn't. He stopped himself.

In the midst of these unbidden and unwanted thoughts, Glaucus realized that this was exactly why Maximinus was keeping him waiting. He was showing Glaucus just who was in control here, who had the power, making him doubt himself and his cause, and so setting him at a disadvantage in the discussion that was to come. It was an old-fashioned negotiating trick. Glaucus had used it himself. Once he understood that, he knew that it could no longer distract him. His own knowledge and experience had defused the tactic. Instead, he settled back down on his couch, smiled to himself and wished that he had brought a book to read.

Abruptly, the morning stillness was broken by the strident sound of a trumpet. There was movement in the camp and, a few moments later, Maximinus stepped out beyond the makeshift gate. He had made no effort at all to dress for the occasion. His robe was old, of uncertain color, and mottled with stains; it was tied at his waist by what looked like a piece of old rope. His hair stuck out at odd angles, he had not shaved and his feet were bare. He looked, at first glance, like one of Glaucus' farm slaves. The only thing that marked Maximinus out as a man of money and rank was his gold signet ring.

He stood there for a moment, looking around, until he caught sight of Glaucus, lounging and at ease in his little pavilion. Then he nodded briefly, as if to himself and swaggered across the grass to Glaucus. Rather awkwardly, and without grace, he flung himself down on his couch, twitched the cloth covering the food aside, grabbed a hunk of bread, dunked it in some oil and began to eat. He had not said a word. Only when he had finished the bread did he turn to Glaucus and ask, "So what's this about then?"

Glaucus waited a moment before speaking. Instead, he placed some sliced sausage and a boiled egg on his plate and plucked out some olives and a hunk of bread. His movements were as understated and precise and Maximinus' had been gross and coarse.

"As I said in my note, it's about the Christian, Hippolytus. I am not as convinced of his guilt as you are and, since he is a member of my household, he remains under my protection. We both know enough law and custom to understand that while you have the power to take Hippolytus by force, whether I wish it or not, to do so would violate my rights as head of this family and master of this house. I have seen him and I note that already you have been questioning him with some…vigor…"

Maximinus interrupted him, "He falls down a lot. He's none too steady on those wonky legs of his."

Maximinus picked up a chicken leg and began to tear at it with his teeth as Glaucus continued, "Tribune, it's clear that he has not confessed to the crime despite all of his…falling over…Otherwise you would have gone by now with both the jewels and the priest."

Maximinus grunted between bites, "Go on."

Glaucus continued. "I do not think that the Christian is guilty for certain, but I am prepared to release him to you. I do have real questions about his guilt. I do not see how he could have done it or why he might have done it. I also know that he is a very convenient suspect because he is a Christian. But it is no good identifying a likely person whom you can pronounce guilty and punish if you do not get the jewels back. I think that you want them back very much too, because if it were my wife's jewels, that is what my first thought would be simply because Lydia would make it so. The Lady Sentia may be very different, but I do not think so."

The tribune stopped eating and thought. Glaucus had touched a sore spot.

"It seems that what is really important to us both is getting this matter resolved; that we are able to identify the culprit without a shadow of any doubt and get the emeralds back. There's no point in squeezing a confession out of the priest if he has no idea where the emeralds are. I have a way to test the priest's guilt. And it has the added benefit that, if the priest is innocent, we will be able to identify the thief and recover the jewels."

Maximinus was interested now, despite himself. He reached over and took another lump of bread, smeared it with sheep's cheese and honey and asked, "So what is this plan of yours?"

Glaucus again made the tribune wait, gathering some more food onto his plate, and then went on, "I will confess not that this is not an original idea. Over a thousand years ago, the Greeks used it to defeat our ancestors at Troy."

"What?" asked Maximinus in surprise. "Are you thinking about building another wooden horse?"

"No, tribune, responded Glaucus. "That's just how they were able to get inside the gate. The reason that the Trojans thought that they could drag the horse inside the city was because they thought that the Greeks had gone. And indeed they had. There were none to be seen, save the liar they left behind who told the Trojans that the Greeks were sailing home. That was when they dragged the horse into their city, breaking the gates in their enthusiasm to capture this great prize."

"You are well educated," remarked Maximinus.

"My father's gift," replied Glaucus, before continuing. "So here is the essence of my plan. Why not make it look as if you think that the Christian is guilty beyond any doubt and that you are taking him on to Petuaria for proper trial and execution. You don't have to tell anyone else that this is a ruse except two trusted men whom you will leave behind. We tell everyone that they are guests of the house until the Christian cracks and confesses. They are to take custody of the jewels once we know where they are and bring them to you."

The tribune had stopped eating now and was listening closely.

"Then, you strike camp. You could do it as early as today. The road to Petuaria goes through the forest. When you are far enough along the road, set up camp and put a watch on the house. Wait there for three nights. If you do not receive a signal from the house in that time, you may move on and do what you will with the priest. That is the proof that he is guilty. But if you do receive a signal—I think a light from the top story window of the tower is best—then return at once to the house. We will present you with both thief and jewels."

"And the two men that I leave behind?"

"They will need to be a part of this little plan. They have to be men that you trust completely—"

Maximinus interrupted him. "I trust all of my men completely. I chose them myself."

"Very good. They are there to protect your interests and, up to a point, mine. They will watch and wait and, should we discover the thief and the jewels, take possession of both until you arrive. While they are with us, they can be as much, or as little a part of the household as they wish. That is up to you, but they can watch us better if they are in the household.

"I am certain that the jewels are hidden in the house. I have no doubt of it. I know that you have searched it thoroughly from the top of the tower to the depths of the bathhouse. But I think that there must be somewhere that we don't know about, some secret place where they have been hidden…"

"So what will you do, then?"

"Watch. Your men are good at it and I can trust my own family also to be on guard for strange movements in the house, especially at night. I don't think that anything will happen on the first night. The villain wants to give you time to get as far away as possible, so that they can make their own escape."

As Glaucus fell silent, he could see Maximinus thinking through the plan testing for weak points.

"And if no one comes for the jewels in those three nights, then I can take the Christian and go?"

"Yes of course. If he did take the jewels, then no one else will come for them."

"What if he had an ally, a partner in crime? Won't they just take the jewels instead?"

"Yes, but then we will catch them in the act. Then you can question them about whether they had a partner in their crime. Either way, you get your answer."

Maximinus sat in silence, working through the options with which Glaucus had presented him. Then he spoke. There was no bluster or bravado. For a change, it was respectful and considered.

"You know, it could work. I can leave you two good men—Aelian and Germanus, I think. We can have the camp packed up and be on the road in a couple of hours, so we could set everything in motion today."

If Glaucus were surprised by just how quickly Maximinus had come around to his plan, he was careful not to show it. He had expected to work harder to convince the tribune. He understood, at that moment, that using Sentia's desire for the return of the jewels had made a particular impact. He wondered what had passed between husband and wife on the topic when they were in private. He relaxed. He realized that he had been holding back a great deal of tension, and was suddenly hungry. Up to this point, he had been too wound up to eat much, only to appear to eat. His stomach had been a tight knot of worry inside him. Now that knot was gone. He reached over, took a hunk of bread, dipped it in oil, and ate hungrily.

Then Maximinus said, "There is, of course, a condition."

Glaucus froze midbite. So it was not going to go all his own way. The tension was back. He forced himself to eat the morsel in his hand and replied, "What's that?"

"While I don't mind waiting in the forest for a few days, I think that Sentia will like it rather less. She is not a lover of the camp life and prefers a floor beneath her feet, four solid walls and a roof, not to mention decent food rather than the endless soldiers' variations on bread, pork, and beans. I would like to leave her with you for those three days. They are her jewels and, if you are right, it is fitting that she is there when they are recovered. Your Christian had a pleasant room in the tower. It is the kind of accommodation that would suit her. Think of it as a favor to me. With my wife well looked after, I can spend the next three days as I please, and I suspect that there is good hunting in that woodland."

Glaucus relaxed again. This was an easy condition to fulfil. Lydia had liked Sentia and enjoyed her conversation. He reached for a hard-boiled egg, shelled it, dipped it in salt and, before taking a bite, said, "I think that we can agree on that. From what I have seen, Lydia and the lady Sentia enjoy one another's company. Since we have been in Britain, my wife also has fewer opportunities to spend time with other ladies of education and distinction."

"Then it's settled," Maximinus said, heartily. "Now let us cease this wretched nibbling and eat our breakfasts like men."

For the next quarter of an hour or so, all that could he heard from the two men was the sound of eating. When they were done, all that was left was the fruit.

Both men leaned back on their couches, belching slightly and scratching their (rather full) stomachs. Sipping from cups of watered wine, they were now completely relaxed. Glaucus, taking a chance, stretched and asked Maximinus, "What made you agree, and so quickly? From your manner this morning, I thought that you were going to eat a few things, hear my idea, and then stalk off. I thought that I would have to work a great deal harder than I did."

The tribune grunted and replied, "You're a good negotiator. I wish that we had someone like you when we are settling treaties with the little Briton communities beyond the wall. You set it up well with your letter. It showed me that you are an intelligent and educated man with whom I can have a decent conversation. There are few enough of those around here for me to turn my back on you easily. Most of the so-called 'society' of Eboracum have never read a book in their lives. They're good to go hunting with, but when we're sitting around the fire afterwards, they can only talk horses and dogs, and that has serious limits.

"Then, of course, you saw through me very quickly. I came here every inch the proud Roman, seemingly ready only to eat, and not to talk. It's a way that I deal with the tribes. You saw through that and matched it in reverse. Where I was rough and crude, you were precise. Where I dressed like a peasant, you dressed according to your station. Now, I might be bored with life here, and I might be itching to get back to Rome, but I'm not stupid. I have been well schooled in both philosophy and strategy, and so when I meet someone who is good at this, I have to respect it. One thing that I have learned in more years of soldiering than I care to remember, there is value in a good plan and I did want to hear yours.

"Then, when you were presenting me with your idea, you grasped my weakest point—my wife—and used it well. You are quite right. Sentia does want her jewels back more than anything. She doesn't care who did it. I still think that the Christian is the most likely suspect, by the way. What she cares about is the return of her property. She has been very clear on that in all of the … discussions … that we have had on the subject. One reason that I am leaving her here with you is to get a couple of days of peace!

"One final thing. Call it a reward, if you like. If we get the jewels back and find the thief, you get the contract. It's not quite a reward. You have a very good operation here, but I could hardly sign a deal with you with the matter of the jewels unsolved. How does all that sound?"

Glaucus was relieved by the offer and surprised at Maximinus' honesty. He nodded his agreement and smiled with relief.

Maximinus grunted and abruptly rose to his feet.

"Now I must get on. We have much to do if we are to be ready to depart by noon."

He walked off, back to the camp. Breakfast was over.

CHAPTER SIXTEEN

THE PLAN

Father Horse woke with the dawn light. Wet and bedraggled, he had finally found sleep in the early hours of the morning when sheer exhaustion overcame his damp misery. This had been the hardest night for him. It begun well enough, but the drenching from Marcellus had also quenched his spirit. It made Hippolytus doubt himself, his vocation, his plan, his everything. The little voices he thought he had banished in Caesarea came back to him, whispering dark words of uncertainty in the secret places of his mind. Every time that they attacked him he sought the refuge of the silence within, but then the dampness of his clothes and the unyielding cold of the stone floor on which he lay brought them back.

He had given up on his bed. The bedclothes were soaked and the straw mattress on which he had lain was wet through and ruined. Instead, he had retreated to the driest part of the cell under the high windows that let in the light. He lay there shivering with cold and self-pity. It was only when he looked up that he paused. There, far above him, and framed by the rectangle of the window's thick walls, was a tiny square of night sky. And in that sky, he saw, high in the distant heavens, the twinkling light of three stars. As he watched them dancing there, so far beyond his little damp cell, the words of a poem that he had learned long ago came, unbidden, to his mind:

When I look at the sky, which your fingers have wrought,
the moon and the stars that you have put in place,
who are we that you think of us at all;
children of flesh that you care for us.

His spirits lifted, there in his small, deep, damp cell. His doubts vanished and, in a few moments, he had fallen asleep.

It had been a deep sleep, dreamless and heedless of the sounds of the house, whether the tiny squeaking of the mice in the roof or the tramp of military boots outside when the guard was changed. He slumbered through it all until the fingers of the dawn light crept through the window above him and bathed his face. He struggled to his feet and stretched. He was stiff and his back was sore from lying on the hard stone of the floor. And he was thirsty. It was the result, no doubt, of his unwanted dunking in salt water in the middle of the night. He thought of going straight to the cupboard and seeing if there were any water there but then he changed his mind. That was too important a secret to be given away by a moment's carelessness. Instead, he stood with his face towards the sunrise, lifted up his arms and began to pray.

His prayers went on for quite some time. Listening to him, it would have been difficult to pick out words since he mostly seemed to mutter under his breath. At times he might have been chanting; at others, singing. He concluded by lapsing into silence and sinking to the floor with his back to the wall and his gnarled legs straight out in front of him. There he sat, eyes closed, and hands palms up on his thighs.

He barely stirred when his cell door clicked open. It took him a moment to surface from that place deep within himself where he had been. When he opened his eyes, Marcellus was standing right in front of him, holding a basket and just watching him. Father Horse felt easy, full of light, and confident in what the day would bring.

"Well, Christian, your luck's in," said Marcellus in that tone of false friendliness that Hippolytus had learned to mistrust long before. "We're off on a little road trip. Some marching, some hunting, a night under the stars. Then to Petuaria and a proper trial for you and a nice little execution to round it off. What do you say?" He did not mean the question to be answered, but went straight on, without pausing for breath. "Now we can't have you fainting from hunger on the way, so the tribune has ordered us to feed you for a while. Nothing special, mind. Just good soldiers' food pork and beans, sour wine and old bread. It's real tucker for titans this. It was men what lived on this that conquered the world."

He set down the basket in front of Hippolytus and signed for him to open it. Inside was a wooden bowl and spoon, a sealed bronze pot, some hard bread and a wineskin.

"Now eat up. I'll be back soon," grunted Marcellus, who turned and left, locking the door behind him.

The first thing that Father Horse did was unseal the wineskin and take a long drink. The sight of the food had brought back his breakfast hunger, but his thirst was more urgent. The wine was indeed sour, and not watered enough for his taste, but he wasn't going to send it back. Before long he had finished both stew and bread and washed it all down with another long drink of the wine. He was cheered, not just by the food itself, but also because of what it meant. It meant that Glaucus had listened, that Maximinus had agreed, and that his plan was working. He gave a little belch of contentment.

Over the next couple of hours, he was brought a bowl of hot water to wash himself and a change of clothes. For the first time in days, he was fed, clean and comfortable. It was almost like freedom except that the soldiers had brought him everything and he had stayed locked in his cell.

It was about noon that Marcellus came back to fetch him.

"Come on, priest," he said, standing at the door. "It's time to take a walk. You'll need your staff. You might have a bit of marching to do."

Hippolytus picked up his staff, took a last look at the little cell with its ruined bed, and followed.

He blinked a little as he emerged into the full light of day. It had been quite a while since he had been outside and his eyes needed to adjust to the glare. Even though the day was overcast, the brightness of the sun seemed to bounce from the clouds. Marcellus did not allow Hippolytus to linger.

"Hurry up, Christian. Time to be moving. No time for goodbyes."

In a few moments, he had left the house, and walked the short path to the soldiers' camp next door. He saw that the tents were all down and the only reminder of the soldiers' presence was the remains of the earth wall and ditch. A baggage cart, harnessed to two grazing horses, stood in the middle of the field. It was a stout, high-sided wagon with two solid wooden wheels and a perch for the driver. The soldiers, for their part, were busy packing and tying up bundles of various kinds and throwing them onto the cart.

Marcellus led him to the wagon and told him to wait there. He was about to walk off, thought better of it, and turned to Father Horse.

"This is where I say goodbye for now, Christian. Aelian and I have a good billet in the house while the lady stays a few more days. But I'll be down to Petuaria in time to see you die, never fear."

He grinned a nasty grin and walked away.

Father Horse was unmoved. He just stood there, by the cart, breathing the sweet air, free of the stench of imprisonment, enjoying the breeze on his face and distant bleating of sheep. His heart and soul sang with joy within him. Even in the midst of his trials, which he knew were not yet over, this was, for him, a golden moment to be grasped, treasured and stored up against any troubles to come.

He heard his name being called. He looked about and saw Silvius coming towards him.

"I'm your new guard, Father," he said. "I'm to stick close to you from here to Petuaria. That's what the tribune said. So, up on the cart!" Silvius gestured to the driver's perch.

"Not the back, then?" asked Hippolytus.

"No Father. There's not a lot of point. We all have horses and you're not really equipped for running." Silvius gestured towards Father Horse's twisted legs.

"Well, don't be too sure," teased Father Horse. "I've walked a long way on these."

"True enough, Father. But it's not walking that you'd be needing to do, but running. And you'd have to run faster than the tribune's horse. None of us can do that." Silvius' word was final.

From his seat on the cart, Father Horse had a good view of the final preparations. The camp had been packed up, the soldiers' baggage rolls organized, and the horses fetched from the stables. He also watched as Maximinus escorted Sentia to the house where she was met at the great door by Glaucus and Lydia. He almost waved but he thought better of it. Germanus was following behind the little party and leading two horses. Once Sentia had been received into the house, Maximinus turned, mounted the larger and glossier of the horses while Germanus (less gracefully) scrambled onto the other. The two ambled their horses over to the cart in slow trot, where the tribune looked Father Horse up and down, seemed about to say something but thought better of it, turned and rode over to what was left of the camp, followed by Germanus.

After a few moments, Hippolytus could hear Maximinus' voice, raised to a thundering, parade-ground pitch. "Assemble at the cart and ready to move in five minutes!"

Within a few minutes, the small, mounted party had assembled around the cart. Germanus took the lead, followed by the tribune, the cart itself with Silvius and Father Horse with Julianus and Victor riding together at the rear. Once they had formed up, the tribune held up a hand, pointed up the track into the forest and called out, "Let's go!"

They were on their way.

Father Horse forced himself not to look back as Hightower grew further away. He wanted to believe that this was no last farewell and that he would be back in a couple of days. Instead, he stared ahead to face his future.

His quiet wondering came to a sudden end when Maximinus threw up his arm. The party reined in, each soldier staying in his place in the line.

"We are not going on the Petuaria. We never were. That was a necessary ruse. We are staying right here in this forest for three nights. We need to be out of sight of the house, but able to keep a watch on it. Germanus, go ahead down the path and find us a place to camp for three nights. There will be no need for the traditional defensive measures. We just need clean water and a bit of shelter. Victor, go back up the path and find a good spot to watch the house. You must be out of sight of the house, but have a clear view of it, in particular the tower. We must be able to see it and its windows. Christian, you just sit tight up there with young Silvius. If you're lucky, he'll tell you some very bad old soldiers' jokes."

The two soldiers cantered off in different directions. As they did, Father Horse felt a tiny drop on his cheek. He looked up and, instead of glimpses of blue through the treetops, he could only see grey cloud. The weather had changed. By the time that Germanus had returned with the news of the clearing and the stream where Father Horse had sat with the children only a few days before, the rain had started and a pleasant afternoon's ride had been transformed into a serious chore.

Before long, Victor also rode up, having located the best watching point. He spoke quietly to Maximinus, whose good humor seemed to be vanishing. Maximinus nodded curtly and ordered him back along the path, along with Julianus so that they would both know the best watching post and take turns standing watch. Maximinus waited in the rain for Julianus to return, and then they all headed down the track to Germanus' bivouac by the stream. By the time that they arrived, the rain had passed and the air was still, damp and heavy.

"Just pitch two tents, boys. The prisoner can sleep under the cart. You," here he pointed to Hippolytus. "Just sit tight up there where I can see you."

The soldiers immediately set to work and the air filled with the sounds of their efforts as they lifted tentpoles, hammered in pegs, tightened guy ropes and shouted short, and often not very helpful, comments to one another.

Once the tents were up, Germanus, who seemed to have taken Marcellus' place as chosen man and commander's orderly, went into Maximinus' tent to arrange it as well as he might while Julianus gathered wood to build a fire. He stored it under the cart to keep it as dry as possible while he dug a small firepit and found the rocks with which to line it. Then he built up the fire so that the larger logs on the top shielded the twigs and kindling underneath. The drizzle came and went, making his task difficult, but he stuck with it and before long a respectable blaze was crackling and hissing in the middle of the clearing. Maximinus looked on the fire with satisfaction.

"Now for something to put on it," he murmured half to himself. Then he turned to the soldiers.

"Silvius stay here with the prisoner and make sure that he does not wander off. In fact, tie him up. Tie him to the cart. Julianus, you stay here until it is time to change the watch, then go and relieve Victor. Germanus and I are going to hunt out our dinner."

Silvius went to the back of the cart and took out a length of rope.

"Loop it around the axle," called Maximinus. "Then tie each of his wrists to an end of the rope. Give him a bit of room, but not too much. And tie the knots hard, not so hard that his hands will fall off, but hard enough to remind this Christian who the lords of this world really are."

"Oh, I know that well enough," Father Horse said softly, but clearly enough to be heard.

"Good," snapped Maximinus. "Now do the job!"

Silvius did as he was ordered, stealing the occasional sheepish glance at Father Horse as if to apologize for doing as he was ordered. He was gentler than he needed to be, and in fact the knots were not too uncomfortable in the end. There was enough play in the rope for Father Horse not to be tied to the cart, but he was tethered to it like a boat at a pier or a dog on a leash.

Maximinus gave Father Horse a quick glance, satisfied himself that he wasn't going anywhere, and then, eager to be off, mounted his horse. Germanus did the same, and the two trotted off down the path, further into the forest. For a moment, the only sound in the clearing was the snapping of the fire and the gurgling of the stream. For a moment, a shaft of sunlight, freed from its shroud of rainclouds, broke through the treetops. The showers had passed, and their little world, heated by the fire, began to dry out. Julianus and Silvius began a dice game. The luck on each side was even and, after an hour, the two were level pegging. Then Julianus stood and went off back up the path towards the house. It was time to relieve Victor.

Again, all was quiet in the camp. Father Horse had watched the dice game without much interest. His mind was elsewhere, and he found himself wondering why it was that Silvius had been as kind and thoughtful as he had, despite Maximinus' evident dislike. With Julianus gone, Father Horse found himself with an opportunity to ask.

"Silvius, may I speak with you a little?" he inquired. "I have been much on my own recently and I would welcome some conversation."

"I'm not sure if the tribune would like it. He's trusting me to make sure that you don't get up to any mischief," the soldier replied.

"How can I? I am well secure. It's just talk. And to make it easy, why don't you do the talking?"

"What do you want me to say?" Silvius was puzzled.

"Perhaps you could answer a question that has been troubling me," responded Father Horse truly enough.

"Me?"

"Oh, yes. You are well able to tell me this."

"What?"

"Why is it," asked Father Horse, "that you do not look at me with the same kind of hate and fear that the tribune does, that there is a kindness in you towards me that I do not find in your comrades. Surely you can tell me that. Is there a story there?"

"Well Father, it's like this," began the young soldier. "I know that the young master thinks the world of you, and that might have been enough, but I have my own reasons. It's because of my growing up. Like a lot of the men from the legion, I'm from Spain. My dad was a soldier and he served in the Sixth too. When he'd done his twenty years, he went back home, to Corduba, and married my ma. I remember him as a big man, maybe because I was so little, but he had bright eyes and strong hands and loved to carry me on his back.

"He'd always been good with leather. In the legion, he ended up mending everyone's boots. He used his discharge to set himself up making sandals and shoes. We had a good living. We had a house that was ours. Then one day, he was a bit careless. He slashed himself right across the back of his hand with a trimming knife. He tried to keep working, but the wound turned bad and started to smell. Then he took a fever and was dead in a week. We had nothing. I was eight, with three younger sisters. Ma just had us and the house. Her family were all gone except a brother who had gone to seek his fortune in Gaul, not that we heard anything from him.

"For the next ten years, it was the Christians of Corduba who kept us going. Every week, there's be a basket of food, and clothes and shoes for us. Sometimes there might even be a few silver coins. They invited us to their homes and they weren't much different from us. They weren't rich, they were just our neighbors, being good to us. Year after year, they kept us going until I grew up and joined the army and could send Ma my pay. Two of my sisters married boys from their houses. They might even be Christians by now.

"With all of that, they never asked us to join. Maybe they would have done if Ma had said anything, but they didn't. They didn't try and buy us with the gifts. They gave because we needed it. So that's your answer. I have never seen what the tribune's seen. I have only seen kindness. Now that's enough. Victor will be back in a moment."

Silvius was right. A few moments later, Victor came down the track. He found Silvius feeding the fire, and Father Horse sitting on the ground, in silence, with his back against the cartwheel.

"Tribune's gone hunting," grunted Silvius.

"Well, who knows what he'll find? Let's get some food on now in any event. Right now, I'm a hungry soldier and I could do with a good feed."

By the time the tribune returned bearing four rabbits, there was a stew of pork and beans on the fire.

"Fancy a bit extra, boys? Give the Christian the army food. We're having fresh!"

Father Horse didn't mind at all. It was his second hot meal in a day.

CHAPTER SEVENTEEN

THE TROJAN POTS

SENTIA HAD BEEN GREETED like an old friend by Lydia. She was immediately taken upstairs to what had been Hippolytus' room to settle in and Aelian brought the trunk containing her belongings to her new room. She was not disappointed at being left behind in the house. She never much liked life under canvas and found the company of a cultured household—even one in which she had been robbed—better than that of the soldiers who surrounded Maximinus. She was also a little excited by the thought that she was part of a plan.

That morning, after he had met with Glaucus, Maximinus had taken Sentia aside into their private tent and given her his instructions.

"Glaucus and I have come to an agreement. We both want the jewels back, and he thinks that the Christian might not have taken them. We both agree that they are still somewhere in the house, and so I want you to go back and keep an eye on things. Glaucus has an idea about how to get them back, but I need you to keep an eye on all of them.

"I have made arrangements for comfortable quarters for you. They are going to give you the Christian's room. That will give you the opportunity to give it a thorough search. Otherwise, enjoy their company. The beds will be softer than on the road and, I daresay, the food better. I am leaving Marcellus and Aelian with you, but I will not be too far away. We will be camped in the forest up the road for three days. If nothing happens by then, then you and the boys will come and find me, and we'll go on to Petuaria and see if we can't get an answer out of the Christian without all of these civilians looking over our shoulders."

She left the trunk unopened while she explored the room. She was excited to find his small library. Reading had long been her secret pleasure but it been difficult to indulge in so far from good book dealers and copyists.

Maximinus did not read much; mostly military manuals and trashy history. When he gave her books, as he did from time to time, he gave her what he thought fitting for a woman; awful stories all written to a pattern about lovesick girls, beautiful young men, and wicked old ones.

It became clear to her very quickly what Hippolytus' interests were. Here were familiar works of philosophy with a heavy leaning towards Plato. But there were books that she did not know by writers of whom she had never heard. Who was Origen? Or Clement of Alexandria? Or Irenaeus, or Polycarp? Not only did these names mean nothing to her, but as she ran her eye over some of their work, she thought it just as silly as the novels that her husband sent her to read. Then, on Hippolytus' big study table in front of the window, she came upon a work apparently much thumbed and read. It was a book with four different but related stories, each like a distinct chapter. Each told the story of a man called Jesus, whom she quickly recognized as bearing the title of "Christ." She had never really wondered where the name "Christian" came from. Now she knew and, against her better judgement, she found herself reading the one by someone called Marcus.

The prose was simple. They were not the words of a philosopher, putting a point of view. They were the words of a storyteller, setting out what he called "good news."

There was a knock at the door and she shut the book, putting it back on the shelf and turning away before she called out, "Come in!"

It was Lois, the slave who served Lydia as a maid.

"My Lady has sent me to tell you that there is lunch downstairs. The whole family is there."

Sentia recognized the importance of the invitation.

"I shall be down at once. I am looking forward to some proper food. I've been on soldier's rations for two days too long."

When she arrived in the dining room, she was surprised to see that the soldiers were there too. There was the usual table bowed with the weight of the many different dishes it carried. Marcellus and Aelian had already piled their platters high with lamb pies, pieces of cold roast chicken, bread and olives. Obedient to both station and manners, however, they had not touched their food, waiting until Sentia arrived to make her own choice and begin the meal.

Sentia settled on a couch opposite Lydia and looked about for a slave to fill her platter, but there was none there. She looked at Glaucus with a question in her eyes. He answered it directly.

"We are lunching today without the help of our slaves. Please lady, allow me to fill your platter."

Without waiting for a reply, he swung off his own couch and onto his feet, taking a platter and serving Sentia with dishes as she pointed to them. Once Glaucus was back in his place, everyone set to eating, and for a time, the only sound in the room was of chewing and the satisfaction of eating good food. Only when everyone had eaten did Glaucus clap his hands for attention.

"You might be wondering why we our helping ourselves without the help of our kitchen slaves. It is because I want no slaves to be here for this conversation. The fewer people in this house who know what I am about to say, the better. Our purpose is to catch a thief, and to do so we have to work together. Maximinus and I both believe that the jewels are still in this house, but he thinks that Father Horse has hidden them and I do not. Maximinus has spent the past few days using military methods to try and persuade Father Horse to give him the information. Marcellus here knows exactly what I mean. And Marcellus could tell you that Father Horse has said nothing. That is because he has nothing to say. Maximinus is less certain but he has given me three days to prove my case. We are going to do that by catching the thief in the act of fetching the emeralds from their hiding place.

"That means a night watch on the courtyard. Now I have dismissed all of the slaves except for Phormio. They have been told to stay out of the house while the soldiers are still here. So we have to do the watching and the catching. Now, whoever the thief is will have to go through the courtyard to get to any part of the house. Gini, Gordi, I have a special job for each of you. You are to be our ears in the midst of the garden. You know the two large empty pots there?"

The children nodded.

"They are big enough for you to hide in. You must stay there and listen. Now this is the difficult part. I don't want you to call out when anyone enters the courtyard. I want you to wait until they are leaving. But when you hear the thief heading out, probably for the front door, make a racket and we will be waiting close by to catch them. If we are right, that will be our thief. Marcellus, Aelian, I need you both with me to help me catch our burglar, and keep him safe for Maximinus' arrival. At Troy, the Greeks hid their secret army in the belly of a wooden horse. We shall hide our secret watchers in big, clay pots."

"So will they be Trojan pots?" called out Gordi.

As everyone hushed him, his father smiled and said quietly, "Well, I suppose they will be."

Glaucus continued. "If we've eaten enough, then it's time to rest. We have a big night ahead of us. We'll need to get as much rest as we can this afternoon."

The family dispersed, each to their rooms and the soldiers to their accommodation in the guest wing.

Lydia walked Sentia back to her room in the tower. Neither spoke, nor was there need. Such was the growing friendship between them. Sentia felt a question growing within her, but the words escaped her and so she was content to say nothing.

When the door had closed behind her, Sentia felt drawn back to the little book that she had left before lunch. It did not take her long to find and finish. She had thought to do so in order to compose her mind as much as possible before sleep, but as she lay upon the couch, the stories that she had read kept returning to her. She was puzzled by so much. Finally, she dozed off, but her dreams, when they came, were of people, some paralyzed, some blind, some raving or dark with inner demons all crying out to be healed.

When she rose in the early evening, she was not much rested, her mind still jumbled with questions. The only person that she knew who might be answer them was her husband's prisoner.

Then, suddenly, she stood, stretched, and went to take a turn around the garden courtyard to walk off her troubled spirit. She found Lydia there, strolling around the little circuit. She fell in beside her, again wordlessly for a moment, and then she found the question that had hidden from her before.

"Lydia, I have been meaning to ask you a question."

Lydia looked back at Sentia, knowing what the question would be and wondering how to put the answer. She decided to let the words just come out as honestly as possible.

"You told me before of your … religion. And that Glaucus does not share it. Why did he agree to employ a Christian as tutor to your children? Is he not afraid that he might steal them away?"

"He tends to leave these matters to me," replied Lydia, and then added, "There is nothing underhanded here. What we needed was a tutor who could get through to the children. We had a succession of well-trained failures. Hippolytus is getting the job done."

"Failures?" Sentia was puzzled. "Your children are so delightful and well-behaved."

"That was not always the case," Lydia responded. "They saw terrible things in Tarsus before we left to come here. It upset them terribly and they simply did not want to learn. They didn't see the point."

"Tarsus? You came from there?" Sentia asked.

"Oh yes. We were there when the Persians came. But it was our slaves. Some remained loyal, but others of the household took their chance and rebelled. The children saw people they had known all of their lives suddenly become terrible enemies."

"How do you manage it?" She asked.

"What do you mean?" Responded Lydia.

"You have all been uprooted from your home; forced to come here that is so far from all that you love. Is this why you are a Christian?"

"Oh no, as I said before, I have been in the Way since I was a child," Lydia replied. "But it gives me a hope to build on, and faith that one day, all things shall be well again."

"And the children?"

"They are still young. They will grow, heal, and make their own choices."

"What do you mean by choices?"

"Well, you have suggested that what I really want is for Father Horse to make the children into little Christians. That is not so, but I do want them to have the freedom and knowledge to choose well."

"Again, you speak of choosing, but that is nonsense. Either things are or they are not. Choosing does not make it true." Sentia was quite definite.

"No," Lydia agreed. "But this is not about choosing what is real. It is about choosing whom you will serve. Reality is too vast even here in our little corner of the world to cut it up into the parts that are agreeable and disagreeable. It is better by far to accept that things are what they are, shabby and imperfect, and then get on with serving the God who is real.

"Don't we all try to do that?"

"In a way. But you try and make deals with your gods. You will give them so many sacrifices in return for their blessings and goodwill. So your altars run red with the blood of slaughtered animals and in return you expect favor or at least that they withhold their anger."

"Don't you believe that?

"Oh goodness me, no," replied Lydia. "That is the 'good news' that we try and bring to people when they listen. That there are not many gods, just the One. And that God is not interested in death or the smell of roasting meat. Our God is interested in us, loves us with the love of a parent, forgives us without the need for blood sacrifice, calls us to serve one another and our world in love and in hope. That is what I believe."

"And so who is this Jesus?"

Lydia might have given a proper answer to this but just then, Marcellus came striding into the courtyard and the moment was lost.

Dinner that night was quiet. Everyone was conscious of the long night ahead, and few of them had slept well. The soldiers had but they were trained to it. The children were too excited by the parts they were to play in the evening's events and Glaucus had been too worried about it all to get any rest. Again, slaves were kept from the meal room and so everyone grazed from a cold buffet. The food was good, but no one except Marcellus and Aelian really tasted it. The soldiers knew the value of a good meal since they so rarely had them. They filled their plates twice over and savored every bite.

Once everyone, even the soldiers, had eaten their fill, Glaucus gave his orders for the night. He had spent much of his sleepless afternoon thinking through the arrangements that he would make, and so he was at least able to give clear instructions. Above all, he had worked out the solution to a problem that no one had raised at lunch—how to get Gini and Gordi inside the pots. He had also worked out roles for everyone else, including himself. If the task of the children was to sound the alarm, then that of the soldiers was actually to catch the thief, and that of Sentia was to signal her husband waiting in the forest, that he might return to the house. Lydia's job was to keep her company so that neither of them would fall asleep. The biggest risk was that the children would fall asleep since they had to stay as quiet as possible and could not talk to one another to keep themselves awake. Glaucus decided that he would keep his own watch on the courtyard just in case.

The summer evening lingered late but when the light began to fade everyone was ready. The rainclouds had gone, and the moon was bright and clear. The family and guests gathered in the courtyard as if to say their goodnights in the evening cool. Everyone sat for a long time on the garden coping making conversation.

"Glaucus, you must get some proper seats in here. This is a very pleasant garden. Why may not one sit here?" Sentia asked.

"I shall tell Septimus tomorrow to make it happen" Glaucus replied. "We have wood enough. I'm sure that we also have sufficient slaves who are skilled in such things to craft us some excellent seats for out here."

The chatter continued in a similar way until the darkness of night descended.

"Well, I'm for my bed," said Sentia, probably a bit too loudly. "Goodnight everyone. Lydia, would you walk me to my room?"

The two women slipped out quietly, leaving only the soldiers and Glaucus for, as the adults had been talking about not very much, Gordi, Gini, Marcellus and Aelian had gone for a wander through the garden. While attention might have been focused on Glaucus and Sentia, the soldiers had quietly lifted the two children into the pots.

Glaucus and the soldiers said their own goodnights and went off leaving the garden courtyard quiet and empty save for its hidden watchers.

Lydia had been wondering for some time if Sentia would want to continue the conversation that had begun in the garden earlier. She was also wondering how she herself might respond. She had imagined—and rejected—all sorts of things, and finally decided just to let the whole thing flow, if it flowed at all. It also occurred to her that Sentia might have been frightened by her own curiosity and stick to talking about the weather and clothes.

That is exactly what Sentia did, at first, wondering if the good weather would hold if it might rain since then the poor children in the pots would be soaked to the skin. Lydia was secretly both relieved and guilty for feeling relieved.

"Who knows?" she replied to Sentia. "Since I have been in this province, I have learned never to try and predict the weather. It changes all the time. All that I know is that, if you don't much like it, you don't have to wait for very long for something else."

"True enough. I have been here for so much longer, and yet I have never learned the way of it, if there is one." Senta said smiling.

Then there was silence, an uncomfortable silence, heavy with unspoken words, rather like that moment just before a storm breaks when everything seems still.

At last, Sentia spoke in a little voice.

"Lydia, tell me about Christ. And, if you can, why my husband and people like him hate him so. He did not seem so very dangerous in the book that I read."

"Well, it depends on what you mean by danger," Lydia replied.

"I don't understand. Danger is danger." Sentia was puzzled.

"Jesus was a dangerous man. He said and did things—the things that you have read about in that book—they were extraordinary. He healed people; he talked about forgiveness; he responded to those who opposed him with wit and words. Everything that he did went against the received wisdom of the world. That wisdom tells us that suffering is deserved; that forgiveness is earned; that opponents are to be beaten by any means. He taught things that were exactly the opposite. That is why he was killed. There is more danger in a man who says and does such things than in any military rebel. The world understands the language of force. It is very good at using it. Jesus refused it. He taught that force is not the way; that problems are not solved with swords; and divisions between people are not healed through punishment.

"So he was killed. He was nailed to a cross. It was a Roman punishment for an escaped slave or a rebel. That seems fair as I think about it. He had refused to serve the Lord of this World, but rebelled against a dull rule based on anger and violence, and called on us all to be better people."

"But that's not all, is it? That book that I read says more," interrupted Sentia.

"That's true. Everything should have ended with Jesus dead and in the tomb. This is where we come to the point where many people find themselves either inspired or baffled. When women came to anoint Jesus' body after he had been dead for some days, they found his tomb empty."

"I read that, and they ran away, frightened. I thought that someone might have stolen the body."

"Did you not read the part where the angel said that he had been raised from the dead?"

"Yes I did. I thought that it was silly."

"Silly or not, that's what we believe actually happened. You said earlier today that things either are or they are not. We believe that this is no mere story but an event that has meaning for us all. As one of our writers once said, if Jesus wasn't raised, then there's no point to any of it and the powers of the world are right. There is no merit in weakness, no virtue in forgiveness, no point to kindness. Everything is random and all of our religion is about trying to make some sense of that. You try and make deals with heaven through sacrifice. But why would the gods listen to that? What kind of gods are they who need the smell of burning meat to become interested in human beings?

"We believe that God—and there is only the one—does not require such things. The single sacrifice that God requires is of ourselves, not on some temple altar, but in our hearts and our lives. God does not require us to come and die, but to come and live. That is what Jesus' resurrection means to us. It is the rebirth of hope in a dark place, and a sure sign that the victory of violence and force does not last forever. It means, in some way, that Jesus is still with us. That is why Hippolytus can go through all of the things that he has. He was tortured in Caesarea years ago, and those soldiers downstairs have, I am sure, been finding ways of inflicting pain on him without making it show. But he bears it all because that's what we do."

Lydia stopped, aware that she might have said too much. Sentia was looking at the floor, and when she looked up, Lydia could see the tears that had sprung to her eyes. After a couple of moments, Sentia spoke, "What you have said truly frightens me, and yet excites me at the same time. I must take time to think. When all this is over, will you write to me?"

"Yes, of course, my dear," Lydia assured her.

"Then come now. We can take turns sleeping so that we can get some rest until something happens. You first. I have some more reading to do."

Lydia curled up on Hippolytus' couch, while Sentia sat in a wicker chair, taking up the little book to read again, and think.

Nothing happened that night. At dawn, Glaucus wearily uncurled himself from beneath his cloak, stretched and staggered over from his own hiding place to the pots. The children were barely awake and glad to be lifted out. They staggered off to bed. Glaucus did the same, all the while hoping that he had not made a huge mistake.

CHAPTER EIGHTEEN

THE THIEF

Hippolytus woke with the sun. He rolled out from under the cart where he had been sleeping and stared at the eastern sky where the light was growing and the sun, at first a bright sliver of light then a semicircle, then the whole orb, emerged in its golden glory. As it blazed upon his face, he began to pray his morning prayers. He closed his eyes and felt the familiar words flow through him and from him, and deep within him, a flower of joy bloomed. Maximinus' voice broke in upon him, "If you are going to talk to the gods, Christian, make sure that you talk to the right one." His tone was one of anger and disdain.

Hippolytus opened his eyes, and turned to face the tribune who stood there, hands on hips and face red with fury.

"There is only one, tribune," Hippolytus replied, softly.

Maximinus grunted and strode off down the forest path.

Once Maximinus had gone Hippolytus finished his prayers, crawled under the cart and out the other side, and sat, watching Julianus at work.

"Where do you come from, soldier?" He asked, pleasantly enough.

Julianus ignored him, so Hippolytus tried again.

"How long have you been in the legion?"

Julianus turned and looked at him.

"We're not to talk to you," he said with quiet certainty. "The tribune says that you have poison in your voice. Just sit there, quiet like, and when it's ready, I'll bring you your food and drink."

Once the fire had turned into hot coals, Julianus took a large bronze pot, went to the creek and filled it with water. When the water was boiling, he threw in some oats, and began to stir vigorously with a wooden spoon. He stopped once or twice to add some salt. When the porridge was thick, and (mostly) free of lumps, he spooned a great, sticky lump of it into a wooden bowl and brought the food, along with a spoon, over to Hippolytus. Once he was satisfied that Hippolytus was eating it, he returned to the stove, added some raisins to the porridge for sweetness, and kept stirring it until Maximinus and Germanus both came back.

All three set to with the hunger of men camping out. It was not meat, but it filled all the hollow places inside them that scraps of rabbit could not reach.

Back at the house, breakfast was a very quiet affair. Everyone (except the soldiers) felt the cost of the long night. For once, the children did not eat much, just enough for the sake of appearance, and then both of them crawled back to their rooms and to bed. The adults felt much the same. Neither Sentia nor Lydia had much energy for talking, and Glaucus was not even there. He had told the kitchen that he was not feeling well, and had Phormio bring some food to his room. When, finally, everyone had eaten enough, they all went back to their respective rooms and sought the comfort of sleep.

So it was for most of the day. With the slaves absent, the house was quiet. Lunch came and went and not much was eaten. The afternoon sleep was taken seriously. It was only in the late afternoon that everyone really began to wake up. The children had recovered their hunger and the adults their desire to talk. Almost automatically, people gathered in the meal room. When Lydia suggested a walk before dinner—not into the forest, but over the farm—Glaucus, Sentia and the children happily agreed. They had been cooped up in the house long enough.

Sentia had not been out in the fields and so had not seen the farm. Glaucus was eager to show her the operation, both for appearance's sake and because he was genuinely proud of it. He showed Sentia all of the buildings in the house paddock that made the farm work: the shearing sheds, the great barn where the fleeces were washed, carded, combed, spun and stored and the even larger shed where slaves worked the looms. They skirted the dyeworks, where the stench of the day's work lingered, and made for the drystone wall that separated the house paddock from the fields beyond. Outside the house paddock, the fields went on almost, it seemed, to the horizon. Some of the fields were being grazed by the black-faced, long-wooled sheep that Glaucus bred. Others lay empty, their pasture recovering.

Glaucus pointed to a line of trees in the middle distance.

"It's mine all the way to those trees. We run five hundred sheep here, give or take, which means that in any given year we can produce about two thousand pounds of fabric."

Sentia was impressed, and said so.

"I don't pretend to understand the farming side of it," added Glaucus. "I don't even have a dog. Septimus does all that. But the business, that's all mine."

By dinner time, everyone was rested, exercised, hungry and ready for the night ahead. The food was good, as usual, but there was little conversation. The ramblers had worked up a hunger and a thirst and attacked their meals with vigor. They agreed on the same arrangements as the night before.

Again, Sentia and Lydia walked together towards the tower room.

"Your husband is a good man," Sentia remarked.

"Thank you," Lydia replied. "I like to think so."

"Is that why he tolerates your religion, I wonder? Mine would not. He would whip me, or divorce me, or worse."

"Any man who would whip his wife does not deserve her," replied Lydia fiercely. "My husband tolerates my religion because he is a good man and we love one another. We didn't at first, of course. It was the usual arrangement between families, but love grew as we grew together. I cannot imagine being without him now."

"Even though he does not share your religion?"

"Even then."

Sentia thought for a while and then said, "I know that Maximinus can seem awful. You all must think him the most terrible man, but ask yourself this, why am I still married to him?"

There was a pause. Lydia began to say something, but, as they climbed the stairs to the tower room, Sentia went on, "He wasn't always like this. When we were first married, he was very proper and old-fashioned, but he could be fun. Our early days were lovely days, and I came to love him too. He has been poisoned by anger and resentment. He has let it consume him. I could have divorced him years ago and gone back to Rome, you know how easy it is, but that would have been a betrayal that I couldn't bear. I made a choice between going back to my boys or staying with the man that I have come to love. It was hard, but I stayed. He knows it too. I hope that one day soon, after this business is over, you will see him a little as I see him. You see a bully who blusters and scorns. I see a man who has been hurt by life and is lashing out because he has never learned to be kind."

"Then we must be kind to him," said Lydia firmly, and they went into the room.

The day dragged for Father Horse. Maximinus would not let him out of the camp, nor off the rope. While his bonds were not too tight to be uncomfortable, the coarse rope was rubbing on his wrists which were becoming sore, red and inflamed. He knew that it was only a matter of time before the skin broke and then there would be the risk of fever. As a result, he kept his arms as still as possible.

He breathed free air, but he knew that he was at the mercy of the tribune and his men. More than once, he found himself praying that his plan would work. Late in the morning, he was given a little reprieve. Silvius had come back from a shift watching the house to take his turn watching the priest. Victor had gone to a tent to catch some sleep, and the tribune and Germanus were still off somewhere in the forest trying to catch dinner. Unlike the others, Silvius had no fear of Father Horse. Once they were alone, Silvius turned to him.

"Let me see your wrists," he demanded. "You have been tied up for a while. It must be hurting by now."

Father Horse extended his bound hands and Silvius looked at the raw and inflamed skin.

"That's not good," he said. "I have something for that. Now don't go away!" He grinned at his own bad joke and went off to his tent.

He was back in a few minutes with a little flask of oil and some rags.

"Hold out your wrists and promise not to run!"

"I promise," said Father Horse, conscious of the fact that he could never have run in any case.

He untied the priest and looked again at his wrists. Taking a rag, he rubbed oil into the skin. It felt cool and it soothed the skin where it was sore and burned.

Then, taking two more rags, he wrapped one around each of Father Horse's wrists, and then tied him up again only now the rags were a barrier against the rubbing of the coarse rope.

"We all know that you're not going anywhere," said Silvius as he finished. "So you might as well be as comfortable as possible while still a prisoner."

"I am grateful," said Father Horse.

"Well, I'm not really doing it for you. It's for all of those families who looked after me and Ma and my sisters. That's who I'm really doing it for."

"Whatever you do for the least of these, you are doing for me," mused the priest.

"What's that?"

"It's just something that Jesus once said about whom it is that we really serve when we do such kindnesses," replied Father Horse.

"Well, I don't know anything about that," replied Silvius. "And I don't really want to know either. I just want to do the right thing."

"And that's all that you need to do," smiled the priest, and that was that.

The day passed slowly enough, marked only by the changing of the watches and the rhythm of the meals. Father Horse sat quietly beside or underneath the cart alternatively praying silently and dozing. Sometimes he wasn't himself sure which one was which.

Maximinus and Germanus came back in the late afternoon, neither of them happy. The hunting had not been good. They had three more rabbits, but otherwise every duck, deer and boar had managed to escape their spears and arrows.

"Next time I come here, I'll bring my dogs," growled Maximinus as he flung the dead rabbits onto the ground for Victor (who was cooking) to deal with.

"That's not going to go far," muttered Victor.

"Why not make stew?" suggested Father Horse. If you have some wine, some onions, some garlic, then you can just throw in whatever else you have and there will be plenty for everyone."

"Nobody asked you, priest," Victor shot back, but then went and fetched water from the stream, a few old onions, a head of garlic that had been dug out of the ground sometime in the reign of a long dead emperor. In half an hour, a pot of rabbit stew was bubbling away on the camp stove. Victor tasted it, added some salt and was satisfied. It would be a decent dinner after all.

The thief had waked soon after dawn. He had kept well away from the house, slept well and was brimming with his own excitement. This was to be the day. This was to be the day of freedom that he had hoped for and had become possible when all that treasure had come into the house. He had a reason, and a purpose. He needed to get well clear of Britain. The jewels would buy him safety. They would see him through to the port at Londinium where most of the merchant ships coming to Britain finished their journeys. They would see him onto one of those ships and away to Spain, or even Africa. A man might get lost in such vast spaces.

Slowly, and without making a fuss, he began to gather the things that he needed to get away. He had little clothing to pack. There was only his savings in a little leather bag, his hooded cloak and boots and a felt beret. He did manage to wander quietly into the kitchen in the middle of the afternoon, while everyone was asleep, fill a little basket with bread, cheese, olives and sausage, and take a goatskin flask of wine. After that, he had kept well away from the big house.

There was an old barn away from the house and out of its sight that he used as a base. He had already stabled a horse there: a stout, farm-born mare, bred to pull the plough or a cart. He knew her well, had ridden her before and knew that what she lacked in lines and speed, she made up for in stamina.

He knew that the army men would be after him and that they had army horses, so he made two decisions. Because she was slower than the army horses, he would collect the jewels early enough in the night so as to give him as big a start as possible; and then get onto the paved road as quickly as possible so that he wouldn't leave any tracks. If he headed due west, he could be on the road south to Londinium in a couple of hours, and in Londinium itself, if he rode hard enough, by the middle of the next day. He was sure of the plan. He had been dreaming of this for years, and now that the moment was upon him, he was completely certain of what to do and when to do it.

When evening came, he took a generous dinner from the house kitchen and ate outside. Afterwards he wished everyone goodnight, although inside he was saying 'goodbye'. Then he waited and listened. Finally, the sounds of the house died to nothing.

He emerged, deep in the night, cloaked and hooded, his face hidden. He knew the house well, every flagstone, brick and cranny, so he could make his way inside silently. He came in through the kitchen door. The fire still gave off heat and the fading glow of dying coals gave him enough light to make his way through the kitchen and out its open door into the covered way.

Up to his left was a little niche in the wall where a lit lamp was left each night. He lit a tallow candle from its flame and, shielding the light moved softly to the plinth. All around him was dark, and he narrowly avoided bumping into one of the large, empty jars that stood by its door. The door itself was latched and it clicked slightly as he opened it. He froze, listening for any sign that someone had heard, but all in that garden courtyard was silent. The next part would make noise, so he had to be as careful as possible, as he had been on the night that he deposited the jewels in their hiding place.

He stooped and went inside, taking a coil of rope from a hook on the wall, and tying it to a little recessed bar on the floor. Then he the threaded the rope through the hook on the ceiling, made sure that the floor was clear and pulled on the rope. The floor opened up, as if hinged, showing, in the soft rose glow of the candle, a set of steps heading down. Once he had tied the trapdoor so that it was open and he could get back out, he went down the steps and into the deep blackness below.

The cellar was stuffy, and smelled of damp and mold. At the foot of the stairs, he had left a filled lamp and he lit this from the candle. With the extra light, he could easily see what he needed to see. The walls were brick, and the floor and much of the roof were stone, except for the trapdoor where he had entered. The room was much larger than the one above and ran some way under the garden.

Using the lamp, he felt his way across the floor until he found the loose stone that he sought. He pulled it up, showing the soft leather bag that held his prize. Setting the lamp down on the floor, he held the flagstone up with one hand and picked up the bag with the other. Straightening up, he let the stone down, not bothering to fit it back in place. It had served its purpose. He opened the bag to make sure of his victory. The green of the emeralds was grey in the light of the lamp, but the glint of the gold gave him comfort.

Closing up the bag, he refused to feel any sense of joy in his success. It was too early, he knew. He had come too far to be caught and had too far to go to be safe. Instead, he clutched the little bag tightly to him for a moment in a little hug of pleasure. Then, he tied up the bag, stowed it in his robe and picked up the lamp. With his sense of triumph mounting with every step, he muffled the light and moved slowly up the staircase. At the top, in the little room inside the plinth, he untied the trapdoor and gently let it back down until it was properly in place. Then he took the rope, coiled it and put it back on its hook. All his movements were still slow and careful. Then, satisfied that all was as it should be, he blew out the lamp, turned and went through the door. He shut it behind him carefully, hearing the soft, scraping sound of metal as the latch fell back in place. He had done it.

Then it all fell apart. As he turned to leave, he heard the sound that turned his blood to ice. Two high-pitched children's voices were calling out very close to him. "Hispana!" he heard them call. "Hispana, Hispana, Hispana!"

He should have run, but panic locked his legs. A moment later, he felt the impact of a body and fell to the ground. One of the armored soldiers was on top of him, keeping him still. Then, one by one, the torches came on around the courtyard, they were the banquet torches used to light the darkest spaces at night.

"Get him up!" It was the familiar, hated, voice of Glaucus.

The soldier pulled him to his feet, holding his arms behind him. It was the hard man, the officer, Marcellus. The other one patted him down in a body search, and pulled the pouch of jewels out from inside the robe.

"Now," ordered Glaucus. "Let's see who we have here. Pull back that hood."

Rough hands grabbed the peak of his hood and pulled it back, revealing the hard, angry, defeated, defiant face of Septimus.

CHAPTER NINETEEN

JUDGEMENT BEFORE BREAKFAST

It was towards the end of his watch when Julianus saw light blaze out from the window of the tower room. That was the signal. Quickly and carefully, he made his way back down the track to the camp. The little square was in darkness except for the fading red glow of the fire. Germanus was sitting sentry at the entrance to Maximinus' tent and looked up as Julianus approached.

"Is it the signal?"

"Yes," replied Julianus.

"The tribune will be surprised. I'll tell him."

Germanus stood up, stretched, stooped a little, and entered the tent.

Julianus heard a low murmur of voices, and then Germanus came back out.

"There's no need to do anything right now. We'll strike camp and go back to the house at first light. The tribune wants you to go back down to the house, let them know, and then come back and get some rest."

"What about the priest?"

"He stays. The tribune gave me no orders for him."

"So what do I say about him?"

"Whatever you like. As I said, he gave me no orders."

Father Horse had woken when Julianus first arrived in the camp. In his improvised cell under the cart, he waited and watched.

He was disappointed not to be going back to the house straightaway, but the morning would do.

Following the departing Julianus with his eyes, he waited until he was out of sight and then turned around and went back to sleep.

He woke before the dawn to the sounds of the soldiers packing up the camp. Above his head, rolled up tents and cooking gear were being tossed into the tray of the cart. He took his chance, rolled out from underneath and tried to stand. He was stiff because he had been sitting and lying for so long, but he struggled to his feet and stood amid the chaos of the shrinking camp.

He caught sight of Maximinus, who was sitting to one side on a folding chair watching his men work. Sensing his gaze, the tribune looked over towards him and called out, "It's not over for you yet, Christian. Not until I know that you had nothing to do with this. So until then, you can continue to consider yourself my prisoner. Silvius here can look after you. He seems to have a soft spot for you."

He grinned, but it was not a kind smile.

Father Horse bowed his head in acknowledgement, replying, "I thank you my Lord."

Then he turned, crawled under the cart and out the other side for his morning prayers.

Two hours later, they were back at the house. They found it busy with morning activity. Five folding chairs had been set up in the entrance hall. A cupboard in the wall had been opened to display the images of the household gods within, and standing before it was a tall, three-legged brazier with hot coals burning in the bowl. Glaucus was preparing to hold court.

Glaucus was dressed formally in tunic and toga. He was waiting to greet the party from the forest, with his family in a row beside him and Sentia already seated in a place of honor. Maximinus himself arrived with some ceremony. Julianus and Victor, in full uniform, marched in and took their places on either side of the front door. Germanus followed, marching to the middle of the room announcing, "The most distinguished Senator Marcus Herennius Faustus Maximinus, tribune of soldiers and quartermaster-in-chief of the Seventh Hispanic Legion!"

With that final word, Maximinus swept into the room. He was in a uniform much adorned with medals and other symbols of bravery.

As Glaucus bowed to his powerful guest, he reflected that if the medals had been truly earned, then the tribune must be a very brave man indeed.

Maximinus nodded at Glaucus by way of returning his bow, then turned behind him and called out, "Bring in the priest!"

Silvius entered, leading Father Horse by the rope that bound his wrists.

Glaucus turned to Maximinus, "Why is he still tied up? I wish for him to join our council here today."

Maximinus glared at Glaucus. "Until I am convinced of this man's innocence, he stays under my power."

Glaucus looked past Maximinus to the priest, who met his eyes and gave a faint nod.

"Very well," said Glaucus and then, looking back over to Hippolytus added, "My apologies Father Horse, but we will have to inconvenience you a little longer."

Then, turning to address the whole group, he said, "So let us begin."

Then he turned to the images of the household gods, murmured a brief prayer, bowed, and, taking a large pinch of incense from a bowl, dropped them onto the coals in the brazier. The room filled with the aromatic smell.

Glaucus then turned to Maximinus.

"As head of this family, it is my intention to deal with this matter myself. I would be glad of the advice of my friends in coming to my decision. Please, take your seats."

Glaucus sat in the middle seat. Maximinus took the place to his right and Lydia, that on his left. Sentia was placed beside her husband, while the fifth chair, intended for Father Horse, was left empty.

Father Horse and Silvius retired to sit on a bench at the back of the large room. The children would have joined them, but they were warned off by Silvius with a little shake of his head. Instead, they sat on another bench, over on the other side of the doorway.

Once everyone was settled, Glaucus called out, "Bring in the prisoner!"

Marcellus led Septimus in.

While he had not known who the thief had been, Father Horse was not entirely surprised. No one knew the secrets of the house better than the steward.

Septimus' wrists were bound with chains that also attached to his ankles. Marcellus had been taking no chances.

"I think that we can unchain him for now, " pronounced Glaucus. "He isn't going anywhere."

Marcellus unscrewed the locking bolt that secured Septimus' chains and the accused man straightened and stretched. Then, and for the first time in his life, Septimus looked boldly into the face of his master.

"Septimus, you were found with the lady's jewels in your possession. A search of the farm's outbuildings also turned up a horse, saddled and bridled, and loaded with food and money. How do you explain this?"

"Glaucus," he said, boldly, addressing his master directly by name. Marcellus immediately drew back his arm to slap him across the face, but Glaucus said, "No! I do not want there to be violence here. I think, in any event, a slave calling his master by name rather than title only serves to add to the weight of evidence that we possess." Turning to Septimus, he added, "And you were going to say?"

Speaking clearly enough to be heard around the room, Septimus began, "I had the jewels because I took them. It was easy enough. No one notices the house slaves coming and going, still less the steward who runs the whole place. I saw where they were, and took my chance when I was certain that everyone was asleep. You did make it easy for me Lady, since you did not lock them away, but simply laid them on the table beside your bed. I can be very quiet when I want to be, and I know this house in the dark. It was a simple matter for me to creep into your chamber, take the jewels and wander out. No one would question my being in the corridors at night."

Maximinus interrupted him, "Did you do this on your own? Or did you have help?" The tribune emphasized the second question with a flick of his wrist towards Hippolytus.

"Quite alone," Septimus emphasized. "It did suit me, I'll admit, for you all to think that the tutor was the thief, and I did see him in the garden that night. Of course, it never occurred to any of you to wonder what I was doing in the garden. You see, I have been so much a part of the furniture of this place that nobody notices my coming and my going."

"Did he suggest this to you, or have any conversation with you about it all?" Maximinus persisted.

Glaucus all but laughed, "Him? Him and those like him don't have the stomach or even the heart for this. If he took the jewels, he'd spend the money on endowing a home for widows or something. No. Even if I thought it would help me, I wouldn't drag him into this. Him and those like him are all too clean for the likes of me. It was good that I could set him up as the villain, precisely because it was clear to me that you wanted him to be guilty."

"How do I know that you are not covering for him?" Maximinus shot back.

"Look, I made a decision last night, while chained up to Marcellus here to tell the truth as completely as I could. It's not for the sake of my conscience. It's because I am eager to delay any pain for as long as possible. I know that you are going to flog me, or worse. I also know that, although you could not legally torture the tutor here (and you went pretty close to the wind there), you can do what you like to me. So if I tell you everything then I delay the pain that will come. And I know it will come."

Glaucus turned to Maximinus, "Does that satisfy you? May I have my children's tutor back now please?"

Maximinus could hardly deny a public request and in the face of the evidence that Father Horse was guiltless. He looked over to Silvius.

"Very well. Free the priest," he ordered.

Silvius drew his dagger and cut Father Horse's bonds so that he was, at last, free.

"Hippolytus," called Glaucus. "Come, here is a seat for you." He pointed to the empty seat beside Lydia. "Join this family council. I think that you have earned your place here."

"I thank you," Father Horse replied. "I trust that the tribune will have no objection?"

Maximinus sat silently, barely containing the frustrated anger that he felt. Then, unexpectedly, he felt Sentia's hand upon his arm. "Husband," she addressed him formally. "What harm can this do? We have the jewels back, we have the thief, and there is no evidence of this man's guilt. If Glaucus wishes for him to join the family council, and he is the head of this house, then surely we must respect that wish. These are the very traditions that we uphold so dearly."

Sentia's words had an effect on her husband.

"Very well. As my wife says, there is no evidence of this man's guilt, and this is your household, so it is your invitation to give."

Father Horse bowed his head, as if to acknowledge the words of the tribune and took his place in the family council.

Attention returned to Septimus.

"What did you do after you had taken the jewels?" Glaucus asked.

Septimus continued, "I hid them in the one place that nobody knew about. I have lived in this house since I was born. My father showed me the hidden cellar when I was a child. He told me that it had been a secret place of the army when Hightower had been a fort. Even Quintus, who stores things in that little plinth has no idea what is underneath it. It was easy for me to go straight from the Lady's room to the garden, get into the cellar and leave the jewels there until I could take my chance to run."

"Why didn't you run there and then?" asked Glaucus swiftly.

"Because I wanted to get away. I took the jewels on impulse because they were there. I knew that if I ran, or even took a horse, then I would have been caught. There were soldiers here with army horses, and they would have been hot on my heels. I knew that my best bet was to wait until everybody had gone and then leave at a time of my choosing. Seeing the tutor in the garden was a bonus. It meant that I could also create a suspect and divert any attention from me. I'm not proud that I did it, but I'm not sorry either."

Glaucus nodded as Septimus made his confession. "But why, Septimus? Am I not a good master? I do not beat my slaves. The whip is not known here at Hightower. You eat well, your life is good. You perform a trusted role and up to now, have done it very well. What possessed you to end all of that, to gamble everything on a bid to get out of here, this home of yours that you love very much? Why would you leave everything, and gamble on this foolish scheme?"

Glaucus' words hung for a moment in the air, and then Septimus spoke, "Glaucus, you have been a good master. You do not beat us, and you try and treat us fairly. That does not change the fact that I am your property. I am still a slave and at the mercy of whatever kind of master that you choose to be. You do not have to be the way you are. You could whip us all, or even worse, for imagined faults and you would be within your rights. So this is not personal. I was born on this farm. My parents were slaves here, so I was born already a slave and as I grew up, this has become the only place I have ever really known. Over the years, I have not left it much, only on business to Londinium or Eboracum, and even then, in the company of a master.

"As I grew, I learned so much about the farm, and its business, that the last master before one put me in charge as the steward. In those days, the masters did not live here, but away in Rome. Then, they fell afoul of some emperor somewhere. They lost their lives and their property was confiscated to the state. For a few years, I dealt with some official from the imperial household until the emperor needed some money, so he sold a whole collection of properties, including this one. He sold it to you, Glaucus. And that was fine. You were off in the east while I ran things here, so I could at least make my slavery seem better by pretending to myself that I was in charge. Then you came to live here, and all that changed. The day that you came and took over was the day that I decided to run and take my chances in the world."

Then Glaucus cleared his throat and spoke to those around him, rather than to Septimus. "This is enough. We have heard this slave's story, his confession of guilt, and of his motives. There is no doubt that this man has broken the basic household laws of trust as well as committing a terrible theft. Before I decide that to do with him, and..." he added, looking at Maximinus,... "as head of this household and owner of this slave, this is my decision to make., I will take advice from those around me as to what actions I should take to punish this man. Maximinus, as senior man present, I call upon you first."

"Thank you, prominent one. This slave deserves severe punishment. A household like yours must have strict discipline, or every other slave will become as bold as this one. I recommend flogging, forty lashes less one. My man Marcellus can do it. He has experience in such things. He can ensure that the experience is very painful without being fatal. Then sell your slave. Not many people will want to buy one like him, but the mines will. There are lead mines in the Brigantian Hills. They'll take him. They always need bodies. He might not live long, but then he's not your problem anymore."

Glaucus turned to Sentia. "And your view, my Lady, as the wronged party? They were your jewels he stole after all."

Sentia stared straight ahead in silence, and then said, in a small voice, "I'm sure that my husband is right. A slave like that can never be trusted again, perhaps never should have been trusted in the first place."

Glaucus then looked at his own wife, "And you, Lydia, what is your advice?"

"Husband, you ask of me something that I cannot give. I know that there must be rules and order. I know that is the way that things are properly set down. It's just that I also remember how kind Septimus was to us when we came here. Do we have to do both? I mean, could we not either flog him or sell him, but not both? It seems a hard enough punishment to send him from his home without adding the terrible burden of a whipping. Or could we not whip him and keep him here? Not as steward, but perhaps as a shepherd or a woodcutter, or to work in the dyeworks."

Glaucus nodded, and then turned to Father Horse.

"And you, Hippolytus, what do you advise? He has hurt you every bit as badly as he hurt anyone else here."

The priest thought for a moment. "I am not going to condemn him for what he has done. He was a man in pain, whose world had come to an end. He had lost the role that he cherished, being the main voice of authority on this farm. A great Roman philosopher once said of slaves that their bodies might be someone's property, but their minds are free. In his mind, for Septimus, this place was his; his life, his only home, and when you arrived, he lost that illusion. That does not mean that it is your fault. He did this himself because, despite his slavery, while you were not here he could pretend—at least to himself—that he was a free and important man. For many years, then, he lived a lie, mostly to himself.

"You can punish the act here and now, flog him and sell him, but that will do no one any good. Think of what Lydia asks for a punishment, but his life. Make no mistake. If he were sold to the mines, he'd be dead very quickly. I think, though, that there is a point here upon which my lady is wrong."

When he said that, he heard a few sharp gasps at his boldness.

"Septimus cannot return to this farm. He has betrayed it and this family and so cannot be trusted, even with a menial task. So, there is a riddle. What do we do with a slave whom we can neither keep, because we cannot trust him, nor sell because we do not wish him dead?"

There was a heavy silence as he asked the question. Then Glaucus, his voice full of hesitation said, "You don't mean …free him?"

"That is the only alternative," answered Hippolytus. "Give him the freedom that he seeks. Give him his savings and bid him farewell, but he can never come back. He must make his own way in the world as a free man, but with no patron, and no home."

"This is weakness," scoffed Maximinus.

"My Lord, I beg to differ. It is strength. It is a harder punishment, and a longer one, than the lash and the mines. Septimus might have his life, and his freedom, but it will have cost him his home. He will be unable to return. He will be an exile from all that he has known."

These words had an effect on Maximinus. He knew exile and its cost. He longed for Rome and to see his sons again.

"You are wiser that I thought, priest. Exile endures longer than the mines and bites harder than the lash. But I cannot agree with you. The old punishments are there for a reason. Their very severity is to deter others from committing a similar crime. And this is personal: this thief has offended against me and my family. I cannot agree with you, but I will defer here to the master of the house."

Glaucus looked at his wife, then at Father Horse, and lastly at Sentia and Maximinus. He cleared his throat, a little nervously and said firmly, "I have come to my decision."

Everyone except Septimus looked at him. Septimus just looked down, bracing himself to hear his fate.

"It shall be as Father Horse says. I shall free Glaucus, but without ceremony. I shall give him the cap of a freed slave and his papers, and then he shall leave and after this day, we shall not see him again."

There was a silence. Then Maximinus stood and made his own declaration. "I accept this verdict although I cannot agree with it. But I have a word of my own to say." He gestured towards Septimus and continued, "From now on I will hold this man my enemy and I will seek my own vengeance upon him. Where he goes, I shall follow. What he attempts, I shall prevent. What he achieves, I shall destroy. He shall never be free of me, or of the fear of me. This I swear by the gods above and the gods below."

The atmosphere in the room seemed heavy with the weight of the oath. It was Glaucus who broke the mood. "Is anyone else hungry? I think that it's time for breakfast."

He stood and left the room, followed by Lydia, Maximinus, Sentia, Father Horse and the children, both of whom rushed up eagerly to their tutor. Septimus stood sullenly between his guards watching them leave.

CHAPTER TWENTY

FAREWELLS

It rained for the next two days. It was not the warm, drifting rain of summer, but hard and sheeting, coming in waves from the west like breaking surf. Septimus left in the early afternoon of the first day. Glaucus made out his papers, gave him his cap and then saw him off the farm. They took the cart, pulled by the horse that Septimus had planned to steal. Glaucus drove, Septimus sat in the back, and Marcellus watched them go, marking the direction that they had taken. When they reached the western boundary stone of the property, Glaucus reined in. He did not look at his former slave. He just waited for him to get down from the cart and begin to walk. The last that Glaucus saw of him before he turned for home was Septimus, hooded and cloaked against the rain, trudging down the track and out of their lives.

The mood at Hightower was as gloomy as the weather. Glaucus was left feeling vaguely angry at another act of treachery from a slave whom he trusted. Sentia, perhaps embarrassed by the curiosity she felt for that little book that she had read in Hippolytus' room, spent little time with Lydia moping in her room. Maximinus, prevented by the rain from leaving, or even going hunting, wrote letters, drank too much and played dice with his soldiers. They, being wise to their futures, let him win.

Lydia felt Sentia's absence and Glaucus' inner sense of betrayal. She ached for them both, and for Septimus whose folly had made all this happen. But she did not sit about feeling sorry for herself. Instead, she sought out the little office from which Septimus had run the farm and began to sort through his papers. Someone had to take his place and it might as well be her. It was the slaves who were most affected. Septimus had betrayed them too. Now they would no longer be so faithfully trusted. There would now be a barrier of suspicion between masters and slaves that would take a long time to break down again. Only the children, and Father Horse, seemed to have emerged from the ordeal of the past few days with their joyful vitality intact.

On that first morning, as the rain began to wash the courtyard, Father Horse had gone, together with the children, to the plinth. Despite the rain that poured down, they scurried (and Father Horse hobbled) along the stone path. They found the door already open and Quintus inside, sheltering from the rain. He looked up at them, ready to be cross at being disturbed in his little haven. When he saw it was that children, he relented a little.

"There's not much room in here, if you want to stay dry," he said with a little smile.

"Oh, there's more than you think," replied Father Horse. "I can't quite reach, Quintus. Do you think that you could take the rope coiled up on that little shelf and thread it through the hook in the ceiling? Now Gordi, can you use one of those knots that Silvius taught you and tie the end of the rope to that little ring in the floor?"

When everything was in place, Father Horse went out of the plinth and back into the rain, bringing the children and Quintus, who had hold of the other length of the rope, with him.

"Now pull on that, Quintus."

The gardener did as he was told, and the trapdoor in the floor opened up wide.

"Now, tie it up. There will be something there to secure it."

The wall was full of hooks and racks for the tools that were stored there, and Quintus found one strong enough to take the weight of the trapdoor.

"Come on then," said Father Horse. "Let's take a look down here and get out of this rain!"

The trapdoor opened onto a set of stone steps leading down into the darkness of an underground room.

"What's this?" asked Quintus, completely astonished that his little garden shed had turned out to be the hidden entrance of a mysterious chamber.

"I believe that it was once the strongroom of a detachment of soldiers. Every Roman fort has one and this building began its life as a Roman fort. It's where they kept their pay chests and anything else of value. Do you have a flint? I wonder if we could get some light down here."

Quintus did have a flint, and an old wool wax candle, which he placed in a horn lantern. The light was not generous but it showed, beyond the steps, a large, stone-lined and stoned-roofed room. They could hear the rushing of water in the walls, filling the lead-lined cisterns under the garden courtyard. The air was damp and stuffy and moisture dripped from the walls and roof.

Gini was definitely not impressed. "Let's get out of here! This place smells!"

It was only when the underground chamber was sealed up again, and Father Horse and the children were drying themselves by the big kitchen fire that Gordi asked the question which had puzzled his whole family. "How did you know where to look, Father Horse? We've all lived here for ages and none of us knew about that room."

"It's because you have lived here for so long that you missed it. What have I always said is the key to true learning?"

It was Gini who answered, "Not looking at new things in old ways, but at old things in new ways."

"Quite right, Gini," agreed Father Horse. "When I came here, I thought from the shape of the buildings, especially the outside walls, that this was an old army fort converted into a villa. Experience has told me that an old fort would have an underground strongroom where the military temple was. The plinth was in just the place where the entrance would have been. Weeks ago, long before the tribune came calling, I had a look at the floor and found that it could be raised, and that settled it in my mind. Since it was the one place that no one, except Septimus, knew about it was the one place that was never searched. But I could not tell anyone. If I had, Maximinus would have been confirmed in his own mind that I was guilty, since I knew about this hiding place. That is why I could not be here when the jewels were found, and the safest place for me was actually up in the camp in the forest with the soldiers. I'm sorry that it was Septimus who took the jewels. I thought that it might have been because he has been here for so long. I hope that he can find a little peace now."

Gordi could stand it no longer and asked, "But why, Father Horse? Why did he risk everything for a few jewels? We trusted him. He was good to us. What did we do?"

"You might think it a puzzle," said the priest in reply. "I can show you how he did it more easily than I can tell you why he did it. Reading the heart is harder than reading a book or the shape of a building. I don't think that your family as such had much to do with it. Septimus simply hated being a slave. He hated being owned by another person. Your father is his third owner. He has been bought and sold with this farm like he was one of the sheds or sheepdogs. He longed, I think, to be his own person, with his own things and able to make his own choices. That is not because of you. It is because he was a slave."

"Well he'll be happy now. He has what he wants." Gini said.

"He thinks that he has what he wants, but he does not. He thinks that he is free, but he is not. He is merely alone. In this world, the opposite of slavery is not freedom; it is service, freely given. No one is truly free, not even Maximinus. He and Sentia are bound by rank and tradition to behave as they do. They must act in certain ways which is why Maximinus had to accept your father's decision and not just do as he wished with Septimus. Sentia must always agree, at least in public, with her husband. They are Roman nobles and as bound to their rank as a slave is to their status.

"That is why Septimus can never really be free. Even though he is alone, he fears the revenge of Maximinus. When Maximinus called him his 'enemy' that was a serious statement, not just bold words. Maximinus will seek Septimus out and try to hurt him in whatever ways that he can, and his reach is very long. That means that Septimus must keep running, and can never really settle. He can never truly make a home. This is not really freedom but a different kind of slavery. He is no longer your father's slave, but slave to his own fear."

All around them, as he spoke, the kitchen slaves who had been coming and going, getting things ready for the midday meal, slowly stopped and quietly listened. Phormio, who would usually have told them to stop dawdling and get on with their work, stopped too. These were important questions that affected them all. When Father Horse had finished speaking, there was a silence, broken finally by Phormio himself who finally remembered what they were all there for.

"Come on then," he called out. "Lunch won't prepare itself." And everyone slipped back into the tasks they had left off a moment before.

The following afternoon, as the rain still came and went, Lydia was busy at the big table in her room trying to sort out the papers that Septimus had left behind. She had transferred all of his records and books there, and was now trying to make sense of them. By her standards, they were a bit of a muddle. He had clearly developed his own system over the years, but to her it was a foreign code that she had to crack.

She was so deep in her work that she did not hear the timid knock at the door. Only when it was repeated a little more loudly, and accompanied by a cough did she notice and turn around. Sentia was standing there, looking not at her, but down at the floor.

"Hello!" Lydia said warmly. She had missed Sentia's company and was genuinely glad to see her. "Please, come in, and find a seat in all this clutter."

And clutter it was. Scraps of papyrus were mingled with little sheets of wood so thin that they curled and baskets of broken pottery with notes written on them. There was mess on the table, mess on the floor, mess on the couch where Lydia normally sat to read. Sentia carefully picked her way to the couch, and sat on the edge, careful not to disturb anything.

"Lydia," she began quietly. "I came to say that I was sorry for all of this and to beg three little favors."

"My dear," replied Lydia gently. "There is nothing to be sorry for. If anything, I should be apologizing to you. It was our slave that stole your jewels, not the other way around. Then you have been stuck here for days waiting for this to be resolved, and for this wretched rain to ease. No, if anything, I should say that I am sorry to you."

"That's very kind but there is much to be sorry for here. I brought those jewels with me to impress you all. I wanted to show what a great lady I am, even out here at the edge of the empire. If I hadn't been so vain and self-important, then none of this would have happened."

"That's very kind of you to say that, but there is nothing really to be sorry for," Lydia was firm. "The cause of all of this is not your vanity, or whatever you want to call it, but Septimus' greed. How could anyone blame you for someone else's act? Besides, if we spend our lives rushing to judgement, whether about ourselves or others, then we can never truly develop friendships or come to love one another in the ways that we should. Now, what are those favors?"

Sentia looked at the floor as she began, "I need to say something first. I came here to visit Hightower, to meet you and your husband, out of a mixture of duty and boredom. Eboracum is an army town. There are not many established families and they are mostly British. The governors and their staff come and go. Life there for me is so limiting, even suffocating. When Maximinus said that he was coming here with Glaucus, I leaped at the opportunity to join him. I could be both the dutiful wife of the mighty Roman commander, and the Roman lady queening around in a country house of —forgive me for saying this—provincial aristocrats."

She stopped there, as if waiting for Lydia to respond. When she did not, she continued, "If that was why I came, it was not what I found. I did not find people who could be overcome by jewels and airs and clever conversation. I found something more important than that. I found someone who might be my friend. I have discovered in you, dear Lydia, a person to whom I can speak openly and without fear of judgement. Friends, anywhere, are more precious than gold. Here, at the isolated edge of empire, they are dearer even than emeralds."

At this she looked up, smiling shyly. Then she drew in a big breath, looked Lydia full in the face and asked, "Would you be my friend?"

Lydia almost laughed out loud.

"Sentia, Sentia, you silly thing. I already am. I have been all along. If that was one of the favors that you wanted, it is given and with joy. I granted it that first night at dinner when I watched as you held yourself back for the sake of your husband."

"He can be a trial," Sentia agreed. "But he is mine to love and I do love him. It's an old-fashioned marriage, but then we are old-fashioned people, and we have come to care for one another very much.

"My second favor is simple. Will you write to me? I do not think that we will see one another often. You are mostly here and I am mostly in Eboracum, but letters can be a great comfort."

"Of course I will, so long as you promise to write me proper letters and not just stories about dinner parties or Eboracum gossip," Lydia responded.

"I don't think that there is much danger of that. They mostly bore me terribly. The ladies I know talk nothing but clothes, or their sons and husbands, or finding matches for their daughters. It is as if they have no life for themselves. I know that you love the life of the mind, that you are interested in real things like philosophy and literature, and I would so love to talk with a friend about what I have read and what I think about it. I'm sure that you would dearly want to do the same. You must feel so cut off here sometimes."

"Yes, that is true. It can be a lonely life here, especially when Glaucus is away. But the children fill my days with a mixture of constant joy and terror. Now that Father Horse is here, it makes it a little easier. He is a strong guide both for them and also for me, although I have never really said so to him. He has a steady wisdom and a deep knowledge that he has only shown to us in flashes. We are very fortunate to have him."

"Well, that's the third favor," Sentia responded. "This is a bit awkward, since I am asking for your help in asking a favor from him."

"Really?" Lydia was intrigued.

"I was absolutely fascinated by that little book of his that I read by Marcus. He does not seem to have another name. It was not like any other book that I have ever read. The style was simple, the stories were strung together in a way that I have never seen before, and he even seems to end very suddenly as if the copyist had forgotten something.

"Despite all of that, it really spoke to me. I found something in me becoming quite excited as I read stories about a teacher in another land in another time. I want to study that book. I want to read it, think about it. To do that, however, I need a copy of the book. This is the favor. Could you ask your priest to let me have his, at least until I can have a copy made in Eboracum. It should only take a few days, and then I can send it back. Your priest has no reason to help me, of course. We have treated him abominably since the emeralds were stolen, and I don't think that Maximinus can still quite believe that he had nothing to do with it. I would not blame him for telling me to go to Hades. Would you help me? Would you ask him for me?" Sentia was almost pleading.

"I can do better than that," said Lydia. "Although the book was in his room, I put it there for him to use. Many of those books in his room are mine. I can let you have that little gospel—that's what that form of literature is called, by the way, and it is new and a bit different, and when you have done with it, you can send it back to me, or even better, bring it back. You will always be welcome here."

"Even if I bring Maximinus?"

"Even then," assured Lydia. Sentia smiled in relief.

"Listen," said Lydia, sharply.

"What?" replied Sentia. "I can't hear anything."

"Exactly!" Lydia smiled. "The rain has stopped."

At much the same time as Lydia was making her observation about the weather, Glaucus was easing himself into the cool water of the pool in his bathhouse. He had spent all day walking the farm. This was not an idle stroll. He had lost his steward, the man who had run the farm for years, and now Glaucus had to learn how to manage without him. At some point he realized that, for years, he had been a businessman who owned farms. Now, with Septimus gone, he had to become a farmer who owned businesses. If Lydia could sort through the accounts and make sense of them, he would do the same with the complex operations of his business. In order to begin, he had to discover just how Septimus had set the whole thing up.

He had to understand the work that was done on his property, down to the smallest detail. He had set out early that morning. By the time he returned, he was that odd combination of being soaked through and hot and bothered. He had the good sense, before he had left that morning, to order that the baths be heated in anticipation of such a return, and so he lay there in the cool water, eyes closed both blessing his foresight, and going over the events of the day.

As he did so, he became aware that he was not alone. He opened his eyes up to see that Maximinus was standing at the edge of the pool, a towel around his waist.

"Mind if I join you?" said the tribune and, without waiting for a reply, dropped the towel and slid into the pool.

"We're off tomorrow," he remarked. "Before we go, we should sign the contract to seal our arrangement."

"We could do that tonight after dinner if that suits," said Glaucus, pleased that the actual reason for the tribune's visit had not been forgotten in all of the unpleasantness.

"I do hope that your cook has something special planned. You keep an excellent table, for all of the isolation of this place."

"That's really Phormio. He has been in my family since I can remember. His father cooked for my father."

"So there's no chance that you will sell him to me?" Maximinus was only half serious.

"None. In fact I am going to do what I should have done when he and his family stayed loyal in that terrible time in Tarsus, and give them their freedom. I don't expect that any of them will leave. But they have been true to me so I should do the same for them."

"You aren't worried that you might lose them to a wealthier employer?"

"Well, that's a price worth paying. Besides, even when they are freed, I remain their patron so they still have some duty to me," Glaucus replied.

"That's true enough. I can see that this fad for freedom has not blunted your business sense. Shall we go and have a sweat?"

The two men heaved themselves out of the pool and went to the hot room, where they slipped on wooden clogs to protect their feet from the heated floor and sat by the edge of the hot tub, letting the sweat pour from their bodies.

"You know," said Maximinus, his voice oddly muffled and echoing in the enclosed space, "I would never have done what you did yesterday, and I will do that man what harm I can for what he did to us, but you did a brave thing to defy my advice and come to your own conclusion. I don't have to agree with what you did to admire it. I think that we shall work very well together." He paused, and then he added "Although it will take a great deal for me to like, or even trust, your priest."

"He's not my 'priest,' as you say. He's my children's tutor, and a very good one too. We had no end of trouble with them before he came. They'd run off; they were disobedient; even insolent. This man has turned all that around."

"Admirable I'm sure, although regular beatings might have been just as effective. My father used a cane on me whenever he thought I needed correction. That was a lot and I turned out all right." Maximinus unconsciously winced at the memory and went on, "But you've made your choice. You have your Christian. Just make sure that he keeps his horrible religion to himself."

Glaucus rolled into the tub, gasped as he hit the warm water, went under and just as quickly emerged, wiping his eyes.

"Of course, tribune. This is a Roman house." Glaucus sounded certain, but inside he was not so sure.

Early the next morning, dawn barely lighting a landscape washed into rich color by two days of rain, the travelling party prepared to leave. Carts were loaded and horses saddled, and soon it was time for farewells. Gordi found it hardest to say goodbye. He had liked having the soldiers around, even when he was tricking them, and Silvius in particular had become a good friend. As the young soldier stood by his mount, tightening the girth strap and making sure that his saddlebags were secure, Gordi sidled up to him.

"Will you come back soon?" He asked softly.

"I don't know. That's up to the tribune. I'm a soldier. I don't get to choose for myself."

Gordi took that in, thought for a moment and replied. "Please try. You'll always be welcome here. I loved my lessons with the sword, but I know I'm still a beginner."

"That you are. Well, we'll see."

While they were speaking, Father Horse had a conversation of his own with Marcellus. The soldier was standing back, watching the legionaries do the packing and loading, occasionally offering a firm word of correction. At first, he did not see the priest, who had approached him from the side and then stood next to him, so he started when he heard Father Horse say, "You know, I bear you no ill will. You were doing your job, following orders."

"Not even for the bucket of salt water?" Marcellus asked softly, unused to this kind of conversation.

"Not even for that," laughed Father Horse quietly.

"Then tell me one thing at least," Marcellus begged.

"What?"

"How did you untie your arms on that first night?"

"What makes you so certain that I did it?" replied Father Horse.

Marcellus was lost for words. Ever since that night, he had quietly been in awe of the priest for enduring everything as he had.

"May God bless you and keep you safe," said Father Horse and slipped away back to the family, leaving Marcellus still struggling for words.

Farewells were exchanged. Lydia and Sentia embraced warmly. Maximinus and Glaucus did so formally, and then the travelling party was on its way. As they watched them leave, Glaucus turned to his family and asked, "Who's hungry?"

Everyone seemed to answer at once.

"Then let's go and have breakfast!"

"Why don't we have it in the kitchen?" suggested Father Horse.

Glaucus thought for a moment and then grinned.

"Why not? I have some matters that I need to talk about with Phormio anyway."

Putting his arm about his son, he turned and went inside. Lydia took Gini by the hand and followed. Father Horse stood back a moment, watched them go in, and then he too went through the great door and joined the family.

www.ingramcontent.com/pod-product-compliance
Lightning Source LLC
Chambersburg PA
CBHW070628310726
48982CB00001B/211

* 9 7 8 1 6 6 6 7 7 1 8 0 0 *